"WOULDN'T THIS MAKE A GREAT PLACE FOR SOME SHOPS?" JO BLURTED OUT.

"You Helfings could sell your homemade noodles, and Mamm and I would have more space to display our bakery stuff and our summer produce—and we could get other local folks to rent spaces, and—and it's on the main highway! Think of how much more business we'd attract here than we do at the roadside stands in our yards."

Her friends stared at her as though she'd sprouted a second head.

"Are you talking about *us* running such a place?" Lydianne asked with a frown. "How would we pay for the property, much less the repairs it needs?"

"And what makes you think a handful of *maidels* could manage a bunch of shops?" Marietta chimed in again.

Jo planted her fists on her hips, grinning despite her friends' very reasonable objections. "What makes you think we couldn't?" she challenged. "We manage quite well without husbands, ain't so? We've been supporting ourselves for years, so we certainly have the smarts to keep a joint business afloat. I think it would be great fun to run a marketplace!"

Morning Star

Charlotte
Hubbard

ZEBRA BOOKS
KENSINGTON PUBLISHING CORP.
www.kensingtonbooks.com

ZEBRA BOOKS are published by

Kensington Publishing Corp.
119 West 40th Street
New York, NY 10018

All Kensington titles, imprints, and distributed lines are available at special quantity discounts for bulk purchases for sales promotion, premiums, fund-raising, educational, or institutional use.

Special book excerpts or customized printings can also be created to fit specific needs. For details, write or phone the office of the Kensington Sales Manager: Attn.: Sales Department. Kensington Publishing Corp., 119 West 40th Street, New York, NY 10018. Phone: 1-800-221-2647.

Zebra and the Z logo Reg. U.S. Pat. & TM Off.
BOUQUET Reg. U.S. Pat. & TM Off.

First Printing: August 2020
ISBN-13: 978-1-4201-4512-0
ISBN-10: 1-4201-4512-6

ISBN-13: 978-1-4201-4515-1 (eBook)
ISBN-10: 1-4201-4515-0 (eBook)

10 9 8 7 6 5 4 3 2 1

Printed in the United States of America

*In memory of Aunt Verna,
the independent, free-thinking, fun* maidel *of
the Hubbard family*

ACKNOWLEDGMENTS

To God be all the glory!

As I begin another new series, I'm grateful to my editor, Alicia Condon, and my agent, Evan Marshall, for shepherding the ideas for these books and for making them happen. It's a joy to work with both of you!

Thank you, thank you, Vicki Harding, my research assistant in Jamesport, Missouri, for answering my questions so quickly—and for keeping your finger on the pulse of Amish life there. Blessings on you and your family, Joe Burkholder, as you pursue a faith path that has been more rewarding but hasn't been easy.

Matthew 22:37–39 (KJV)

Jesus said unto him, Thou shalt love the Lord thy God with all thy heart, and with all thy soul, and with all thy mind. This is the first and great commandment. And the second is like unto it, Thou shalt love thy neighbour as thyself.

Chapter One

Spring had painted the Missouri countryside with a palette of vibrant greens and gentle pastels only God Himself could have created. The pastures were lush with new grass, and the dogwood and redbud trees added splashes of pink, cream, and fuchsia to the untamed landscape. Jo Fussner and her four *maidel* friends were on their usual afternoon walk on a visiting Sunday, soaking up the midday sunshine. An occasional car passed as they strolled alongside the county highway, but otherwise, Morning Star seemed to be nodding off for its Sunday nap.

As they reached the edge of town, Jo gazed at a dilapidated white stable that sat back from the road, surrounded by a few acres of land. The plank fence around it was also in a sorry state of disrepair. She couldn't recall the last time she'd seen horses in the pasture, or any sign of the English folks who owned it. The harsh winter hadn't done the stable any favors, and Jo thought the place looked sadder than usual as the April breeze riffled some of its loose shingles.

The wooden sign posted on the fence alongside the gate startled her. "Did you know this place was for sale?" Jo blurted. "I haven't seen this sign before."

"Me, neither," Molly Helfing replied. She glanced at

her rail-thin twin sister, Marietta, who was recovering from chemo treatments. "Last I knew, that Clementi fellow who owned this property died in the nursing home—"

"And his kids have been squabbling over the estate," Marietta put in. Despite the spring day's warmth, she pulled her black cloak more closely around her. "I still haven't figured out how the English can bear to put their parents in places like the senior center. It seems so cruel, separating older folks from their families."

"*Jah*, Mamm exasperates me, but I could never shut her away in a care facility—especially now that Dat's passed on," Jo agreed. An idea was spinning in her head—an adventurous, totally impractical idea—as she gazed at the long white stable with its peeling paint and missing boards. Her longtime friends would think she was *ferhoodled*, yet her imagination was running wild with possibilities.

"The kids must've decided to sell the place rather than keep it in the family," redheaded Regina Miller remarked. "I can't think it'll bring much, though, run-down as it is."

"Anybody who bought it would have to invest a lot of money to make it usable as a stable again. And replacing the slat fence would cost another small fortune," Lydianne Christner said with a shake of her head. "Folks around town have been hoping the family will just tear this eyesore down—"

"But wouldn't it make a great place for some shops?" Jo blurted out. "You Helfings could sell your homemade noodles, and Mamm and I would have more space to display our bakery stuff and our summer produce—and we could get other local folks to rent spaces, and—and it's on the main highway! Think of how much more business we'd attract here than we do at the roadside stands in our yards."

Her friends stared at her as though she'd sprouted a second head.

Molly's brow puckered. "How could we run a store on this side of town—"

"—while we were making our noodles in our shop at home?" Marietta finished doubtfully.

Regina appeared more positive, yet she shook her head. "Would Bishop Jeremiah allow that? He's always preaching about how we should keep our businesses to a manageable size. When some of our men have talked of expanding their shops, he's reminded them that bigger isn't better."

"Are you talking about *us* running such a place?" Lydianne asked with a frown. "How would we pay for the property, much less the repairs it needs?"

"And what makes you think a handful of *maidels* could manage a bunch of shops?" Marietta chimed in again.

Jo planted her fists on her hips, grinning despite her friends' very reasonable objections. "What makes you think we couldn't?" she challenged. "We manage quite well without husbands, ain't so? We've been supporting ourselves for years, so we certainly have the smarts to keep a joint business afloat—especially since Lydianne's a bookkeeper. I think it would be great fun to run a marketplace!"

"Puh! Your *mamm* would never go along with that!" Regina teased.

"*Jah*, I can already see Drusilla shaking a finger at you," Molly agreed as she shook her own finger. "And I can just hear her saying, 'No *gut* will ever come of such an outrageous idea, Josephine Fussner! Who ever heard of unhitched women doing such a thing?'"

Jo laughed along with her friends at Molly's imitation of her widowed mother. "You've got her pegged," she said, even as she gazed wistfully at the stable. The weather vane on the center cupola had lost its rooster, and enough boards were missing that she could see daylight on the structure's other side. Even so, she could imagine the building glowing with fresh paint. She could hear the voices of shoppers who'd be delighted to discover the products Plain folks from the Morning Star area would display in their tidy open booths.

"We've got our homes and our work—not to mention the *Gut* Lord and our church family to sustain us—and we get by just fine," she continued in a voice that tightened with unanticipated emotion. "But haven't you ever wanted to do something just for the *fun* of it? Something *new*? Whatever happened to sayings like 'Where there's a will there's a way'—and Bible verses like 'With God, all things are possible' and 'I can do all things through Christ who strengthens me'?"

Her friends got quiet. The four of them stood beside her in a line along the fence, gazing at the forlorn stable and the pasture covered with clumps of green weeds, yellow dandelions, and the occasional pile of dried horse manure.

Regina finally broke the silence. "You're really serious about this."

After a few more moments of contemplation, Lydianne squeezed Jo's shoulder. "I can see how opening shops might be fun, but—"

"It sounds crazy and impossibly expensive," Jo admitted, "and it would take an incredible amount of carpentry work and elbow grease and commitment and organization, but I just thought . . . "

As her voice trailed off into a frustrated sigh, Jo gazed at the long barn with the three cupolas along the top of its roof. "Without a house on the property, I can't think many folks will want to buy this place. It would be such a shame to tear the stable down—"

"We know plenty of men who could fix it up," Regina said, "but why would they want to?"

"—and maybe it's just *me*," Jo continued softly, "but come springtime, when Mother Nature puts on her pretty, fresh colors, I wish I could take on a whole new appearance, too—like the rebirth Bishop Jeremiah preached about on Easter Sunday. When I turned thirty last year, I accepted that I'll never have a husband or kids, but some days I long for something different. Something *more*. You know?"

Her four closest friends *did* know. For one reason or another, each woman believed marriage wasn't an option for her. Jo didn't regret her unwed state, yet the way Marietta sighed when Molly hugged her angular shoulders, and Regina gazed into the distance, and Lydianne pressed her lips together told Jo that sometimes they, too, grew weary of their solitary state . . . and a future that held little opportunity for change.

Even though Plain *maidels* enjoyed a few more freedoms than their married friends, their faith placed limitations on them. They weren't allowed to train for careers or travel to faraway places or break out of the mold of conformity. Amish women who'd been baptized into the Old Order knew their place—and they were expected to stay there.

Jo turned to continue on their walk. "Well, it was an interesting thought, anyway."

For the next few days, however, Jo couldn't let go of the idea of a marketplace. She was so engrossed in her vision—even thinking up possible names for the new shopping area—that she planted rows of onion sets where Mamm had intended to put the hills for the zucchini and other summer squash.

"Josephine Fussner, what's gotten into you?" her mother demanded in exasperation. "You might as well be living on another planet, for all the response I've gotten from you lately!"

After she endured a talking-to about the garden chart Mamm had drawn, Jo headed into town to do the week's shopping—and to pay a visit to Bishop Jeremiah Shetler. If the leader of their church district refused to go along with her idea about refurbishing the old stable, she would put it out of her mind and move on. It was a big stretch, thinking the property could ever be brought up to the glowing images she'd seen in her daydreams.

And yet, as they sat in wicker chairs on his front porch, Bishop Jeremiah listened patiently as Jo described her ideas for shops—and about how she and her four friends would manage the place. She hadn't exactly gotten full agreement from Lydianne, the Helfings, or Regina, but she felt the bishop would be quicker to approve if she presented an organized business plan, which she'd devised over the past few days.

"Wouldn't it be *something* if we transformed the Clementi stable into shops where local folks could sell what they make?" Jo began excitedly. "It would take a lot of work, but can't you imagine Amish stores along three of the walls, with an open central area where shoppers could gather at tables and enjoy homemade refreshments? With some fixing up and a fresh coat of paint—maybe some colorful shutters and flower boxes at the windows—it could become a big attraction for Morning Star, don't you think? If we rented out the shop stalls, we could make money for our church district."

The bishop sat forward, as though Jo's last sentence had snagged his attention. "*Jah*, I saw that the Clementi place was up for sale," he said, "and I can tell you've given your idea a lot of thought, Jo. Who do you suppose might want to rent space in this new marketplace?"

Jo blinked. Instead of waving off her dream as something only a silly, impractical *maidel* would come up with, Bishop Jeremiah was nodding as he listened to her. He was a patient, forward-thinking leader—younger than most bishops, with dark brown hair, expressive brows, and a matching beard. His deep cocoa eyes seemed to search the soul of whomever he was talking to.

Jeremiah's steady gaze made Jo answer carefully. "The Helfing twins could sell their homemade noodles. Mamm and I could expand our baking and produce business—and sell those refreshments I mentioned—"

"And what does your mother say about this?"

Jo laughed when she caught the twitch of the bishop's lips. "Well, Mamm doesn't know about it yet. I figured if you wouldn't go along with our idea, there was no reason to mention it to her.

"But think about it!" she continued brightly. "We have a lot of local folks who make toys and furniture and such! Maybe Anne and Martha Maude Hartzler would want to sell their quilts, and maybe the Flauds would put some of their furniture in a booth—and we could advertise for more Plain crafters from this area! We could have the marketplace open only on Saturdays, so nobody would have to mind a store all during the week. That would really cut into a family's daily life."

Bishop Jeremiah stroked his closely trimmed beard. "What about the land? There's about five acres with the stable, and we'd have to maintain it somehow."

Jo hadn't thought about the pasture, but she hated to admit that when the bishop seemed sincerely interested in her idea. "What if we used it for our annual mud sale to benefit the volunteer fire department—or even for big produce auctions in the summer, like other Amish districts have?"

This was an all-or-nothing proposal, so Jo gathered her courage as she presented the idea that would make it or break it. "Truth be told, I'm hoping our church district will use the land somehow, because while we *maidels* could organize the shops, we have no way to pay for the property or for rebuilding the stable. Maybe the church would help with that part, too."

After giving the bishop a few moments to contemplate her proposal, Jo held his gaze. "I'm asking for a lot, ain't so? And maybe nobody but me will see any benefit to this marketplace. But I had to ask."

Bishop Jeremiah's smile brought out the laugh lines around his eyes. "If you don't ask, you probably won't receive," he pointed out. "If you don't knock, who will know to open the door for you?"

When the bishop rose from his chair, Jo took his action as her cue to leave—yet she felt greatly encouraged. "*Denki* for listening," she said as she stood up. "I appreciate the way you've heard me out, because some men wouldn't have given my idea even a minute's consideration."

Jo immediately wondered if she'd sounded too critical, too much like a *maidel* with a habit of complaining.

The bishop chuckled, however. "Some folks—men and women alike—pass over new ideas because they'll have to put out extra effort or change their habits to make their dreams a reality," he remarked. "I'll pray over what you've told me today, Jo, and we'll see what happens. When you skip a little stone across a lake, you never know how far the ripples might travel."

Chapter Two

As the final prayer of the Sunday service ended, Regina Miller opened her eyes. She reached for the *Ausbund* under her pew bench. Across the room on the men's side, Gabe Flaud sang the first phrase of the concluding hymn in his clear, melodious voice to establish the pitch and the tempo.

I could listen to Gabe sing all day, Regina thought as she joined in with the others.

She would never tell Gabe that, of course. Five days a week she worked as a finisher in the furniture shop his *dat* owned, staining and varnishing the dining room and bedroom sets the male employees built in the factory. Gabe was the foreman and he was single, but he looked at Regina as though she were a fixture in the shop—just one of the boys. She'd heard rumors that he dated English girls despite the fact that he'd joined the Old Order, yet the church leaders had never called him on it.

He's way too adventurous to give a mouse like me a second glance, she mused as she looked at the stained hands holding her hymnal. *Why do I waste my time thinking about him? Must be that springtime thing Jo was talking about, wanting something different—something more—in my life.*

Regina had a more compelling reason for not entertaining notions about Gabe, but it was a secret she didn't dare think about during church. God was undoubtedly displeased with the part of her life she kept hidden away. She'd probably be inviting a visible sign of His judgment—perhaps a lightning bolt shooting through the roof to strike her down—if she allowed her mind to wander to her sinful pastime while she was supposed to be worshipping Him.

Regina sang louder, focusing on the words. As the congregation plodded through the thirteenth verse at the methodical pace with which they sang their hymns, Regina's stomach rumbled loudly. She often wondered what had possessed the Amish songwriters of the sixteenth century to ramble on at such length.

Beside her, Jo Fussner rolled her eyes as they began verse fourteen. Regina stifled a laugh. In front of them, Lydianne Christner rubbed the small of her back while the Helfing twins leaned into each other and began to sway subtly to the beat. The five of them often joked about having calluses on their backsides from a lifetime of endless Sunday services—it was another detail that bound them together as the *maidels* of Morning Star, a bit of irreverent humor they shared only among themselves.

Regina and her friends let out a sigh of relief as the final note of the hymn died away. When Bishop Jeremiah stood to give the benediction, they bowed their heads to receive his blessing. The five of them took their Old Order faith seriously, even if they sometimes muttered about its inconveniences.

"I know you're ready to devour the common meal," the bishop said after the benediction, "but I'm calling a

Members Meeting. An opportunity has presented itself in the form of property that's gone up for sale."

Regina's eyes widened. Had the old stable caught the bishop's eye? If he'd decided to buy the land for himself, he wouldn't be bringing it up at church—yet she couldn't imagine Preacher Ammon Slabaugh or her uncle, Preacher Clarence Miller, buying that dilapidated building or the pastureland surrounding it.

"You're all familiar with the Clementi place at the edge of town," Bishop Jeremiah continued, "and I've heard an intriguing idea about how the stable might be turned into shops where our members and other Plain folks could rent space to sell their wares, as well as a suggestion to use the pastureland for mud sales, produce auctions, and other events."

Regina elbowed Jo. "You talked to the bishop?" she mouthed in amazement.

Jo's tight, hopeful expression confirmed Regina's assumption.

"When I approached our preachers and Deacon Saul, they hesitated—until I suggested that our church could collect a commission from the shops' sales, which would go toward building a new schoolhouse," the bishop continued as he looked out over the crowd. "Preacher Ammon pointed out that we often run short of parking space at our mud sales—"

"Are you saying our church district would buy the property?" Elva Detweiler asked loudly. She was hard of hearing, and she spoke as though everyone else was, too. "Won't that deplete our emergency aid fund?"

"Why would we waste money rebuilding that rickety old stable when we could build a new one cheaper?" Gabe's *dat*, Martin Flaud, challenged.

"What with that big Plain gift shop just down the road

in Willow Ridge, why would we open the same sort of store here?" Gabe asked.

Bishop Jeremiah held up his hands for silence. "I'm pleased that you're questioning this idea, rather than rejecting it flat out," he said. "I'm surprised the Clementi family doesn't want more money for this property. They're hoping to unload the place quickly to settle the estate, and because we could pay cash up front, they've agreed to accept less than their listing price. Deacon Saul feels it would be a *gut* investment—"

"*Jah*, I'd sell my pastureland for twice as much," Saul Hartzler chimed in from the preachers' bench. "We wouldn't be out anything but some grass seed to make it look better. Mowing it before mud sales and auctions would be the only other maintenance."

"I'm in favor of refurbishing the stable rather than tearing it down because the main structure is basically sound, and we wouldn't have to replace much wood," Preacher Ammon replied to Martin. "It also has a character about it you don't see in modern-style stables."

"I'm hoping to hire my nephew Pete to do that carpentry work for us," the bishop said with a knowing smile. "Maybe it'll set him onto a straighter path than working at the pet food factory. And maybe it'll get him to church more often, too."

Regina and several other folks chuckled. Pete Shetler was in his late twenties, seemingly stuck in perpetual *rumspringa*. He tended to frequent the pool hall after working the night shift, so he sometimes came to church wearing clothes that reeked of grease and cigarettes.

"I also believe English shoppers will flock to a quaint stable with cupolas on top, and colorful shutters and flower boxes—not to mention plenty of parking space," Bishop Jeremiah continued, painting them a bright picture. "And because our shops would be individually operated by folks selling their own products, only on Saturdays, I don't think we'd be competing against the Simple Gifts store in Willow Ridge."

"Sounds like you've got this all figured out and you're ready to put money on the table, Bishop. So why're you bringing this up to *us*?" Elva asked. "We pay you such a princely sum, you can surely afford it on your own."

The room erupted in laughter. Because Amish bishops serve without pay, Bishop Jeremiah was laughing the loudest of all.

"The preachers, Deacon Saul, and I are bringing this matter before the congregation because we see it as a possible way to support the construction of a new schoolhouse—to replace the current one, which is becoming too crowded," Bishop Jeremiah replied patiently. "We could even build it on the new property, where we wouldn't face flooding like we had last spring."

Several parents of school-age children nodded. They all recalled the terrible mess they'd had to clean up—and the days of school the scholars had missed—because several inches of water from the Missouri River had inundated the little white building.

"Is there more discussion, or shall we vote about whether to buy the Clementi property?" the bishop asked.

Martin Flaud quickly spoke up. "With all due respect, Jeremiah, I can't imagine that *you* will take charge of these shops—or that you came up with the idea for them. Who's going to manage this place?"

"*Jah*, and who would rent space there?" Gabe chimed in. "No sense in proceeding with this purchase unless several folks are willing to invest themselves in making it work."

Regina held her breath, noting how intently Jo was

focused on the bishop—probably concerned about having to convince the local men that her plan had merit. The idea Jo had blurted on the spur of the moment during their walk last Sunday had become a full-blown business possibility in a very short time, mostly because Bishop Jeremiah seemed sold on it.

When Lydianne, Molly, and Marietta turned to look at Regina and Jo, their faces were lit with hopeful excitement— as though Jo's idea suddenly felt more appealing because it had a chance to succeed.

"One of the first names that came to my mind as a potential renter was *yours*, Martin," Bishop Jeremiah replied. "You and your employees produce some of the finest furniture I've ever seen, yet your showroom's too small to do it justice. What would it hurt to display some pieces where new customers could run their fingers over your glossy tabletops and picture one of your beautiful bedroom sets in their homes?"

Regina's eyes widened at the bishop's praise. Customers had no way of knowing that she and Lydianne did most of the staining and finishing at the Flauds' factory, yet she and her friend took pride in giving each piece all the time and attention it deserved before it left the workroom.

"And what about you, Glenn?" Preacher Clarence asked. "The wooden toys and rocking chairs you handcraft would be a big hit at a Saturday marketplace. I see these shops as something akin to a flea market, except the items would all be new, top-notch Amish products instead of antiques or estate sale stuff that vendors have hauled from one place to another."

Jo chuckled under her breath. "Who knew your uncle would ever get so excited about *shopping*?" she whispered.

"I had no idea *any* of these men would support your

plan," Regina murmured. "The bishop's really enthusiastic about this!"

"He's being smart about it, too, keeping my name out of it," Jo remarked softly.

Meanwhile, Glenn Detweiler had stood up to survey the crowd. "All right, I'm in!" he exclaimed. "I've sold several things through the consignment shop in Willow Ridge, but I'd much rather attract shoppers to Morning Star! Who'll join me?"

Regina and Jo sucked in their breath, and the Helfing twins turned to look at them. "Can you believe this?" Molly whispered. "Your idea for saving the stable is taking off like a shot!"

Without warning, Marietta rose to her feet. "We Helfings will rent a booth to sell our noodles," she declared.

From a couple benches in front of them, Martha Maude Hartzler—Deacon Saul's mother—stood up, too. "This sounds like a fine opportunity to get some of my quilts out of the closet and sell them—"

"Amen to that," Saul put in with a roll of his eyes.

"—and I'd be delighted if any of you other quilting ladies would join me," she continued.

"What a great idea!" her daughter-in-law, Anne, chimed in. "I'm already feeling inspired to make some *new* quilts to sell!"

As three other women waved their hands above their heads, Regina got caught up in the energy that filled the room. Folks were whispering excitedly, looking around to see if anyone else might volunteer, while a dangerously daring thought came to her mind.

Don't even think about it! Don't you dare say a word! Regina's inner voice warned.

Beside her, Jo stood up. "You know, Mamm and I could

sell a lot more baked goods and produce at a stall in this marketplace than we do at our roadside stand," she stated as she focused on Bishop Jeremiah. "Maybe we could even sell refreshments to the shoppers! I'd be willing to organize and manage this endeavor—perhaps instead of paying rent on a shop?"

"And I'll keep the books!" Lydianne put in as she, too, rose from her seat. "And if you Flauds decide to rent a space, I could help you oversee it."

"Wait just a minute, Josephine!" From the second row, Drusilla Fussner stood up to face her daughter. "I'm busy enough with our baking and gardening—and redding up the *dawdi haus* for tourist rentals—without you piling more work on me. This sounds like some crazy half-baked scheme that blew in out of nowhere, and I want no part of it!"

Jo clasped her hands in front of her. "I understand your concerns, Mamm, and I'll assume the additional work it'll take to maintain a stall at the new marketplace," she said calmly. "I see this as a way to increase our income while we also support a new school building—by donating a percentage of everyone's sales," she added for clarification. "It was never my intention to force you into this. We'll discuss it more when we get home."

"*Jah*, you bet we will!" Drusilla clucked.

As Jo's *mamm* sat down, Regina caught a conspiratorial sparkle in the bishop's eyes.

"I think the new marketplace will be in *gut* hands if Jo and Lydianne manage it," he said as he looked out over the congregation. "Does this make you feel better about acquiring the property, Martin? As your bishop, I intend to keep an eye on how things are done. I'm greatly encouraged by the enthusiasm folks are showing—"

"Put Flaud Furniture down for a double-sized stall, maybe in a corner so we've got more room," Gabe called out. "I'm all for trying something new—and meanwhile we'll be funding the schoolhouse. Seems the least we can do, as one of the largest family businesses in Morning Star."

Regina counted on her fingers. Five stalls had already been spoken for.

If Martha Maude can sell the quilts that're stacking up in her closet, why can't you empty out your attic the same way?

Regina's cheeks went so hot, she thought her freckles might pop off. She hoped Jo wouldn't notice how antsy she was getting as these forbidden thoughts raced through her mind.

This is a bad idea! How can you possibly hope to pull this off? Imagine the consequences if anyone finds out—

Even as the warning voice in her head was wailing like a fire siren, Regina stood up to speak before she lost her nerve. "I'd be willing to help Lydianne staff the Flauds' stall, and I'll help Jo with the organizational stuff, too," she began in a halting voice. "And I have a—a *friend* who's looking for a place to display some of his pieces. So that's already six stalls we've accounted for."

"That's all well and *gut*," Martin objected, "but why are we rushing into such a major undertaking before we've thought this through? Why don't we call another meeting after church in a couple of weeks, and see some signed agreements from folks who'll commit to renting stalls? And why don't we make sure Pete's willing to do the carpentry work—or get other men to say they'll rebuild that stable? And why don't we see some concrete plans from our volunteer managers concerning rental contracts and how they'll advertise this marketplace?"

Bishop Jeremiah smiled as though Martin had played into his plans. "Excellent ideas," he said. "How about if all the interested parties meet with me after we've eaten our lunch, and we'll set a time to discuss the nuts and bolts of making this marketplace happen? We'll report back to the congregation in two weeks."

"I like that idea, Martin," Deacon Saul chimed in. "You and I know that a business needs a plan if it's to succeed."

Regina agreed with Saul, because his carriage shop employed even more Amish men than Flaud Furniture and was the most lucrative Amish business in Morning Star. The new marketplace would only succeed if the entire community stood behind it—and it would fail if Martin or Saul spoke against it. Several folks were nodding as the meeting adjourned. The women rose to set out the food for the common meal.

As they headed toward the kitchen, Jo nudged Regina with her elbow. "So who's this *friend*, Miss Miller?" she teased.

"*Jah*, Regina," Molly joined in from behind them. "What juicy secrets have you been keeping from us?"

Regina's throat closed up. Already she was paying for her impulsive decision, and she suddenly needed to concoct a plausible story that wouldn't get her into deep trouble. "It's no one you know," she insisted. "Just a—a guy I met a while back who was looking for a place to display his nature paintings. He might not even agree to rent a space—"

"Do you suppose we should allow English to participate?" Marietta asked as they entered the kitchen.

"Unless we have more Plain shopkeepers than we have space for—and unless the bishop thinks English items are a bad idea—I'd hate to limit renters this early," Jo replied. "It would be *gut* to offer a variety of merchandise, especially if this man's pieces sell well and bring in a lot of commission. Funding a new schoolhouse was Bishop Jeremiah's idea, and I'm glad he thought of it!"

"*Jah*, the marketplace takes on a higher purpose if some of the proceeds are dedicated to such a worthwhile project," Lydianne agreed. "Did you see how everyone was nodding, agreeing that we need a bigger schoolhouse in a safer location?"

Relieved that her curious friends' conversation was no longer focused on her, Regina busied herself with filling water pitchers at the kitchen sink. It was only moments later, however, that her aunt Cora was at her elbow to take the filled pitchers.

"So this *friend*," she began with an expectant smile, "is he a nice Amish fellow who makes a *gut* living from what he sells?"

Regina kicked herself. Why had she blurted out that the potential stall renter was a male? Why had she even opened this can of worms, which was leading her into deeper spiritual quicksand than she already struggled with?

As Cora's three daughters smiled at her, carrying trays of sandwiches, Regina reminded herself that she was setting an example for her cousins Emma, Lucy, and Linda— and that her well-meaning aunt deserved a straightforward answer. Aunt Cora and Uncle Clarence had helped Regina recover after her parents died in a nasty bus accident ten years ago, and she was grateful for all they'd done. Where would she be if they hadn't helped her through her grief?

But you can't tell them the truth.

Regina put a patient smile on her face. "No, Aunt Cora, he's an English fellow. Merely an acquaintance whose paintings I've admired."

Her aunt's smile fell. "Oh. I was hoping—"

"Sorry," Regina put in softly. "No need to plan a wedding."

As her aunt carried the pitchers toward the front room, Regina regretted disappointing her aunt yet again. Even though she was content living her *maidel* life—and had remained in the house on her parents' acreage and supported herself with her earnings from the furniture factory—traditional women like Cora Miller didn't understand how a woman of thirty-two could possibly feel fulfilled without a husband and kids.

If you had any idea why I insisted on staying in my parents' home rather than coming to live with you, Aunt Cora, you'd be appalled—and you'd find my secret much more unsettling than my decision to remain single.

During the course of the common meal, if anyone asked about her "friend," Regina stuck to the sketchy details she'd given about the mysterious artist so she wouldn't incriminate herself further. The meeting with Bishop Jeremiah only took a few minutes, because when he suggested they hold their first organizational talk at his place on the following Wednesday afternoon, everyone agreed. After she bid her *maidel* friends goodbye, Regina pedaled her bike to her single-story home on Maple Lane, situated at the edge of town. She'd firmly decided to call her masquerade to a halt—to announce on Wednesday that her artist friend had no interest in renting a stall.

What was I thinking, exposing myself this way?

She entered her bedroom, stepped onto her large metal trunk, and then opened the short, narrow door in the wall so she could climb the wooden stairs to the attic.

What if nobody wants my paintings, or, worse yet, people ridicule them? And what if folks figure out that I'm

*the artist—and that I've been living a lie for years? Best to
nip this in the bud before I have to tell any more whoppers
and get caught in them.*

And yet, as Regina stood in the center of her secret
studio, something deep inside her longed to display the
work that so satisfied her soul. Nearly every evening, after
a day of staining furniture, she spent a few hours in her
hideaway, painting nature scenes. Her more recent paintings hung from strings suspended across the studio, except
where her easel sat by the small windows on the front of
the house. Her older work was carefully stacked upright in
bins—and the bins covered half the attic's plank floor.

Regina needed to paint the way most folks needed to eat
and breathe. Her schoolteacher had complimented her
artwork when she'd been young—and because composing
scenes and working with color had come so naturally to
her, her parents had allowed her to take a short watercolor
class at Koenig's Krafts when she'd entered *rumspringa*.
Dat's brother Clarence was a preacher, however, so he'd
been adamant about Regina's joining the church at an early
age. She'd secured her salvation at seventeen by being
baptized, but she'd forfeited her innermost soul: in the
Morning Star district, members were forbidden to create
art for art's sake. Unless her painting decorated something
useful like milk cans or housewares, it was considered
worldly, something that called attention to the artist.

Regina had obediently tucked her paints and brushes
into her wooden trunk, but she'd felt the loss of her art
acutely. After her parents had died when a train collided
with the bus they were all riding in on the way home from
a wedding, Regina had kept herself sane by taking up her
paints again, setting up her easel in the attic—where it
would be out of sight when anyone came to visit. At

twenty-two, she'd been rather young to live alone on her family's small acreage, but she'd instinctively known that moving in with strict, stern Preacher Clarence, Aunt Cora, and their young daughters would kill her spirit forever.

Bishop Jeremiah had taken her side and had dropped in on her often until she'd gotten a little older. Martin Flaud had hired her because her father had been one of his finest craftsmen—and because Regina had proven herself to be more meticulous at staining and finishing than any of his male employees. She'd survived the rough, lonely times by working hard at the factory, and by surrounding herself with the quilts and curtains Mamm had made and the furniture Dat had built for their cozy home.

And so the last ten years had passed . . .

Regina had willingly given up any chance for marriage—because she couldn't reveal her sinful pastime to a husband. Her solitary state bewildered Aunt Cora and Uncle Clarence. Her three nieces, however, were intrigued by her relative freedom and independence, which made family dynamics difficult when she spent time at her aunt and uncle's house on visiting Sundays.

Gazing at the nature paintings that surrounded her on that Sunday afternoon, Regina felt torn. Why had God given her a keen eye and the talent to render woodland scenes, flowers, and wild creatures on paper if He wouldn't allow her to paint pictures of His creation openly and without guilt?

She flipped through the paintings in the nearest bin . . . a pheasant on the riverbank; a collapsing barn surrounded by the first wildflowers of spring; an enlarged study of a dogwood blossom. Each scene brought back the wonder and awe she'd felt as she'd sketched and painted it. It saddened her greatly that she lived a double life that was unacceptable to God and to her family and friends, but painting was a habit she couldn't seem to kick.

Once again she told herself to back away from displaying her work at the new marketplace—to preserve her secret rather than risking exposure that would surely get her shunned. Wasn't it exciting enough to be helping Jo, Lydianne, and the Helfings by creating new shops in what had been a dilapidated stable?

Regina sat down at her easel. She brushed water on a section of the painting in progress and added a few more ribbons of pink and peach to a sunrise she'd begun. Watching the colors run together and take on the delicate hues of an early-morning sky caught her up in the magic of creating. If it was a sin for her to paint, picking up her brush on Sunday surely compounded her transgressions in God's eyes, yet she was in such a quandary she didn't know any other way to handle her opposing emotions.

She should tell her friends that her artist friend had declined the offer to display his work. And she should pack up her paints and dispose of the evidence of her wayward nature.

But *then* what would she do?

Chapter Three

Jo felt downright bubbly as she approached the bishop's front porch on Wednesday afternoon. "Hey there, Margaret," she said as Jeremiah's mother opened the door for her. "*Denki* for allowing us to invade your kitchen when you're most likely starting dinner."

"Sounds like you *businesswomen* have a lot to discuss if that old stable's to become a place for shops," she said. "I've got a chicken casserole in the oven, and if your meeting runs long, I'd appreciate it if you'd take it out."

"Will do." Jo smiled, recognizing the same undertone of disapproval in Margaret's voice that her mother had expressed several times since Sunday's Members Meeting. "The final decision on buying the Clementi place rests with the entire congregation—"

"Puh! Martin and Saul have been here to have their say about it, so I already know how the vote will go," Margaret remarked as they entered the kitchen. "You've got coffee and a few cookies on the counter, so I'll leave you to your planning."

Bishop Jeremiah chuckled as he came in from the front room with a stack of papers. "It's no secret that God's will and church business proceed faster when the movers and shakers put their influence behind it," he remarked. "*Gut* to see you, Jo. I was hoping to speak with you before the others arrived."

"I'm early," she admitted, intrigued by what she'd just heard. "I've sketched some plans for the arrangement of the shops and—well, I'm *excited*, so I couldn't wait to get here."

"Your enthusiasm and organizational skills will go a long way toward helping this project succeed, too." Jeremiah laid out his armload of papers on the kitchen table. "I hope you don't mind that I didn't give you credit for this marketplace idea on Sunday. Saul had been eyeing the Clementi place as additional pastureland for his cattle, and Clarence had remarked about how crowded the schoolhouse has become. When I suggested that we could build a new school on higher ground if the church acquired that property, Ammon jumped on board. Please don't think I was downplaying your part in this project—"

"Our church leaders are much more invested in it now because they think it's mostly their idea—and yours," Jo put in.

The bishop met her eye gratefully. "*Denki* for understanding that. With you and your friends planning the shopping area, I believe we can create an appealing attraction that will benefit our district and the whole town of Morning Star. It's an exciting way to support the schoolhouse, and an opportunity for women and men alike to be involved in the growth of our community."

As Margaret greeted more folks at the front door, Jo glowed with the bishop's compliment. Because he'd lost his wife a few years ago and his widowed *mamm* kept house for him, Jeremiah had more time to devote to new projects—although everyone sincerely hoped he'd find a second wife. Jo had never entertained fantasies that he would ever want to court *her*, so she and the bishop worked well together on church matters without the complications of a potential romance.

Within the next few minutes, the Helfing twins and Lydianne arrived, and so did Glenn Detweiler and Gabe.

"How's Dorcas doing? And your new baby boy?" Jo asked as the two men took their seats.

Glenn composed his answer carefully. "Levi's better now that we're supplementing Dorcas's milk with some goat milk," he replied softly. "The doctor says she's extremely anemic. He's put her on vitamins and told her to stay off her feet until she's stronger. Having this baby has really depleted her body and her strength, so Mamm and Dat are helping us out. *Denki* for asking."

"She's in our prayers," Jo murmured as the front door opened again.

In the front room, Martha Maude Hartzler exchanged pleasantries with Margaret before joining them in the kitchen, and Regina slipped in last. She was clutching a large brown folder to her chest, and her freckled cheeks appeared flushed.

"Sorry I'm late," she murmured. "What have I missed?"

"We're just getting started," Bishop Jeremiah said as he took his spot at the head of the table. "I asked Pete to stop by before he went in for his shift, so we'll see if he makes it. Considering how unreliable he can be, I hope I haven't set us up for delays with the stable renovation—"

"But our other carpenters can help," Gabe pointed out. "Pete's a whiz at plumbing and ductwork, though."

"He is," the bishop agreed. "And I hope you understand why I'd like to guide him away from his apartment in Higher Ground and his after-work pool hall habit by involving him on this project. Shall we open with a prayer?"

Jo and the others bowed their heads as Bishop Jeremiah invoked God's guidance. Higher Ground was a new town a few miles down the road from Morning Star. It had been hastily founded by a renegade bishop who'd been excommunicated from Willow Ridge—and who'd subsequently died—so for the local Amish, its reputation was overshadowed by a black cloud. The residents weren't part of an organized church district anymore, which was another strike against Higher Ground.

"Amen." The bishop held up a stack of pages. "Since our meeting on Sunday, Martin has provided for us these forms from Byler Printing, where Flaud Furniture gets their invoices and receipts. He's also suggested that we could have them handle our advertising, both print and online."

Glenn took a packet of forms before passing them along. "I've had the Bylers design flyers and a simple website for my carving business," he remarked. "Couldn't hurt to involve them and other Mennonites in our new project, for better exposure."

"*Jah*, because it's English shoppers we're trying to attract," Gabe pointed out. "Probably three-quarters of our custom furniture orders come from our online presence. We wouldn't have nearly the reach if the Bylers weren't maintaining a site for us."

Jo listened carefully as she took a packet of the forms and then handed them to Molly and Regina. She was quickly realizing that her enthusiasm for the new shops wouldn't be enough to make them successful. "I'm grateful that you fellows are sharing your experience," she said. "These ready-made forms are helpful. How much commission do you think we should collect on our sales?"

"The shop in Willow Ridge gets ten percent," Glenn

replied as he took a pen from the center of the table. "I've sold several rocking chairs and toys there, and adding ten percent doesn't raise the prices enough to discourage folks from buying them."

"And it would equate to a tithe, if you want to get biblical about it," Bishop Jeremiah said with a chuckle. "The tougher question is what to charge vendors for renting space with us. I'd hate to cut into their income too much, but we'll have to cover utility payments and building upkeep, not to mention advertising expenses. Would forty dollars a month be fair? Hopefully everyone will sell enough on four Saturdays to afford ten dollars a week."

Jo stilled. She sensed the Helfing twins were doing some mental calculations as well. She would have to sell a *lot* of pastries, bread, and refreshments to cover that amount and make any profit—and Mamm would consider forty dollars an exorbitant sum, because their little roadside stand didn't cost them *anything*.

"Is everyone okay with me managing the refreshment area instead of paying stall rent?" she asked softly.

"And what if Marietta and I take charge of the building's cleaning and upkeep in lieu of paying rent?" Molly asked. "I'm excited about having a shop, but we'll have to sell *several* bags of dry noodles to clear forty dollars. Just saying."

"We have other commitments to bulk stores for orders, too," Marietta put in. "And they don't charge us for display space."

"I think that's only fair," Martha Maude stated with a nod. "You gals are supporting yourselves with your home-made products, and you'll be investing quite a lot of time and effort to keep your shops going. Rose Wagler, Anne, and a couple of other ladies are going in on our quilt shop, so it'll be no burden for us to come up with rent."

"*Jah*, quilts sell for a lot more than noodles and cinnamon rolls," Bishop Jeremiah agreed. "I'm fine with this arrangement. How about the rest of you?"

Jo felt greatly relieved when Glenn, Gabe, and Regina nodded their consent. It was a plus to have Deacon Saul's *mamm* and his wife running a shop, because their beautiful quilts were sure to sell well—and even if they didn't sell a single quilt, the family would still have food on their table.

Lydianne cleared her throat. "Regina mentioned something earlier that we should probably clarify before we go any further," she said. "Bishop, you and the preachers seem very positive about opening a marketplace, but you've often warned us about expanding beyond the work we can do while still having time for our families. Do you see a problem with adding the commitment of this new venture to our workloads?"

"Someone has actually listened to my sermons!" Bishop Jeremiah teased before he resumed a more serious demeanor. "You've asked an important question, Lydianne."

He sat back in his chair, pondering for a moment. "Because we're setting up our marketplace to fund a new school, and as a place to hold the auctions and mud sales that support our firemen and other community causes—and because several members will be involved—I don't feel any one family will be burdened by extra work," he finally replied. "If the shops succeed, we Amish all benefit. If they don't, we'll still have a better place to build the new schoolhouse and host our outdoor auctions."

"Even if we weren't setting up these shops, our members would step up to cover the cost of a school," Gabe pointed out. "We'll be sharing the work, but nobody will lose his shirt if it doesn't work out."

Folks around the table nodded, and Jo agreed. She, the Helfings, and Glenn would still be supporting themselves with their handmade items even if they gave up on the shops after a while. "Chances are we could rent out the stable for parties and special events if the marketplace doesn't succeed—or even if it does," she added. "English and Plain folks alike would benefit, since Morning Star doesn't have any other large halls available."

"That's a fine idea!" Martha Maude said as her face lit up. "It could be a place for family reunions, or even weddings and funerals for families who'll have bigger crowds than they can handle at their homes."

Encouraged by their progress, Jo reached into her tote bag. "I, um, sketched out my idea for how the interior of the stable might look when it's been renovated," she began nervously. "I envision the shops being positioned along the outer walls around an open central area, where we could maybe have tables and chairs for serving refreshments. We'll need restrooms, of course—"

"Pete can install those for us, as well as the water lines and such," the bishop put in with a nod.

"—and we'll need an office for keeping our records," Jo continued. "I'm also hoping for a small kitchen in my stall, so I can bake those refreshments I mentioned on-site. I think the aroma of homemade goodies and fresh coffee will be a big draw."

"Oh, I think we should go for a full-sized kitchen," Martha Maude insisted as she turned Jo's diagram so she could see it better. "Any group who'd hold a family gathering there would want to be able to cook."

"I agree," Bishop Jeremiah said as he stood behind Gabe to look at the diagram. "We might have to check health department rules for compliance on that, but I can already smell the cinnamon rolls and imagine folks sitting and chatting over their coffee. Most likely, it'll be a place for husbands to gather while their wives spend their money in the shops!"

Laughter filled the bishop's kitchen as Gabe pointed to a section of the floor plan. "I want the two spots in this corner for Flaud Furniture," he said. "I'll fill out my rental form right now."

"I think your kitchen should be right here across from the main entry, Jo," Molly put in, pointing to the spot. "It'll be centrally located that way, close to where you want to serve refreshments—"

"And the restrooms could be in this tack storage area that sticks out from the back of the building," Glenn suggested. "Close enough to share the water pipes and drainage system the kitchen would need, yet separate from the eating area."

"Pencil that in!" Jo said. "These are great ideas!"

"*Jah*, they are," Gabe agreed enthusiastically. "Dat's been talking about this place a lot the past few days, so I'll convince him that we should provide some basic tables and chairs for this central area. It'll be *gut* advertisement for us, after all."

"And if you build them, we know they'll be top-notch," Jo said.

Lydianne pointed to the words Jo had carefully written at the top of the diagram. "Is this what you think we should call our new shops—The Marketplace at Morning Star?"

"Or just The Marketplace, for short." Jo glanced at the folks around the table to gauge their reactions. "Maybe somebody else has a better idea—"

"It has a nice ring to it," Marietta said as her slender face lit up with a big smile. "The Marketplace."

"Simple, but it states our case," Gabe chimed in with a nod.

"I like it!" Glenn put in. "How about if I build signs to mount on the front and the side of the building that faces the road, as well as one to post on the fence—assuming we plan to keep that slat fence and the gate."

Everyone got quiet, thinking.

"Well, it'll take some doing to replace the missing slats and paint that long stretch of fence," Bishop Jeremiah said. "But we need a way to keep folks off the property during the week when the shops aren't open."

"*Jah*, and if it's kept the place secure for the Clementi family these past few years, it'll probably work for us," Gabe added. "I say we include the fence renovation with the stable work."

"I'm *gut* with that," Jo agreed. "And I think we should open at nine and close at five. It'll give us time to set up our shops beforehand, and we'll still have the evening to take care of things at home before Sunday comes."

"And we agree to have Glenn make the signs?" the bishop asked.

As everyone nodded, Jo felt a real sense of accomplishment. Their committee members were already working well together, and the church leaders were solidly behind this new venture. Glenn, Gabe, Martha Maude, and Molly were filling out rental agreements for their stalls, so Jo reached for a blank form, too.

When she realized how quiet Regina had been—and noticed some papers sticking out of her folder—Jo gently elbowed her redheaded friend. "Have you spoken with your artist friend, Regina?" she asked as she looked around the table. "Has anyone thought of other potential shopkeepers we should invite?"

Regina opened the plain brown folder. "He—he sent

along a few samples, and he says it's okay if you don't think his paintings will fit in, what with the rest of the shops carrying Amish products—"

"Ooh, look at this little squirrel with his cheeks full of food!" Marietta interrupted gleefully. She reached for the painting on top of the pile. "He looks so real, you can just *feel* how silky his fur is!"

"*I* like this picture of the old broken-down barn in the field of wildflowers," Martha Maude put in, leaning forward for a closer look. "The warmth of that sunny spring day comes right off the page."

Within moments every person at the table had snatched up a painting. Jo was immediately attracted to a pair of cardinals in a snow-frosted cedar tree. "What kind of paintings are these?" she asked. "The details are so distinct, yet some of the colors blur together."

"These are watercolors," Regina explained. "None of them are framed, so he wasn't sure folks would be as inclined to buy them—"

"Frames are a matter of personal taste," Glenn put in. "And his pictures might be easier to display without frames on them."

"And you could offer frames in your shop, Glenn," Gabe pointed out quickly.

Regina was nodding, yet she seemed doubtful. "Is it all right if he's English, then? Do you think the preachers will object—especially if all the shop spaces fill up and we have to turn away Plain shopkeepers?"

Bishop Jeremiah considered this question as he looked over everyone's shoulders to study each painting in turn. "Your friend paints nature scenes—renderings of God's creation," he summarized softly. "We still have several spaces open, so I'd like to give him a chance. I suspect customers will have the same immediate reaction to his paintings that we've had."

"Me too," Jo agreed. "Why not take a rental form, Regina? If he needs time to decide, that's all right. That said, we need to figure out a date when we'll be open for business. Any idea how much time the renovation might take?"

Bishop Jeremiah chuckled. "If we set a date, Pete—and whoever else helps—will have a reason to get moving on the work." He went to the wall calendar and flipped its pages. "June first is a Saturday. If the congregation votes *yes* on Sunday, May fifth, can we be ready in about a month?"

"We should make the most of the summertime, when we'll have more daylight hours," Gabe replied. "If we wait too long to open, we might lose our momentum—"

"And it'll mean Pete has to apply himself right off the bat," the bishop remarked as he glanced out the front window. He smiled at Jo. "As for where he'll live, would you and your *mamm* consider renting him your *dawdi haus*? I know you have tourist traffic in the summertime—"

"No! Mamm will fry my hide if I agree to that," Jo blurted.

The kitchen got quiet, as though folks were startled by the tone of her immediate response.

Bishop Jeremiah nodded. "I didn't want your *mamm* to think I'd passed her over with my offer of paying Pete's rent through the summer," he said. "But I can understand why she wouldn't think of him as the ideal tenant."

Marietta and Molly were looking at each other, communicating without the need for words in that special way twins had.

"Would it be proper for Pete to stay in one of our *dawdi hauses*?" Marietta asked.

"Mamm had a second one built to allow for the renters we get during the mud sales and auctions," Molly reminded everyone, "but sometimes—"

"It would be nice if one of them was bringing in a steady income this summer," Marietta finished. "As long as Pete understands that we only provide breakfast—"

"And we won't be cleaning his room every day, like in a motel," Molly put in firmly, "but we'll change his sheets once a week."

"—I'd be all right with him staying at our place," Marietta continued. "He'll be out working, after all. It's not as though he'll be underfoot while we're busy in our noodle shed each day."

The bishop nodded. "I'm fine with everything you've said, ladies, and I appreciate your willingness to help me out. We'll settle up before you leave, all right?"

The twins nodded together, and Jo chuckled as she got back to filling out her rental agreement form. The Helfings' conversations reminded her of playing a game of leapfrog, and their innate understanding of each other's ideas amazed her.

Martha Maude signed her form with a flourish and put it in the center of the table. "What if I post notices on the bulletin boards of Plain stores, asking for more shopkeepers and letting folks know about our new marketplace?" she offered. "I'd wait until the vote at church is official, of course, but meanwhile I could be writing out the note cards."

"I think we should have the Bylers print out some posters about our opening, too," Gabe put in. "We want our advertising to look professional, so English shoppers take us seriously. Maybe you could put those around in May, when we're sure the stable will be ready on time."

Folks were nodding, finishing their forms—and taking a last look at the delightful paintings Regina was gathering up.

"We've covered a lot of ground, even if Pete apparently couldn't join us today," Bishop Jeremiah said. "Shall we meet next Wednesday, same time, to check our progress before I conduct a vote the following Sunday? I predict we'll get a lot of enthusiastic response when folks around Morning Star see what we've cooked up for this property."

Everyone agreed as they rose from their chairs. The aromas of chicken and cheese reminded Jo to take Margaret's casserole from the oven. "Here's your dinner, Bishop," she said as she set the steaming glass pan on a trivet. "Be sure to thank your *mamm* again for tolerating us as we talked everything through."

"*Denki* to all of you for your ideas and your enthusiasm," Bishop Jeremiah called out to everyone. "We're off to a fine start."

Jo agreed wholeheartedly. She couldn't help smiling as she descended the porch stairs. It was sprinkling, and Mamm would be pleased that her garden was receiving God's *gut* rain. Jo decided not to mention that she'd saved them from Pete Shetler's presence in their *dawdi haus* all summer. It was best to enjoy her mother's rare good mood without bringing up any extraneous details.

Chapter Four

Thursday morning, Regina was applying walnut stain to a hutch, a large table and its eight leaves, and the twelve chairs that went with it. As she focused on keeping her brush strokes smooth and even across the table's top, her thoughts buzzed like bees. After hearing her friends' exuberant admiration of her paintings, she was floating on clouds of euphoria.

Yet her heart thudded heavily. Displaying her watercolors at The Marketplace would shift her private sin to a public one. Not only would she still be defying the rules of the Old Order—she'd be lying to Bishop Jeremiah and her closest friends about who'd painted those pictures.

Lord, I'm in a bad place, she prayed as she worked. *You really should give me an unmistakable sign—like that proverbial thunderbolt coming through the roof—that I'm on the wrong road with selling my paintings, before I get myself into deeper—*

"That's a mighty serious expression on your face, Red. Are you finding flaws in the table you're staining?"

Regina blinked, raising her wet brush from the table's surface. How long had Gabe been watching her?

"No, no—just lost in thought," she stammered. She was suddenly aware of the dark walnut stain lining her fingernails, and her faded gray dress, and the brown kerchief she wore at the factory so she wouldn't splatter stain on her white *kapps*. "This is going to be quite a nice roomful of furniture when it's done."

"It's for a family in St. Louis," Gabe remarked as he assessed her progress. "You're such a patient and thorough finisher, Red. It was a *gut* decision when Dat and I hired you—and then Lydianne—for this job."

Regina sucked in her breath, unaccustomed to such praise. "I—I'm happy to have the work," she admitted. "Cooking and keeping house were never my callings, I'm afraid."

When Gabe chuckled, dimples came out to play on either side of his clean-shaven face. "Seems we'll have a new calling when The Marketplace opens. I wasn't too fired up about it at first, but now I think that renovated stable will bring a breath of fresh air to Morning Star. And on that note, what do you think about these tables and chairs for Jo's refreshment area?"

Even though the designs were very basic, Gabe's sketches were precise and refined—as artistic in their way as her watercolor paintings. "I like them," she replied. "They're simple and compact."

"And they fold up, so we can pull extras from the storage area when we need them—like for those family gatherings Martha Maude mentioned," Gabe explained. "Dat was so taken with the idea of renting the stable for events, he thought Flaud Furniture should provide several of these tables and chairs as a contribution to the community's new venture—with our business cards attached for some advertisement, of course."

"That's a generous gesture," Regina said.

Gabe nodded. "I suspect my parents are looking ahead to a family wedding, thinking it'll be easier to host the

dinner in that big stable instead of at home. Well, carry
on, Red."

As suddenly as he'd appeared, Gabe strode away. For a
moment Regina stood in a daze, wondering what had just
happened. Martin's son was a hardworking shop foreman,
but when had he ever complimented her work or asked her
opinion about anything? She'd worked in the Flaud factory
for nearly ten years, and Gabe hadn't seemed to know she
existed.

As Regina resumed her work on the dining room set,
however, she wondered about what Gabe had said. His
sisters, Kate and Lorena, were too young to be dating. If
Delores and Martin Flaud anticipated a wedding in the
near future, did that mean Gabe was courting a young
woman who lived somewhere else?

*She's probably very pretty, and a fine cook and seam-
stress, and most likely she comes from a family that's well-off.
What other kind of wife would Gabe want, after all?*

Gabe focused for a moment before humming the pitch
he heard in his head—which was not too high for the
basses, and would also keep the tenors from becoming
shrill during the song the men were practicing. On Friday
nights, the fellows from church who enjoyed music often
gathered at Bishop Jeremiah's place to sing. As the group's
unofficial leader, Gabe usually suggested a few hymns
from the *Ausbund* as warm-ups, then directed them in the
finer points of harmonizing gospel songs.

As he and Glenn Detweiler carried the melody of "I'll
Fly Away," Gabe's spirit soared. Everyone enjoyed this
tune—which was much snappier than a hymn—and it was
a joy to hear his father and Glenn's *dat*, Reuben, pulsing
along on the bass part that came in on the chorus. Bishop

Jeremiah began to clap to the beat, and Deacon Saul joined in, and soon the front room rang with the song's enthusiasm about leaving this earthly life behind for a heavenly home. As the tune ended, Gabe directed its slowing down and reveled in the four-part harmony that resonated so clear and sweet on the final note.

"*Jah, that*'s how you sing that one!" Matthias Wagler called out when they'd finished. Matthias had relocated to Morning Star a little more than a year ago with his harness-making business—and then he'd married Rose, acquiring her little Gracie as a daughter. "Just think how folks in church would smile if we sang from the gospel songbook we men are using, instead of ancient German hymns."

"I think that's a fine idea," Gabe chimed in, already knowing what the church leaders' response would be.

Preacher Ammon raised his bushy eyebrows. "It's one thing to sing some rousing tunes during a social time like this one," he pointed out, "but quite another thing to cut loose during a worship service. Next thing you know, we'd be bringing in a piano—"

"Or a pipe organ, like they've got at the Methodist church in town!" Deacon Saul teased. "We'd sound high and mighty then, ain't so?"

As the discussion continued around him, Gabe *yearned* for the chance to sing more progressive songs during church services—and to have instrumental accompaniment, as well—but in the Old Order, that would never happen. As it was, Preacher Clarence didn't participate in the men's Friday night songfests, because he considered the newer gospel tunes too worldly and improper. He felt that music about God and His kingdom should remain respectful, reflecting the Lord's majestic, omnipotent power.

Gabe sighed inwardly. He wished their worship services could be more cheerful and uplifting—wished Old Order

leaders would be more open to *change*. He didn't want to
believe the God he loved would deny the Amish their eternal salvation if they made a joyful noise instead of singing
hymns more suited to a funeral.

"So how're plans for the stable renovation coming?"
Deacon Saul asked. "How'd your organizational meeting go?"

Bishop Jeremiah smiled. "We're off to a fine start—
don't you think, Gabe?"

Gabe came out of his woolgathering and nodded.
"We've got several spaces spoken for already, and a wide
variety of items to be offered for sale," he replied. He decided not to mention the English watercolor artist until
he'd submitted his rental application and fee.

"I'm excited about the idea of using that space for big
social events," Gabe's *dat* chimed in. "Morning Star doesn't
have anyplace for that now. I think a lot of English will
want to rent it from us."

"And what's Pete think of the idea, Jeremiah?" Preacher
Ammon asked.

The room fell silent. Unfortunately, the bishop's best
efforts to shepherd his nephew over the past few years
hadn't made Pete any more reliable.

"He'll be at our meeting on Wednesday," Bishop Jeremiah stated firmly. "We've set our opening date for June
first, and Pete knows what has to be accomplished by then.
He'll also be moving into one of the Helfing sisters' *dawdi
hauses*, so we'll be able to keep a closer eye on him."

"Let's hope he doesn't wear out his welcome with
Molly and Marietta before he completes the renovation,"
Deacon Saul remarked.

"Maybe he'll hitch up with one of them," Reuben blurted.
When he burst out laughing, his belly strained against his

shirt and black suspenders, and soon the others were chuckling at his unlikely idea as well.

After a bit more conversation, the men started for home, some of them in buggies and some of them walking to enjoy the pleasant April evening. Gabe strolled alongside his *dat*, once again immersed in his thoughts about how the Amish—their music and their conversations alike—never changed. Folks in the older generations were determined that anyone over the age of eighteen should be married and raising a family, and they never tired of matchmaking.

Gabe would never say it aloud, but he sometimes envied Pete Shetler the relative freedom of working at the pet food factory, living in his own apartment, and driving an old pickup. Remaining in *rumspringa* had some advantages that Gabe had given up when he'd joined the church, probably sooner than he should have.

"Maybe *you* should head over to the Helfing place and take a shine to one of the twins, before Pete does," his father suggested. "Or there's Jo Fussner, who's a *fine* cook, or—well, *gut*ness knows you've been working with Lydianne and the Miller gal for years, and nothing's come of it."

Gabe let out an exasperated sigh. "How many times have we had this conversation, Dat? And how many times have I said I'll know the right girl when I see her?" he snapped. "End of conversation."

Chapter Five

Bishop Jeremiah's kitchen was filled with fresh energy as everyone took seats around the table on Wednesday afternoon. While the others helped themselves to cookies and coffee, Regina slipped her rental agreement form onto the stack in the center of the table, desperately hoping no one would quiz her about its details or the artist she'd named Hartley Fox. Despite her earlier misgivings, she was all in, committed to a space where she would display—and hopefully sell—her work. There was no backing out now.

As Martha Maude entered the kitchen with her daughter-in-law, Anne, along with two other women, the attention shifted to them. "Lenore will be going in on our quilt shop, and Rose will be selling her candles there, too," Martha Maude said as she gestured for them to sit down. "With all that merchandise, we'll need two slots in the corner opposite the Flauds' shop so we'll have plenty of display space—which means we'll pay double rent, of course."

Regina smiled as the two new participants sat down. Lenore Otto had moved to Morning Star from Cedar Creek, and she lived with her daughter, Leah, and her son-in-law, Jude Shetler, who was Bishop Jeremiah's brother. She created quilts with bolder colors and patterns than many Amish women used, so Regina was pleased that she wanted to offer her unique work at The Marketplace.

"Hey there, Rose, have a seat," she said as she pulled out the chair to her right. "I think your new candle business will be a great addition to our shops!"

Rose had moved to Morning Star with her little girl, Gracie, when she'd married Matthias Wagler. She was in the family way, due in the fall, and she glowed with health and happiness. "I was so excited when Martha Maude asked if I'd be interested," she said. "The four of us can take turns running our shop—much more manageable for me, come time to welcome this wee one," she added as she curved her arm around her modest bump.

"I've also brought the completed rental form from the father and son who own Wengerd Nurseries, over by Queen City," Anne put in as she placed it on the growing stack. "We've known Nelson and Michael for years, and they've agreed to maintain the window boxes and any other plantings we may want around the building. Come summer, they also want to participate in produce auctions."

"That's great!" Jo exclaimed. "If lots of vegetables—and flowers—are displayed outside the building, they'll draw in folks who're passing by on the road."

"Glad to hear it." Bishop Jeremiah sat down at the head of the table, nodding at everyone. "The two preachers and Deacon Saul went with me yesterday to speak to the Clementi family and look at the stable. They feel confident that this project is on the right track, and that it'll be a worthwhile investment for our church district."

"Dat's on board, too," Gabe put in as he handed the bishop a copy of his sketches. "We're donating several of these collapsible tables and chairs for the refreshment area—and any group events we might schedule—so I have a feeling that very few folks in the congregation will vote against our project. The fellows in our shop are talking about The Marketplace already, pleased that we can build the new schoolhouse on that property with the percentage we'll collect on sales. They see it as a win-win situation."

"And I'm calling it a win-win-*win*," Bishop Jeremiah said. "We'll have the shops, we'll be supporting the new school, *and* I've convinced Pete to move to the Helfings' *dawdi haus*, away from Higher Ground. He wants to keep his night job at the pet food factory, but he knows he'll have to prioritize his time so the stable's ready several days ahead of June first. This'll be a *big* step forward in steering my nephew back onto the Amish path."

Marietta looked less convinced. "Today's the first of May, and we haven't heard a word from Pete about moving in—"

"So do you really think he's going to?" Molly finished.

The bishop sighed. "My nephew has always kept his own schedule. He'll show up when—"

Outside, a big engine rumbled and then backfired loudly. Through the window, Regina saw a black pickup lurch to a halt in the driveway. A muscular blond fellow slid out of it—along with a golden retriever, which barked excitedly and ran around him in circles.

"He's here," Regina announced softly. "And he's got a big—"

Boisterous barking filled the front room as the door flew open. "Riley, stop!" Pete called out. "You've got to behave yourself when—"

The rowdy dog had already planted his large paws on the kitchen table, however, right next to the cookie plate and Bishop Jeremiah. By the time Jo had snatched the goodies away from Riley, Pete was entering the kitchen.

"Sit *down*, boy!" he commanded. "Get away from that table right *now*, Riley!"

Jeremiah slipped his arm around the retriever. "Riley, *sit*," he murmured.

Riley obeyed immediately. His tongue lolled out of his mouth as he gazed adoringly at the bishop.

Pete brushed his shoulder-length blond hair back from his face as he looked around the table. He was wearing a snug black T-shirt with the logo of a rock band on it, along with faded jeans and lace-up work boots. Aromas of grease and cigarettes came in with him, as though he'd recently spent some time at the pool hall. "Sorry I'm late—"

"Take a load off, Pete," Gabe said, pulling out the empty chair to his right. "Your new landladies were just wondering when you were moving in."

Pete maneuvered the chair so its back was against the table between Gabe and Glenn and then straddled it. He grinned at the Helfings as though his good looks and charm would make up for any inconvenience he'd caused them. "How about now? All my stuff's in the truck."

Regina thought the twins did a fine job of controlling their exasperation.

"We'll get you moved in after the meeting," Marietta said with a frown. "But when we agreed to let you stay at our place, we didn't know—"

"You have a big *dog*," Molly stated sternly. "I'm informing you right now that Riley won't be allowed on the *dawdi haus* furniture—"

"And you'll have to keep him away from our noodle shed, or the health department will be shutting us down," Marietta said without missing a beat.

"And we can't be stepping in any *poop*," Molly added.

Pete's eyes widened as though their demands were unreasonable. "Anything else?"

"We'll think of something!" Molly blurted.

Everyone else burst out laughing, and Gabe slapped

Pete playfully on the back. "You'll have to toe the line now, buddy—but we're glad you're here," he added emphatically. "Say, Dat and some of the guys at the shop are wondering about installing solar panels on the roof of the stable to run the lighting and the kitchen equipment."

"And we'll all need plug-ins—along with those gadgets to swipe customers' credit cards," Glenn put in.

Folks got quiet. No one had considered the possibility of using solar power.

Pete thought for a moment. "Depending on which way the building's situated—"

"It faces north," Bishop Jeremiah said.

"Well then, we could install solar panels on the south side of the roof," Pete said with a nod. "I assume there's already electricity to run the stable's lights. But if you're wanting to stay Amish and not use that, you might want a gas backup along with your solar power."

"Let's keep our options open until the renovation gets underway," Bishop Jeremiah suggested. He handed Pete a sheet of paper. "Here's the sketch of how we'd like the shops to be arranged in a U around a central open area. Does that seem feasible?"

Pete glanced at Jo's drawing. "Depends on where the supports and the weight-bearing walls are located. We can reconfigure whatever's in place," he added, "but it'll take longer if we have to do that."

Nodding, Bishop Jeremiah pressed on. "Once the congregation votes to buy the property on Sunday, several men will probably be interested in helping with the work. You're in charge, Pete," he insisted, "so it's your call whether or not you accept their assistance. And it's on *you* to complete the renovation a week before our June first opening date, so our shopkeepers can set up their spaces. *Jah?*"

Defiance glimmered in Pete's brown eyes, as though

he'd had all the bossing he could handle. "Today's May first—and the vote on buying the property isn't until the fifth," he noted as he looked at the bishop's wall calendar. "That's not much time to work, considering I have a full-time job."

"We've talked about this, Pete," Bishop Jeremiah stated, holding his nephew's gaze. At forty-one, he was younger than most bishops, but he had a presence about him that couldn't be denied.

Pete rose from his chair. "I'm outta here," he muttered. "Let's go, Riley."

After the front door slammed behind him, folks at the table stared at one another. Outside, Pete's pickup rumbled to life. He roared out of the bishop's lane, and his tires squealed as he raced down the paved road.

Martha Maude cleared her throat. The hair beneath her *kapp* was silver-gray, but there was nothing elderly or submissive about her demeanor. "Jeremiah, you'll be finding someone more dependable to do our carpentry work."

Chapter Six

As Gabe joined the men gathering outside Elam Stoltzfus's home before church, all the talk was about The Marketplace—how quickly the plans were coming together, as well as some speculation about whether Pete Shetler would be the lead carpenter.

Everyone *liked* Pete, and they believed he had the skills to do the stable's renovation. But they agreed that it was time for him to grow up and accept adult responsibilities.

"We all feel bad that Pete grew up with a *dat* whose brain disease turned him violent and shattered his family," Jude Shetler said of his nephew. "But we've been helping him as best we can—and at twenty-eight, Pete's long past the acceptable age for clinging to his *rumspringa* and his freewheeling bachelor ways."

Gabe wasn't surprised by Jude's remark. Still single at twenty-seven, Gabe was the target of similar remarks—except he'd joined the Old Order nine years ago. He'd been courting a girl at the time, so church membership had been a necessary step toward marriage. After she'd changed her mind, Gabe had often wondered if he'd locked himself into the Amish lifestyle too soon.

But he could never admit his secret doubts or yearnings. It was too late for that.

After the men and women had settled themselves on their respective sides of Teacher Elam's front room, Gabe sang the first phrase of the opening hymn to set the pitch and the tempo. As the congregation joined in, Bishop Jeremiah, Preachers Ammon and Clarence, and Deacon Saul removed their hats in one sweeping motion. Shortly after that, the four ordained leaders left the singing congregation to gather in another room, where they would decide which Bible passages Deacon Saul would read and who would preach the service's two sermons.

As they began the fifth verse, Pete slid onto the end of the bench next to Gabe and Glenn. His black broadfall trousers and white shirt appeared clean but rumpled. His blond hair was still wet from his shower.

Gabe flashed Pete a thumbs-up, noting his taut expression as he grudgingly joined the singing. The two of them had been friends since their early grades in school, when Pete had come to live with Jeremiah and his wife, Priscilla, before she'd passed. Pete's *dat*, Jacob Shetler, had contracted Lyme disease, and it had advanced into a brain infection that had turned him so violent, Bishop Jeremiah had had Jacob committed to a care facility. Jacob had died there several months later and Pete's *mamm* had remarried. Pete had been dead set against leaving Morning Star to live in Indiana with a stepfather he didn't get along with—so he'd stayed with Jeremiah and Priscilla until he'd moved out on his own.

No one really knew how much emotional and physical abuse Pete and his *mamm* had suffered at the hands of his *dat*. At the very least, Gabe figured his longtime friend deserved his continued support, and a chance to do the carpentry work he was so skilled at.

During the second hymn, the church leaders returned to the front room and hung their hats on the wall to signal that the worship service was about to begin. Bishop Jeremiah's eyebrows rose when he caught sight of Pete, who warily held his uncle's gaze—as though the two of them had recently exchanged some tough words.

All signs of discord eased from the bishop's face, however, as he rose to begin the service. "May the grace and peace of our Lord Jesus Christ be with you on this Sabbath day, the fifth of May," he began in his resonant voice. "Let us never forget that we're here to worship God and to submit to His will."

Gabe believed the Morning Star district was particularly blessed to have Jeremiah Shetler as its bishop, because he had a positive, relatively progressive attitude. He could set aside his personal preferences to embrace the wide variety of personalities he dealt with—yet church members knew they were expected to uphold the tenets of the Amish faith, without exception. Pete would receive no special treatment because he was Jeremiah's nephew.

As Preacher Clarence rose to deliver the opening sermon, Gabe sighed to himself. Clarence Miller spoke in a singsong voice that lulled folks into a daze as he meandered from topic to topic, so after about ten minutes Gabe found himself gazing absently between the older men's heads to the women's side of the room.

Red was nodding off. Her head drifted lower and lower until she jerked and sat upright again—and the cycle repeated. Gabe chuckled. What might keep a quiet mouse like Regina Miller from getting her rest? Did she stay up late into the night reading romance novels? Was she a light sleeper, easily awakened by traffic noise?

And how did she come to know the guy who painted those amazing nature pictures? He doesn't live here in town . . .

The remainder of the prayers, hymns, and the second

sermon that Preacher Ammon Slabaugh delivered went by a lot faster because Gabe was speculating about his reclusive redheaded employee. Red had been very quiet during the most recent meeting at the bishop's house—had she turned in a rental form for her artist friend? It occurred to Gabe that he went for days at a time without talking to her because she worked in the staining room, which was enclosed to prevent sawdust from drifting onto the wet furniture. Before they'd become involved in developing The Marketplace, they'd had little in common, it seemed.

Maybe Red had a date with that artist last night! All this time we've thought of her as a quiet, unassuming maidel *when she might really have an English boyfriend—which is totally forbidden!*

Gabe stifled a laugh. It was far more likely that Red and Lydianne had gone out for Saturday night supper together, considering that they preferred talking to each other during breaks rather than to the male employees.

"May God bless us and keep us and make His face to shine upon us," Bishop Jeremiah intoned in his benediction. "Amen."

Folks sat up taller, anticipating the Members Meeting— and the vote about buying the Clementi property. Deacon Saul rose to speak, gazing first at the men and then at the women.

"At our previous meeting, some of you had reservations— and rightfully so—about buying the Clementi place on such short notice," he began. "Jeremiah was excited about acquiring the property, so he's asked me to report our findings today, to present a second opinion, as it were."

Folks around the room nodded. They respected Saul Hartzler, not only because he was in charge of the district's finances but because he was one of the foremost businessmen—Plain or English—in Morning Star.

"After Ammon, Clarence, Jeremiah, and I looked that stable over closely and walked the pastureland," Saul continued, "we concluded that the property is well worth the asking price, and that it would be a suitable place to set up rental shops and to build our new schoolhouse. We have also studied Jo Fussner's proposed floor plan—and in answer to Martin's request for a commitment from potential shopkeepers, we have already received seven signed rental agreements."

Saul paused, allowing folks to absorb what he was saying. "Because two of those renters want double-sized spaces, and we're asking forty dollars a month in rent," he continued, "those nine stalls would bring in three hundred sixty dollars each month. Assuming these shopkeepers stay for a year, that total rent would be four thousand three hundred and twenty dollars—and in addition to that, our church district will receive ten percent of the shops' gross sales. The committee is proposing to call this project The Marketplace, and they've already devised an advertising plan."

Bishop Jeremiah rose from the preachers' bench to stand beside Saul. "Does this satisfy your need for more commitment, Martin?" he asked as he gauged the congregation's reaction to Saul's report. "Does anyone else have any questions before we vote on whether to buy the property?"

"*Jah*, we need a reliable carpenter committed to renovating the stable in time for our June first opening date," Martha Maude said loudly.

Pete stiffened. He scowled, looking away from the women's side, where Martha Maude sat near the front.

Bishop Jeremiah picked up some papers from the preachers' bench. "Pete realizes our opening date is approaching very quickly, so he has signed a contract for installing the plumbing, the restrooms, and the electricity required by the health department, as well as some solar panels. He will also lead a construction crew, which will include volunteer carpenters from the congregation, to re-furbish the stable's main structure," the bishop announced. "Glenn Detweiler has also signed a contract to head up the interior finishing work, in lieu of six months' rent on his shop. We don't usually require contracts for such things, but we felt folks might be more comfortable seeing these agreements in writing."

"We Flauds and some of our furniture crew will be help-ing," Martin put in. "And as you know, Martha Maude, we're also providing the tables and chairs for the central re-freshment area—because we believe The Marketplace will benefit our church and the entire Morning Star community."

"*That* ought to shut her up," Pete muttered.

Gabe elbowed him playfully. "Hey, we all want this to work out—and we're glad you're still in on it," he added softly.

Pete shrugged, frowning. "I get tired of the Hartzlers throwing their weight around just because they're the wealthiest family in the district," he shot back under his breath. "I'll uphold my end of this bargain, but you'd better keep Martha Maude—and Saul—out of my hair. I won't tolerate them watching my every hammer stroke or telling me my work doesn't suit them."

"Not to worry," Gabe murmured, squeezing his friend's shoulder. "Dat and Glenn and I will be working right alongside you. We've got your back, buddy."

"*Jah*, and I'm glad you're to be the foreman," Glenn put in, leaning in front of Gabe to focus on Pete. "Saul builds a fine carriage, and his money comes in handy for the expenses a project like this requires—only he's a man you can work *for* but not *with*. That's the way some of his employees tell it, anyway."

Gabe nodded. "He told Dat he's had an influx of orders for buggies and wagons this spring, so I doubt he'll spend much time around the site anyway. It's all *gut*, Pete," he added with a smile. "You'll do us proud."

Meanwhile, folks around them were murmuring as Martha Maude and a few others looked at the contracts. When Bishop Jeremiah called for a vote, the *ayes* bounced along the rows of the men's side like a rubber ball and did the same as the women expressed their opinions. A big cheer erupted when the district's youngest member—Gabe's teenaged sister Lorena—spoke the final vote in favor of The Marketplace. As folks rose from the pew benches, talking and laughing, a new sense of energy filled the big room.

When Gabe saw Red and her friends heading toward the kitchen, he turned to Pete. "How's it going, living at the Helfing place?"

Pete rolled his eyes. "It's a *gut* thing I still have a full-time job and that Riley goes with me," he replied. "At ten months, he's still got a lot of puppy in him, so he's full of energy. Molly gave him what-for after he snatched one of her dresses off the clothesline on Friday."

Glenn laughed. "At least he didn't go after her under-wear, *jah*?"

"I suspect the twins are hanging their skivvies indoors now that I live there," Pete replied with a shrug. "Or else they don't wear any."

As the three of them laughed together, Gabe felt some of the tension draining from Pete's attitude. "So how's the breakfast they cook for you? What's their *dawdi haus* like?"

"The food's okay—and seeing how my uncle has paid my rent ahead, the price is right," Pete remarked. "It's putting a cramp in my style, though. Living alongside two *maidels* is different from having an apartment where nobody was aware of my comings and goings. It beats living with Uncle Jeremiah and Mammi Margaret, though," he added emphatically. "That was the alternative he offered me if I didn't sign the contract."

Gabe had wondered if there was more to the story behind the contract than Bishop Jeremiah had mentioned. Pete was old enough to go his own way, however, so Gabe was surprised that Bishop Jeremiah thought he could control his nephew's lifestyle . . . unless Pete was too broke to get by without his uncle's help.

Regina was standing in the aisle, waiting for Lydianne, so Gabe set aside his musings about Pete. "Hey there, Red!" he called out. "Did you convince your artist friend to rent a stall at The Marketplace?"

Her eyes widened as though the question had startled her. "*Jah*, I—I turned in his form at the meeting."

She seemed eager to get to the kitchen to help set out the meal. Gabe felt compelled to ask more questions about this English guy she might be dating, so he followed her closely along the crowded aisle. "I'm looking forward to meeting this fellow," he said. "His paintings are so life-like—"

"Oh, I doubt you'll ever see him," Red put in quickly. "He—Hartley's very shy. He doesn't like to be around when folks are talking about his work."

Hartley? What kind of a name is that? Sounds like a rich English snob, Gabe thought. He noticed how Red's auburn bun was quivering beneath her *kapp*.

"If he hears any criticism, he curls up in a ball and can't paint for days," Red continued with a shake of her head. "Artists are sensitive that way, you know."

"Who could possibly criticize the way he paints?" he

asked in a puzzled tone. "I'm no expert, but those pictures you showed us Wednesday were—well, they seemed like perfection on paper. His subjects appeared almost better than the real thing."

Regina's head swiveled quickly. When she looked at him, her hazel eyes were wide and her mouth was an O. "I'll tell him you said that," she whispered.

Gabe was suddenly aware of how close Red was standing—and how, when she hurried forward with the other women, he wished she hadn't seemed so intent on setting out the meal.

"So this artist's name is Hartley?" Glenn asked from behind him. "Do you suppose that's his first name or his last name? I'm curious about him—and about how Regina knows him."

"I have no idea," Gabe replied as he watched Red disappear into the kitchen. "You know as much about this guy as I do."

But I intend to find out more.

Regina clutched the baskets of bread she was carrying to the tables, hoping not to drop them and call more attention to herself. Her cheeks felt so hot, they surely had to be blazing red.

Perfection on paper.

Never had she heard such glowing remarks about her work—but then, she hadn't shown it to anyone since she'd completed her art classes years ago. She had to get a better grip on her emotions, and she had to keep track of what she told folks about her imaginary artist, Hartley Fox.

This wouldn't be a problem if you hadn't rented a space in the stable—and if you weren't lying to cover up your secret.

Gabe was setting up tables on the far side of the front room, and Regina made sure not to look at him. She remained among the other women before the meal and sat among her *maidel* friends, who were happily chatting about how they'd organize the bookkeeping and keep track of commissions when The Marketplace opened.

Jo seemed especially excited about their dream coming true. "I think I'll keep the larger items—like loaves of bread, and pans of cinnamon rolls, and cakes—in the shop on display racks," she said, "and I'll serve separate items like cookies and pastries out in the center area. I'll have to keep a big pot of coffee hot—"

"You should get one of those thirty- or sixty-cup coffee makers like we've seen in the bulk store," Marietta suggested. "The bishop says we'll have electricity—"

"And that way folks could serve themselves at a coffee counter," Molly put in. "It would leave you free to serve your goodies and collect all the money you're going to make!"

Jo waved the twins off. "Let's don't count our cash before it's in our hands," she said with a laugh. "We have a lot of logistics to figure out between now and June first."

Regina sighed inwardly. Her girlfriends had asked a few casual questions about Hartley, but they had *no idea* how many answers she had to make up before her shop opened, or how she'd have to control her facial features whenever she talked about him.

When she got home, Regina went up to gaze at the paintings hanging on the strings that crisscrossed her attic—and at the many bins of her older pictures. How much should she charge for her work? Which pictures should she take to the shop first? How would she keep explaining to her customers—and her friends—that she was selling these paintings on behalf of an artist who was too reclusive to face his customers?

Lord, I know You don't approve of what I've set myself up for, but I hope You'll help me keep my stories straight so I can earn a lot of commissions for the new schoolhouse, Regina prayed earnestly. *And then I hope You'll guide me out of this web of deception before anyone—especially me—gets caught in it.*

Chapter Seven

On the following Saturday, Jo convinced her *mamm* to ride to the stable with her to see how its reconstruction was progressing—and to help with the snack and the lunch the churchwomen were serving the construction crew. When Jo first caught sight of the stable, she sucked in her breath. The rumble of generators and the *zap-zap-zap* of nail guns filled the air as she drove their wagon through the open gate. Riley bounded out to greet them, barking exuberantly.

"Look at all the men up there! They've removed the old shingles and they're already putting on the new roof," she said excitedly. "They must've gotten an early start."

"Hush up! Stop that barking!" Mamm cried out, pointing at the golden retriever.

Riley's face fell, but he sat down quietly and let them drive past him.

Jo's mother gazed up at the men silhouetted against the morning's bright sky. "Some of those men are awfully old to be climbing around like monkeys," she remarked. "If somebody falls and gets hurt—"

"Let's figure that Pete has assigned the elderly, unsteady fellows to jobs on the ground," Jo said quickly. "See? Glenn's *dat* and Martin's older brothers are at the side of the stable, shoveling the torn-off shingles into that wagon.

Everyone here's excited about this project, Mamm, so let's be excited with them, shall we?"

Her mother shook her head as she determined that Reuben Detweiler and the Flauds—all of them in their seventies and eighties—were indeed cleaning up the debris. Jo parked beside the other flatbed wagons, where women were setting out a midmorning snack.

"Fine," Mamm muttered as she stepped down, "but I'll never understand why the church wants to take on all the responsibility of running shops in this old place. What if you can't get rid of the smell of horses and manure? Who'll want to buy all those pastries you're planning to bake, Josephine?"

Sighing inwardly, Jo focused on the smiles of the friends who'd already arrived. "Hey there, Anne! And Rose, it's *gut* to see you this morning—and you too, Gracie!" she added as Rose's blond daughter ran up to her.

"We baked brownies and sticky buns—and for lunch later, Mamma made a big ole pot of chili," Gracie blurted out. "And I helped!"

"Of course you did, sweetheart," Jo replied. "You're the best helper ever—and we're glad your *mamm*'s going to sell her candles in your *mammi*'s quilt shop, too."

"She says I can help in the store—until I get to start at the new school!" Gracie, who would soon turn six, beamed like the sun. "It's gonna be so much fun, Jo."

"*Jah*, it is. I loved school," Jo agreed as she took two pans of coffee cake from a box on the back of the wagon. She glanced at her mother, happy to see that she'd struck up a conversation with Martha Maude. After she cut the warm coffee cakes into large squares, she pulled the big cooler full of lemonade to the edge of the wagon and arranged some cups, plates, and forks near them.

Cora Miller, Preacher Clarence's wife, rang a cowbell

to get the workmen's attention. "Come on down for coffee and treats," she cried between blasts of their air drills.

As the men on the roof clambered down their long extension ladders, a few other fellows emerged from inside the stable. Glenn, Preacher Ammon, and Teacher Elam brushed cobwebs and sawdust from their hair as they approached. Jo noticed dark circles under Glenn's eyes and wondered if his wife—or baby Levi—had kept him up most of the night.

"Here's apple cinnamon and chocolate zucchini coffee cake," she offered. "Rose brought sticky buns and brownies, and there's plenty of coffee and lemonade. Looks like you fellows have made great progress this morning."

"Shoo! Get away from this food!" Jo's mother said, stomping her foot as Riley approached with a hopeful look on his face.

Glenn smiled as he lifted a large square of chocolate coffee cake onto a plate. "We hauled all the old hay out of the loft earlier this week, and we've swept out the entire interior," he said as Ammon and Elam nodded. "I suggest you put your office and some storage room upstairs, so the main floor will have more space for shops."

"*Jah*, the loft floor's solid, and you'll have a window or two up there," Preacher Ammon remarked as he poured coffee. "Wouldn't take much to put up a few walls and doors so you could close that area off."

"It would keep you warmer in the winter, too," Elam added. "And shoppers couldn't wander into your office."

Jo liked that idea. "I'll ask Lydianne what she thinks when she comes for the lunch shift."

Pete, Gabe, and the other men who'd been on the roof joined them, talking and laughing as they loaded their plates. Jo was pleased that so many men had come today, because they all worked well together—and because The

Marketplace would be ready for its grand opening. When Reuben stepped up to the cooler with his cup in one hand and a big brownie in the other, Jo pressed the spigot lever for him.

"What's Elva doing today?" she asked as he watched the liquid rising in his cup.

"Whatever she wants!" he replied without missing a beat. The men around them burst out laughing. It was a local joke that Reuben lost few opportunities to get out of the small *dawdi haus* at Glenn's place, where he and his out-spoken wife lived.

After Reuben gulped his lemonade, however, he sobered. "Truth be told, the wee one was fussy last night," he said softly. "Elva's looking after him and Billy Jay today while Dorcas gets some rest."

"Dat and I will head home in another hour or so to help her out," Glenn put in wearily, but then he brightened. "Before I leave, though, would you come inside and show me how you want things arranged? We can pace off the area for the shops and put down some markers so the rest of the crew knows what's going on if I can't be here all the time."

"We'll do that whenever you're ready, Glenn!" When Jo saw her mother nearby, she slipped an arm around her shoulders. "Would you like to go in with us, Mamm? It'll give you a better idea about—"

"It'll give me a nose full of dust and dirt, and I'll be sneezing the rest of the day," Mamm objected. "I'm not setting foot in there until the shops are ready to open—and even then, Josephine, I'll not be working in your bakery."

"*Jah*, so you've told me," Jo murmured patiently. "I've got ideas about who might help me—but meanwhile, Glenn, I'll give you all the help I can this morning."

About fifteen minutes later, the men were tossing their

plates and cups in the trash, thanking the women for the snacks. When Jo started toward the stable with Glenn, Preacher Ammon, Elam, and Martha Maude joined them— and so did Anne, Rose, and little Gracie.

"It'll be *gut* to get an idea of how much display space we'll have," Martha Maude remarked. "What with Lenore Otto joining us, we'll have quilts from the three of us, as well as tables and shelves for your candles, Rose."

"If we have room, we could put a quilting frame in the shop—or just outside it," Anne suggested as they all approached the stable doors. "I think folks would enjoy watching us work when we have a few spare minutes."

"What a great idea!" Jo agreed.

"And it'll help us keep up with our quilting so we'll have more pieces to sell," Martha Maude pointed out. "Our closets might empty out faster than we anticipate!"

As they stepped into the large building, Jo stopped to look all around her. The men had cleared a lot of debris and old straw since she'd sketched her floor plan, and with only the stalls remaining in place, it was much easier to picture how The Marketplace would take shape. She felt deliriously excited, even though a lot of work was still ahead of them.

"Can we reuse these sturdy beams and partitions?" she asked, running her hand along the top of a stall. "If we could clean up this wood—"

"We'd save a lot of money, and it would preserve the look of an old-fashioned stable," Glenn said with an enthusiastic nod. "If we follow your plan of having the shops in a U around three of the walls—mostly open, except for the stall dividers between them—and we put down some easy-to-clean flooring and paint the wood and the walls to freshen them up, that's all we'd really need to do, ain't so?"

"Let's keep it simple," Martha Maude agreed as she

walked partway down the center aisle. "This stable's a *lot* bigger inside than I'd imagined, so even the painting will cost us some cash. Will it look . . . underwhelming if we only have seven shops in here?"

Jo shrugged. "We have to start somewhere. I really like your idea about renting out the center space for parties—"

"Maybe, if store owners in town see how much room we have," Rose put in eagerly, "they'll rent space for some of their merchandise, too. Matthias might want to sell his leatherwork and saddles here."

"And who knows?" said Martha Maude. "Saul could park a wagon or two, or a buggy, here. A lot of English folks use farm wagons like we build in the carriage factory, after all, but they seldom come in to see what we Amish have to offer."

Gracie's face lit up as she grabbed her *mammi*'s hand. "And Dawdi could give the kids rides in his special carriages!" she sang out. "And I could ride up on top while he was drivin'!"

Everyone chuckled at the little girl's exuberance—but Jo could envision Gracie's idea as a big attraction on special days. Ordinary Plain buggies, farm wagons, and courting buggies were the bread and butter of Hartzler Carriage Company, but Saul also built very ornamental, specialized vehicles for theme parks and businesses that offered horse-drawn carriage rides around historic areas of their towns.

"That would be great fun, Gracie!" Jo said as the little girl hopped and whirled in circles around them. "This stable has given us a lot of inspiration—and *denki*, Glenn, for taking charge of our interior," she added. "It's going to be wonderful!"

"See where those red rags are tied?" he asked, gesturing toward the far side of the building. "I've marked off a space that's twenty by twenty. That'll be about right for my own shop—but how about for your kitchen area, Jo? And your quilt shop, Martha Maude?"

They crossed the concrete floor to the area Glenn had measured out. Jo tried to imagine ovens, a sink, and a refrigerator in place, as well as storage for her equipment and glass display cases for her baked goods. "I think this'll work for me if I make efficient use of the space," she said.

"And if we double this area in the corner, we'll have plenty of room to hang quilts," Martha Maude replied.

"If you need more display space for your goodies, Jo, you could put them on rolling shelves that you wheel out in front of your bakery," Rose suggested.

Jo nodded, trying not to become overwhelmed by the planning she had to do—and the equipment she'd need to purchase—in the next few weeks. "We all have a lot of ideas spinning in our heads now, ain't so?"

The *zap-zap-zap* of nail guns reverberated inside the stable as the men on the roof resumed their work, so the women took that as their cue to return to the wagons. Jo heard Riley barking again. As she followed the dog's progress toward the front gate, a couple of men she didn't recognize were approaching in a buggy.

"Do we need to ask Pete to keep his dog at home?" she asked her companions.

When the long-legged passenger of the buggy hopped down to play with Riley, however, Jo felt relieved that he hadn't been put off by the dog's ruckus. He was a nice-looking young man, slender yet muscular—and when the driver stepped down from the buggy, it was immediately apparent that they were father and son.

"Ah, it's the Wengerds!" Martha Maude said as she hurried in their direction. "Nelson and Michael, welcome! It's *gut* you could come today!"

"These guys own the nursery over near Queen City," Jo explained to Rose. They followed Martha Maude, who was gesturing toward the wagons where the refreshments had been laid out.

"We still have some goodies left—and lunch will arrive around noon," Martha Maude was saying. "Please help yourselves and we'll show you around. This is Rose Wagler—and Jo Fussner, who's managing The Marketplace. Jo, Nelson and Michael Wengerd have come to look things over."

Jo nodded at the two men, immediately liking their cordial smiles. "And this is my mother, Drusilla Fussner, who baked some of that coffee cake you see."

Mamm had been following the conversation with her usual scrutiny. She nodded at the Wengerds. "I'm surprised you fellows left your nursery on this fine Saturday. I'd think your store would be very busy now that spring's set in."

"You've got that right, Drusilla," Nelson said. When he smiled, dimples and laugh lines bracketed his mouth. "We wanted to see the stable today while it's open, so we left our assistants in charge."

"Ah. Your wife and daughters, no doubt," Mamm remarked.

Jo sighed. Would the Wengerds think her mother was impossibly nosy?

The men's faces fell a bit, however. "No, my Verna went to be with her Lord a couple of years ago," Nelson replied softly. "My daughter, Salome, married and moved to Ohio to live with her husband's family. We have a couple of young folks from our church who work for us through the busiest months."

"Well, we're glad you've come today," Jo put in quickly,

"and we're *really* glad you'll have flowers and vegetables to sell with us."

"Can't you picture the stable with its new black roof and black shutters, along with a fresh coat of rustic red paint—and window boxes of your colorful flowers?" Martha Maude asked as she gestured toward the building. "We think it'll be a big draw for folks passing by on the highway."

"Sounds fine to me," Nelson said. "We plan to bring hanging baskets, as well—"

"And we'll plant some flower beds around the building as soon as we know what the other plans for the grounds are," Michael added. "It's great that there's so much room for parking, and that we're outside of town where there won't be a lot of traffic noise. Morning Star's a bigger, busier city than I expected!"

Jo nodded. "It's basically an English town where we Amish and some Mennonites have found some affordable farmland to settle on," she said.

Nelson was studying the property immediately around the stable. "If possible, I'd like to position our flowers on the side of the building facing the road, and have space inside for selling gardening supplies and seeds," he said, pointing toward the end of the building. "Do you suppose I can use that door on the end? And have our shop space right inside there?"

"I'll write you into the floor plan," Jo said happily. "Nobody's spoken for space on that end yet."

Nelson's face lit up, and he looked years younger, pleased that his requests were already being granted. "What shall we plant in those window boxes to make them pop, Drusilla? What are your favorite summer flowers?"

Mamm looked stunned. Jo, too, was surprised at

Nelson's question—and secretly pleased that he'd managed to stump her mother.

"Well, you can't go wrong with geraniums," Mamm replied after a moment.

The Wengerds were both nodding. "The boxes will be in full sunlight," Michael pointed out, "so how about some white geraniums, purple petunias, and bright green sweet potato and vinca vines to hang down a bit—and big yellow and orange marigolds?"

Mamm blinked. "Sounds awfully flashy for a Plain—"

"A rainbow!" Jo blurted out. She was delighted that the nurserymen wanted to put such bright colors in their boxes, because her mother would've stopped with the geraniums.

"And if we build a pergola near the building for the hanging baskets, that'll give us more display space so customers can select what they'd like—and more color to attract folks from the road," Michael suggested.

Jo wasn't sure what a pergola was, but she really liked the way these men were thinking. "We'll have some wood you can use for that pergola after we dismantle some of the stalls inside the stable," she said. "Let's go inside so you can meet Glenn. He's remodeling the interior for us, so he—or our other foreman, Pete Shetler—can build whatever structures you'd like, once they've finished remodeling the stable."

As the rest of the morning passed, Jo was gratified by the sense of teamwork and excitement everyone shared. The Wengerds met people easily and talked with Glenn and the other men over Rose's chili and the creamy chicken and noodles the Helfing twins brought for the men's lunch. Delores Flaud and her girls stopped by with large bowls of fruit salad and coleslaw. Lenore Otto provided pies and a fresh urn of hot coffee, while Lydianne brought a big chocolate cake. Regina furnished wet wipes and trash bags, and she cleaned up after everyone ate.

By the time Pete and his men shut down their air compressors that afternoon, the stable's roof was covered with fresh black shingles. Glenn and his crew had removed the stall posts and gates, so they were ready to construct the basic skeleton of the shop area. Folks went home with a real sense of accomplishment.

"Let's stop at the bulk store for a few things," Mamm said as she took her place on the wagon seat beside Jo. "I've spent my whole day here, so I have no idea what we'll have for supper—or what to cook for tomorrow's meals, either."

Jo suppressed a sigh as she urged the horse forward. Her mother complained anytime her routine was interrupted, so her remark about cooking was probably the first of many to come. And Mamm seemed to forget that she wasn't the only capable cook in the family.

"Tell you what," Jo said as they turned onto the county highway. "I'll spring for supper in town, and we'll order enough extra food to take home for tomorrow. I'm celebrating how far we moved toward making a dream come true today!"

Mamm's glance was doubtful. "I'm glad this marketplace thing is *your* project and not mine! It could turn into a nightmare mighty fast if—"

"But what if The Marketplace becomes the best new thing Morning Star has seen in a long time?" Jo countered quickly. "Do you think Martha Maude and Glenn—and the Wengerds—would invest their time and effort if they didn't believe we'd succeed?"

Mamm looked off into the distance, temporarily silenced. When they'd parked at the Mennonite bulk store, they went inside and Mamm grabbed a grocery cart.

"Go ahead and start your shopping," Jo said. "I want to check the bulletin board."

After her mother headed down the produce aisle, Jo went to the corkboard that was covered with notices about upcoming events and items that were for sale. She immediately spotted a colorful sheet of paper with a photo of the stable on it. COMING SOON—THE MARKETPLACE! AMISH SHOPS AND LOCAL SPECIALTIES!

The stable photo had been enhanced with flower boxes and lush green grass—computer magic that made Jo even more enthusiastic about how wonderful Morning Star's new shopping area would be. Martha Maude had obviously instructed the printer to drum up excitement with the poster, and her heart was beating faster just from looking at it.

Another notice caught her eye, too. CAFÉ GOING OUT OF BUSINESS. MUST SELL ALL EQUIPMENT. The list included ovens, sinks, dishwashers—all the items Jo needed for her new bakery to be in compliance with the health department. The address was in Higher Ground, just a few miles down the road, so she dug a scrap of paper from her purse and jotted down the phone number.

Jo had no idea how she would pay for such equipment—and maybe it would be too large for her shop area—yet she sensed that God's hand had led her to the bulk store to find the sale notice. He had a way of providing what His children needed when they called on Him.

In her mind, Jo heard Bishop Jeremiah's voice. *If you don't ask, you probably won't receive. If you don't knock, who will know to open the door for you?*

"You've got it right, Bishop," she murmured as she caught up to her mother. "It'll all work out the way it's supposed to."

Chapter Eight

Two weeks later, Regina was amazed at how much had been accomplished at the stable. She'd been avoiding the work site so no one could quiz her about her mysterious artist friend—and because she'd been painting late into the evenings. Her fingers had been afire, as though a new and wonderful inspiration was prodding her to produce more pictures for her shop. She'd even painted the name of her store—NatureScapes—on an artsy, irregular piece of wood from the furniture factory's scrap box. She planned to hang it above the doorway.

"Can you believe how well everything's falling together?" Jo asked as Regina approached the center of the stable. "Next week at this time, we'll be open for business!"

"It looks awesome," Regina agreed as she gazed around. The shops were separated by open, slatted walls that resembled horse stalls, and they were painted a fresh shade of ivory. The flooring was imitation hardwood, and the stable's tall interior walls were painted a warm shade of beige. "The colors in here are quaint and homey," she remarked, "and they won't detract from the items we're selling,"

"Come see my kitchen!" Jo said, grabbing Regina's

elbow. "Pete and Glenn installed my equipment yesterday evening."

Regina waved at the Hartzler women, who were helping Glenn arrange long quilt poles on their walls. Gabe and his *dat* were pulling a cart loaded with tables and chairs through the double entry door, and the Helfing twins were painting the shelves in the shop next to Jo's.

"Who made your sign, Jo?" she asked, smiling up at the simple wooden oval with FUSSNER BAKERY carved into it.

"Glenn did. Isn't he just the handiest woodworker?" Jo replied happily. "And would you believe I found all this equipment at a little restaurant in Higher Ground? The owners wanted to liquidate everything quickly, so it only cost me half what I would've paid for new pieces."

Regina's eyes widened. Two lighted glass cases formed an attractive countertop. Behind it, a large stainless steel refrigerator stood against one wall, a deep sink was positioned near a dishwasher, and two ovens sat side by side opposite the fridge. Roller tables, stacks of baking pans, and other kitchen equipment were waiting to be put into place. This kitchen was far more efficient and modern than the one Jo and her mother had at home.

"Wow," Regina whispered as she stepped behind the glass cases for a closer look. "Your appliances look brand-new—and they're all electric."

"*Jah*, Bishop Jeremiah was okay with that because of the sanitation requirements—and because they're connected to our solar panels, with electrical backup," Jo explained. "*Please* don't tell Mamm, but I borrowed the money from the church to buy this stuff. Jeremiah and the preachers agreed to let me repay the loan each week from my sales."

"It's not as though any of us would have enough money

out of pocket to buy all this," Regina remarked. "And think of the possibilities for family gatherings and parties now, because you've provided folks a kitchen."

"That's the way Deacon Saul sees it, too—as an opportunity for more income." Jo grinned like a little kid at Christmas as she stood in the center of her new shop. "It's all falling into place, Regina—which makes me believe The Marketplace was meant to be. We five *maidels* were in the right place at the right time that Sunday afternoon we spotted the FOR SALE sign on the fence."

As Regina carried bins of her watercolor pictures into her shop, she thought about what Jo had said. If she and her friends had made good on a timely business opportunity, was it God's will that she should sell her paintings now?

You know that's not the way the Amish church sees it!

Sighing over the tug-of-war she'd had with her conscience the past few weeks, Regina began displaying her pictures on the back wall of her shop. Using little wads of poster putty on the upper corners of each sheet wasn't very professional, yet it seemed the most practical way to display groupings of unframed paintings—and it would be very easy to put up new pictures whenever she'd sold some. The pale beige wall at the back of her shop brought out the colors of nature in her paintings, and she became so caught up in arranging them that she didn't realize someone was standing behind her.

"These paintings look even better on the walls than they did at the meeting, Red."

Regina nearly jumped out of her skin before turning to face Gabe. "I—I was thinking the same thing," she stammered. "You scared the daylights out of me."

"Sorry. I didn't mean to interrupt your concentration." Gabe stepped over to look at the pictures she'd already hung. "I still think your artist friend should be here next week for our grand opening. What was his name again? I'd like to meet him."

Regina's heart pounded. She reminded herself to be calm, to give the responses she'd practiced so carefully at home. "His name's Hartley Fox—and besides being really shy, like I told you before, he has trouble getting around," she explained. "He—he's confined to a wheelchair, and his health issues keep him at home. Painting keeps him from going crazy."

"Ah. Artistic therapy, eh?" Gabe stepped closer to study a painting of a pair of mallard ducks. "His colors and brush strokes are amazing. This drake looks like he ought to fly right off the pond."

Regina focused on hanging pictures, hoping Gabe didn't notice her shaky hands. His praise was music for her soul to dance to, even if his nearness—and the way he studied her work so closely—was nerve-racking. She'd never dreamed that her shop foreman, a member of the Old Order, would have an interest in anything artistic.

She searched for a safer topic of conversation. "Did I see you and your *dat* bringing in tables and chairs for the entryway area? How'd they turn out?"

"Dat's really gung ho about them," Gabe replied with a chuckle. "He and I spent several hours putting them together so they'd be ready in time. I think he intends to be Jo's first customer when her shop opens Saturday morning, so he can sit at one of the tables with coffee and treats, watching the customers come in."

Regina smiled. "That might be a *gut* idea, so our shoppers know they're welcome to do that."

"Huh. I just noticed that Fox doesn't sign his work."

Regina's hands froze on a picture of a chipmunk. Just as she knew art for art's sake was a forbidden hobby for an Amish woman, she believed that signing her work was prideful—it would be yet another black mark against her, the way Old Order folks would see it. And it just seemed dangerous, having her name on so many forbidden paintings.

She cleared her throat, stalling. *What would Hartley give as an answer?*

It occurred to her that playing dumb was the most appropriate response for an Amish *maidel*. "Was he supposed to put his name on these?" Regina asked with a shrug. "I have no idea why he didn't."

Behind her, Gabe remained silent for several moments.

Had she said the wrong thing? Regina hung a couple more pictures, wishing he would find something better to do than scrutinize her.

"Well, Fox is a lucky man, having a *friend* like you to display his work—and who has a real knack for arranging it, too," Gabe remarked softly. "So . . . are you dating him, Red? If you are, I won't tell a soul—I mean, with him being English and all."

When Regina spun around, Gabe was standing so close that she nearly bumped into him. Her face was blazing, and he could surely see how his remark had caught her off guard. "Of course I'm not! What kind of question is that?"

Regina caught a flicker of emotion on Gabe's handsome face that she couldn't name. He backed away, as though he suddenly realized he was standing so close that he could . . . kiss her.

The idea of kissing him made her mouth drop open. She clamped it shut again, dismissing such a ridiculous notion. Gabe Flaud was desirable enough to court any young woman he wanted, yet his social life was a complete mystery to her. The way she had him figured, he was keeping plenty of his own secrets. And he would never be interested in a plain Jane who wore faded, stained clothes and a kerchief every day, much less in kissing her.

"You're right, Red," he murmured. "That was a nosy question, and I had no right to insinuate that you'd do anything forbidden. I'm sorry."

When Gabe left her shop, his footfalls echoed in the large, central area of the stable. Soon she heard the rhythmic clicking of table legs locking into place. When Regina glanced out her door a little while later, about a third of the stable's entryway was set up with square tables and folding chairs that shone in the glow of the gas-powered light fixtures suspended from the high ceiling.

Gabe had left the building, apparently. Regina relaxed, breathing deeply to settle her jittery nerves.

She set the remaining bins of her pictures in a corner. When she came again, she would bring some simple tables to set the bins on so customers could flip through the pictures—assuming anyone would come in and look at them. Deep in the fragile recesses of her artist's heart, she still allowed for the possibility that no one would think her paintings were special enough to pay for.

When she heard Gabe and Martin's voices—saw that they were hauling in furniture to display in the shop next to hers—Regina quickly headed down the short hallway by the restrooms and out the building's back exit. Why had she ever volunteered to oversee the Flaud Furniture shop, anyway?

No, that was a perfectly honorable thing to do. The real question is why you opened a shop for your paintings—and how long you think you can get away with selling them.

Chapter Nine

By seven o'clock on the morning of June first, Jo had slipped two large pans of brownies into one of her ovens and was spooning peanut butter cookie dough onto other pans. She wanted the building to smell like homemade goodies when the doors opened at nine—and she planned to have her day's baking done by then so she could focus on her customers.

"Hey there, Jo!" Molly called out as she and her sister entered the adjacent shop with boxes of their bagged flat noodles. "Are we ready for this?"

"We'd better be, *jah*?" Marietta teased. "Everything looks really nice!"

"When did the Wengerds get the flower boxes planted?" Molly asked. "Nothing looks prettier than colorful flowers against a red building, ain't so?"

"Those hanging baskets on either side of the door are gorgeous, too," her sister put in.

Jo spooned the last few balls of cookie dough onto the pan. "Pete and some of the other men spray painted the building on Wednesday and Thursday," she replied. "Nelson and Michael did their planting yesterday afternoon, and they stayed the night in our *dawdi haus* so they could be here early today for the grand opening. It saved them from getting up in the wee hours to drive from Queen City."

After Molly set down her boxes, she peered between the wooden slats that separated the Helfings' shop from Jo's. "Really now?" she teased. "And what did Drusilla think about *that*?"

Jo laughed. "Well, it was a night's rental income," she pointed out. "I think Mamm was happy to make their breakfast, knowing they'd head home after The Marketplace closes today. Pretty easy, having guests who eat and then leave to go about their business, you know."

Marietta laughed. "*Jah*, there's that—and then there's Pete, who gets home from his job when most folks are starting their day."

"And how's that working out by now?" Jo glanced between the slats to watch the twins stock one of their shelves. She wondered if the Helfings were having second thoughts about a renter with a noisy pickup—and a boisterous dog—intruding upon their peaceful daily routine. Although Bishop Jeremiah had asked the twins about moving his nephew to their place, he hadn't left them much chance to say no.

Molly and Marietta shrugged at the same time. "He's been busy working here at the stable during his off hours these past few weeks," Marietta pointed out.

"We'll see how it goes now that he's finished with The Marketplace," Molly continued. "At least he fulfilled his commitment here, so folks know he can be reliable when he puts his mind to it."

Jo nodded as she slid the filled cookie sheets into her second oven. "Could be Bishop Jeremiah will get him started on the new schoolhouse—"

"Did someone say my name?" a loud voice called out from the stable's central area.

Jo laughed as the bishop peered first into the noodle shop and then into her bakery. "*Gut* thing we have only complimentary things to say about you, *jah*, Bishop?" she teased. "Are you here to be our very first customer?"

Jeremiah stepped up to the glass display cases and scrutinized Jo's pies and cupcakes. "I came to congratulate you all," he replied, "and to wish you a *gut* grand opening. I stand amazed at what you gals and our construction crews have accomplished here in a very short time. We've got a sunny Saturday, and I predict we'll have more shoppers today than any of us have anticipated."

"*Denki* for all you've done to help make this place possible," Jo said.

From the adjacent shop, the twins agreed. "You convinced our church members to go along with our original idea," Molly put in. "You could've told us we were getting too big for our britches—"

"Or you could've shut down the whole idea of The Marketplace before we even got started," Marietta finished. "Help yourself to a bag of egg noodles or lasagna or flat dumplings before you leave today!"

"And your first pastry or cookie or slice of pie is on me, too," Jo put in eagerly.

Bishop Jeremiah chuckled. "I'll collect on your offers at the end of the day—if you have anything left," he added. "I'll go say hello to Glenn and our quilters, and see you ladies later. If I can help you somehow—get more change at the bank, or whatever you need—I'll be around."

As her oven timer dinged, Jo called out her thanks again. "I'll be coaching your nieces soon, and I think they'll be excellent help."

Laughter rang in the back hallway, which shop owners would be using as their entrance before hours. Alice and Adeline Shetler—Jude and Leah's daughters—entered the bakery with bright smiles that immediately confirmed Jo's decision to hire them.

"Are you ready to welcome folks today?" she asked as the seventeen-year-old twins studied the baked goods in the glass case. "In those apple green dresses and white aprons, you look as fresh and pretty as our new flower boxes! Our English customers will be delighted that you're greeting them—and you'll be allowing me to handle the sales and the restocking."

"What exactly would you like us to do, Jo?"

As she gazed at the identical expressions on their flawless, slightly freckled faces, Jo wasn't sure if it had been Alice or Adeline who'd spoken. With their reddish-brown hair tucked under fresh *kapps* and their trim, feminine figures modestly covered in new cape dresses, the Shetler twins were everything Jo had never been: attractive and outgoing. Before they'd joined the church a few months earlier, they'd caused their *dat* and their beleaguered new step*mamm* all manner of heartache, running around with troublesome English boys during their *rumspringa*.

Their experiences in the outside world had given Alice and Adeline a confidence that would make them the perfect hostesses, however. And by hiring them to work in a Plain environment, Jo was giving them some worthwhile responsibilities—and a chance to earn spending money.

"If you girls will serve our shoppers coffee and goodies out in the central commons area, and collect the money—and keep the tables clean," Jo replied, "you'll be doing every one of our shopkeepers a favor. Where else in Morning Star can folks chat over treats, shop for specialty items, and support our new schoolhouse, all at the same time?"

The sisters smiled, nodding. "So you'd like us be waitresses, mostly?"

"And bus girls?"

"And friendly faces," Jo said. "We'll attract some folks who've never dealt directly with the Amish, and we want them to feel welcome—and to come back!"

Alice and Adeline grinned at each other. "It's the same sort of thing we do at Dat's auctions—" one of them began.

"—except we're getting paid for it!" her sister finished.

Jo laughed along with them, noting that this set of twins shared an effortless, unspoken communication system like the Helfings did. "Let me show you how the big coffee makers work so you can start the second one if we need it," she said as she led them out of the shop. "The cups, plates, and dish bins are out here in the cabinet. And you'll be responsible for replenishing the supply of cookies and pastries in this area."

"Wow, it already smells like coffee and brownies out here," one of the girls said, sniffing the air.

"We'll be starting that second coffee maker sooner rather than later," her sister put in. "Folks all over town have been talking about The Marketplace and how they plan to come out here today!"

Jo sighed happily. "That's exactly what I wanted to hear."

Around eleven, Gabe glanced between the slats that separated Flaud Furniture's shop from NatureScapes. His *dat* was chatting up a couple who were shopping for a new dining room set, and Red was slipping a trio of paintings into a paper sack for a happy customer—so neither of them noticed that he was once again spying on the young woman who'd piqued his curiosity.

He wasn't a bit surprised that Red had been too busy in Hartley Fox's shop to help in his as she'd originally intended.

Gabe *was* amazed, however, at how the quiet young woman who stained furniture in his factory every weekday had come out of her shell once folks began exclaiming over the watercolors on her walls. He'd never seen Red smile so much, although he wondered how she'd become so knowledgeable about the paintings she was selling. Her customers listened, caught up in her explanations of the animals and countryside scenes Hartley Fox had rendered so perfectly. More often than not, they bought the piece Red had told them about.

A few moments later, Lydianne returned from her short break. She'd been helping him and his *dat*, and she'd occasionally slipped over to handle Red's cash box when customers were lined up to buy artwork.

"This place is *swarming* with shoppers!" she exclaimed as she came to stand beside him. "The Wengerds' hanging baskets are selling like crazy, and Glenn's wood shop is crowded—and I just saw a lady leaving the Hartzlers' shop with *two* quilts."

Gabe nodded. "It didn't take Dat but half an hour to declare that renting space here was the best thing he's done for the business in a long while," he remarked. "We've already sold both bedroom sets in our display, and we've taken some orders for tables, chairs, and hutches."

"And who knew that there was an artist nearby painting such beautiful nature scenes?" Lydianne asked as she, too, peered between the slats into the NatureScapes shop. "Of course, I don't know many English folks around here well enough to—"

"This Hartley guy's making money hand over fist today," Gabe remarked softly. He wondered if he should quiz Lydianne about her best friend's connection to Fox, but he didn't want her to think he was interested in Red. Ultimately, however, his curiosity won out.

"So, do you know anything about Red's artist friend?"

he asked nonchalantly. "She's told me he's in a wheelchair and his other health issues keep him at home."

Lydianne shrugged. "Before we opened these shops, I hadn't heard a word about him. I've been as surprised as everyone else that she knows an artist."

At the sound of voices entering the shop, Gabe turned. "Ah—better get back to work. Looks like Dat's writing up another order."

For the next hour, he greeted the people who came into the shop and gave them the details about what species of wood they were seeing, or about how the furniture from the family-owned Flaud factory was all meticulously finished by hand. When he mentioned that Lydianne was one of their finishers, folks seemed even more impressed with the display pieces and with what they saw in the Flaud Furniture catalog.

Around twelve thirty, there was a lull in the traffic. Gabe had planned to get coffee and goodies from the Shetler twins—until Bishop Jeremiah showed up with sandwiches and soft drinks for all the shopkeepers.

"You folks haven't even had time to eat your lunch!" he said as he entered the shop with his wheeled cooler and his insulated bag of sandwiches. "Feeding you is the least I can do, considering how much money you've raised for the schoolhouse already."

"It's been incredible," Gabe agreed as he chose a thick roast beef sandwich and a can of cola.

"You can say that again!" his *dat* chimed in as he approached them. "I had my doubts about whether all our work on this dilapidated stable would be worthwhile, but today's sales have made me a believer."

"I've heard the same thing from every shopkeeper here," Bishop Jeremiah said as he sat down at a dining room table with them. "Nelson and Michael don't have a lot left to sell this afternoon, so they'll be taking orders for what they'll bring next Saturday. The Helfing twins are planning to double their noodle production this week, too."

"Sales during the warmer months will be a lot better than in the winter," Gabe's *dat* pointed out as he unwrapped a fat pastrami sandwich. "After all, how much can the Wengerds sell after they've harvested their vegetables and closed down their greenhouses for the season?"

"Michael's on it!" the bishop replied with a chuckle. "He's already talking about expanding into hothouse tomatoes and maybe even hydroponic crops. Seems our shopkeepers are considering ideas they would never have dreamed of before today's success—and to God be the glory for that! Tomorrow's church service will be a real celebration."

As they ate their sandwiches, Gabe and his father took turns greeting customers. Around four thirty the crowd thinned out and the noise level in the commons area died down. Gabe decided to chat with Red about how her day had gone.

She wasn't in her shop, however—and Gabe couldn't help but notice several blank spaces on her walls. He caught sight of her at one of the empty tables out front, resting her head on her folded arms while the Shetler twins tidied up around her.

"Hey there, Red—you okay?" he asked as he slid into the chair across from her.

Her low groan worried him, until she raised her head. "I have never been so tired in my entire life," she murmured, although she was smiling. "Who knew I'd sell so many of—of Hartley's paintings today? I haven't even had time to tally up the sales."

"Maybe you should hire help, like Jo did," he suggested. "Or I could pay a fellow from the shop to come in each

Saturday, and Lydianne can be your full-time assistant. Would that work for you?"

Red's grateful expression made his insides tingle, a reaction he wasn't expecting. "I appreciate your understanding, and your offer, Gabe. I really did intend to help in your shop today."

He shrugged, unable to look away from her hazel-eyed gaze. "I didn't want to miss the grand opening—and Dat was having so much fun, I didn't tell him to sit down," he remarked. "Won't surprise me if he dozes off during the sermons tomorrow."

Her soft laughter teased his senses. "I might do that myself. I'm heading straight home to put my feet up—and I'll probably fall asleep in my recliner."

Gabe had the sudden urge to drive her home—to pick up some carryout on the way and be sure she ate something while she relaxed. He pictured himself staying with her for most of the evening, even if he'd be across her front room, at a safe distance.

Safe distance? Since when have you kept your distance from a woman who attracted you?

Gabe blinked. He had no idea where such thoughts were coming from. And dating an employee would be a bad idea.

Since when have you wanted to date Red? If the guys at the shop find out, they'll give you no end of grief about it. And her closest male relative is a preacher. Do you really want to go down that road?

Gabe stood up before he could do something dangerously impractical, such as asking Red if she'd join him for dinner in town sometime soon. "Well—see you tomorrow for church," he said, noting how thin and adolescent his voice sounded. "Rest well tonight, Red."

Chapter Ten

Rest was the furthest thing from Regina's mind when she got home. She was achingly, desperately exhausted, but she was too excited to kick back in her recliner. While she ate a quick peanut butter and jelly sandwich at her cluttered kitchen table, she totaled her day's sales.

Her sandwich lay forgotten on her plate as she gaped at the final figures. She'd charged what she considered exorbitant prices—perhaps secretly hoping no one would buy her work, so she could close her shop before she got caught at her painting and the lies that covered it. Even so, Regina's customers had insisted that other artists charged far more. They'd snapped up entire groupings of her ducks, flowers, and other natural subjects.

According to the receipts she'd scribbled out, she'd sold forty-eight seven-by-ten-inch paintings for fifty dollars apiece, and twenty-two that measured fourteen by twenty, for which she'd charged a hundred dollars. When Regina counted the money in her cash box, the amount she'd collected matched the receipts she'd be handing over to Jo and Lydianne for their records.

She was absolutely stunned. *Four thousand six hundred dollars!*

Who could believe she'd sold so many paintings in a single day? She'd been telling herself not to be disappointed if no one bought her work, so Regina felt elated beyond belief—and she grabbed her pad of watercolor paper and her sketching pencil.

As she sat in her recliner with her feet up, she quickly blocked out several scenes that were similar to the ones she'd sold. Because she painted the final details on a whim, no two pictures were ever alike, even though several might be of the same animals or flowers or barn. Many of her customers had remarked that they loved her four-seasons paintings—such as the same horse barn and silo painted with autumn foliage, with snow, with the bright yellow-greens of springtime, and with the contrasting sunshine and shade of a summer afternoon.

Regina sketched quickly, on instinct, so the outlines of animal forms, rustic fencerows, and trees appeared without much effort. The idea was to build up a stack of sketches she could paint this week—starting Monday, because Sunday was a day of rest. Even though her painting was forbidden no matter when she did it, Regina believed it was best to observe the Sabbath.

She was too tired to paint, but when she carried her sketches up to the attic, she thumbed through her bins, picking out pictures to display on the following Saturday. After she'd chosen about a hundred, Regina realized how few paintings remained in her bins. It gave her the incentive to work very hard every evening so she'd have enough pictures for customers to choose from in the future.

Regina went to bed with a big smile on her face. She prayed for God's forgiveness even as she hoped He would be so pleased with her contribution toward the schoolhouse that He would overlook the way in which she was earning it . . . and the lies she was telling her friends.

Weary as she was, however, sleep eluded her. In her mind, Regina kept replaying her conversation with Gabe. It had seemed perfectly ordinary on the surface, yet his body language had sent messages she hadn't read before. He'd seemed concerned because she was tired, yes, but he'd also acted . . . *interested*, in her as much as in her paintings.

It would be a dream come true if Gabe wanted to court me, she thought as she tossed and turned. *But why now? If he gets too close, or asks too many questions, it'll mean big trouble.*

Regina went to the kitchen for a drink of cold water. As she stood by the open window, letting the night air soothe her, she sensed she needed to create several more convincing details about Hartley Fox to keep Gabe and her girlfriends from ferreting out the truth.

The next morning at church, Jo's hips and leg muscles reminded her that she'd spent a long Saturday standing on hard floors. But who could allow aches and pains to overshadow the huge success she and her friends had enjoyed at the grand opening?

After Bishop Jeremiah gave the benediction, he called a Members Meeting. "What a day we had at The Marketplace yesterday!" he crowed as he gazed at the nodding congregation. "It was a fine grand opening for our shopkeepers, and it was *gut* to see a lot of you there to support them—not to mention hundreds of our Mennonite friends and English customers."

"Do we have any idea how much the shops grossed yesterday?" Deacon Saul asked. "While I was there in the morning, I saw a great many quilts, bags of noodles, and wood items being carried out—not to mention hanging baskets and the treats folks consumed in the commons arca."

Jo held up her file box with a grin. "Lydianne and I just received some of the shops' receipts this morning before church, so we haven't tallied an exact figure—"

"But because we sold several big-ticket items like furniture sets and quilts, we took in thousands and *thousands* of dollars," Lydianne chimed in.

"We ran out!" Molly crowed. "Every last bag of our soup noodles and lasagna flew out of the store!"

"And I sold more chairs, rocking horses, and small toys in one day than I usually sell in a month at the store in Willow Ridge," Glenn put in happily.

"We quilters are very pleased with how many of our pieces sold, too," Martha Maude said. "And Rose's candles were a big hit."

Chuckling, Saul held up a pocket calculator. "Just for fun, we could do a quick accounting so folks would know how much commission we collected for the schoolhouse by the time they've finished eating," he suggested. "Or, because this is Sunday, should we hold off until tomorrow? Your call, Bishop."

Jeremiah pondered the deacon's question as he glanced at the eager faces around him. "Considering how excited we are about our new venture, I guess it wouldn't hurt— just this once—to do a little math on the Sabbath."

"*Jah!* You number crunchers go to it!" Martin called out. "You're excused from setting up tables and setting out the food today."

Laughter filled the room as folks stood up. Jo glanced down the row to catch Regina's eye. "Got your receipts?" she asked beneath the chatter that surrounded them.

"*Jah.* Am I the last one?" Regina pulled a couple of bundles of paper from her handbag. "Sorry I didn't get these to you sooner. I was brain-fried when I got home yesterday."

"You had a lot of folks in your shop," Jo agreed as she

accepted the receipts. "I was so busy keeping my glass cases and the goodies out in the commons replenished, I didn't have a chance to visit with you."

"You're smart to have the Shetler girls helping you," Regina remarked. "Who knew I'd have so much traffic in my—Hartley's—shop."

"Gabe suggested that I help you out," Lydianne put in from behind Jo. "I'll be happy to do that, if you'd like me to."

As Jo made her way toward the aisle, she wondered why Regina had been so subdued all morning, and why she looked as if she hadn't gotten any sleep. Maybe Regina's pale complexion made her exhaustion more obvious—or maybe she was coming down with a summer bug. Considering all the people they'd been around at the grand opening, she could've caught something. Saul was gesturing at Jo so eagerly, however, she didn't have a chance to ask Regina if she was all right.

Church had been held in the Hartzlers' large home, so Saul led her and Lydianne into his office at the back of the house. Jo wasn't surprised that the deacon immediately took charge of the receipt tallying. He already had his hand out as he sat down behind his big walnut desk.

Jo gave him Regina's receipts first. "Ordinarily, Lydianne will take care of the accounting, you know," she remarked politely as the two of them sat down.

"*Jah*, we've got a desk, file cabinets, and a calculator in our office at The Marketplace," Lydianne added.

Saul's fingers flew over the keys of the small calculator as he flipped over one receipt after another. "I'm sure you'll do a fine job of it," he murmured. "But as the district's deacon, I'm ultimately responsible for what we collect for the church district—to repay what we've invested in the stable's renovation, and to build the new schoolhouse."

Jo glanced at Lydianne. They both knew Lydianne was

a competent bookkeeper—just as they knew better than to challenge Saul's insistence on totaling Saturday's income.

"Well now!" the deacon said as he rebundled Regina's receipts. "That artist fellow took in forty-six hundred dollars, which means four hundred and sixty for us. I'll have to check out his pictures next Saturday, to see what all the fuss is about."

"He paints beautiful nature scenes and animals," Jo remarked as she handed Saul the receipts from Quilts and More.

"And it's nice that he's already covered his shop rent," the deacon said as his fingers clicked the keys again. "With those artsy types, you never can tell. Let Regina—and your other shopkeepers—know that their monthly rent should come out of their income on the first Saturday of each month. Just so everybody's clear about the payment date."

Once again Jo and Lydianne glanced at one another as Saul did his figuring. "Don't forget that we've agreed to forgo the first six months' rent for Glenn and Jo because of all the carpentry and setup work they've done," Lydianne reminded him in a low, firm voice. "And the Helfings are doing our cleaning, so they don't pay rent, either."

Saul let out a whistle. "All hail and hallelujah!" he said with a chuckle. "My wife and my mother have finally found a way to make a profitable hobby from all that fabric they buy! It's a fine thing they do, donating lap robes to folks in the senior center, but I'm happy to see some return for the hundreds of dollars of quilting materials I've paid for over the years."

Jo held her tongue. She could imagine Martha Maude's reaction if her son had made the same remark to *her*—and it seemed like one more good reason not to get married. A husband would probably say the same thing about all the flour, sugar, and other ingredients she and Mamm bought for their baked goods—even if baking was the way they supported themselves.

Of course, if you had a husband, you wouldn't have to work to keep a roof over your head. You could quilt or do whatever you enjoyed during your spare time, the way Martha Maude and Anne do.

Jo reminded herself not to envy the Hartzler women— or to feel disappointed about never getting married. What with renting out their *dawdi haus* and selling their produce, eggs, and baked goods, she and her mother got by just fine, and they didn't have to answer to a man. It was a situation that suited her *mamm* as much as it did Jo, so she saw no reason to change it.

Within fifteen minutes Saul had completed his calculations. He handed Jo the stacks of receipts with a satisfied smile. "Twenty-five thousand three hundred and fifty dollars," he announced, "which means two thousand five hundred and thirty-five dollars in commission for the district. Congratulations, ladies! We had a very profitable day!"

Lydianne sucked in her breath. "We did!"

"Wow," Jo murmured, rising from her chair. "Aren't we glad the Flauds agreed to sell furniture with us? Most of that money probably came from their sales—"

"Don't you dare underestimate your own contribution," Lydianne insisted softly as she followed Jo out of the office. "You and the Helfings and Glenn and Regina— everybody at The Marketplace—made our success possible. And it was *your* idea, Jo. Remember?"

Jo slung her arm around her friend as they stepped out into the front room, where folks were just beginning to eat. "I guess it was," she murmured. "We *maidels* can accomplish amazing things when we put our minds to it, ain't so?"

Chapter Eleven

The next two Saturdays, Gabe marveled at the continuing customer traffic at The Marketplace. During a lull at the furniture shop, he headed outside to chat with Nelson and Michael Wengerd—very pleasant fellows who arrived each week with lush hanging baskets in a riot of colors that attracted folks in from the road. They had some pint boxes of produce on a table in the shade as well.

"Has it been worth your time to sign on here in Morning Star?" Gabe asked them. "It's a bit of a drive from Queen City, *jah*?"

Nelson shrugged amiably. "We come in on Friday afternoons so we have time to unload and arrange our stock," he explained. "Makes it pretty handy that we can stay in the Fussners' *dawdi haus*—"

"And we get much better meals than we would cook for ourselves at home!" Michael put in with a laugh. "We were happy to see the posters Martha Maude's going to put around town advertising our first produce auction on the twenty-ninth. By then our garden plots will be putting out a lot of veggies."

"What with other area farmers bringing produce as well, it should attract a lot of buyers," Nelson remarked as he watched cars turn in off the county highway. "Might depend on the weather, as to whether we drive in for every Saturday during the winter. We've decided to build some special greenhouses for hothouse tomatoes and other fresh produce you couldn't otherwise grow in the colder months."

"It's *gut* to try something different," Michael remarked, waving as folks approached them. "And we like meeting all these new people as well."

Nodding, Gabe let the Wengerds greet their customers. Back in the building, he saw Bishop Jeremiah and his *dat* sipping coffee and eating brownies at one of the tables in the commons area. He was glad one of the men from the shop was coming in to help for a few hours midday, so his father wouldn't be on his feet for so long. Gabe waved as he passed Glenn's wood shop. His friend appeared pale and drawn, which made Gabe wonder if Dorcas or the new baby might not be doing so well.

He told himself to return to the furniture shop—so Red wouldn't think he'd rather spend time with *her*—yet his feet went their own way. As Red and Lydianne rang up a nice four-seasons collection featuring a buck, a doe, and a fawn, Gabe admired the artwork on the shop's walls. When the bishop came in to stand beside him, he glanced up.

"This guy's paintings are really something," Jeremiah said, stooping for a closer look at a pair of wood ducks on a pond. "If I were one to hang artwork on my walls, I'd certainly buy a few of these watercolors."

"Dat says the same thing," Gabe remarked. Amish folks didn't display a lot of decorative stuff in their homes. They hung calendars and clocks, mostly, along with a list of family members beside the front door, because those served a purpose and reinforced the importance of each and every member of a family. "For a guy who's got health problems and is confined to a wheelchair, he has a real talent—and he gets a *lot* of painting done."

Bishop Jeremiah nodded, scrutinizing a few of the pictures. "I don't know much about art, but I thought it was customary for the artist to sign his work."

Gabe recalled mentioning that subject to Red, and the way she'd acted as though she wasn't aware of such a tradition. He didn't respond to the bishop—because he was too engrossed in watching the animated way Red's hands moved and the radiance of her face as she spoke to a customer.

How does Red seem to know every little thing about these watercolor paintings—and the way Fox portrays his nature subjects—yet she's not aware of the signature thing?

Gabe's doubtful thoughts flew from his mind when Red caught him watching her. He waved, hoping he didn't look like a lovestruck puppy.

"*Gut* afternoon, Bishop—and Gabe," she added breezily. "Looks like we're all having another great day."

It would be an even greater day if you'd join me for dinner—

Gabe caught himself before he could say those words out loud. He'd have to be very careful if he wanted to come across as a fellow worth dating instead of a clueless kid. "We haven't moved as much furniture today as we did that first Saturday," he remarked, "but I figure any exposure to potential customers is *gut* exposure."

Was Red chuckling at his choice of words, maybe getting private ideas about *exposure*? Why had he used that word twice? Or did she look so fetching in her rust-colored dress and her fresh *kapp* that he'd been temporarily *ferhoodled*? "So how's it going for *you* today, Red?" he asked quickly.

"You've had a constant stream of folks in your shop—well, Fox's shop—all day."

"Are you sure we couldn't convince your artist friend to make an appearance?" Bishop Jeremiah put in. "Everybody's eager to meet him."

Red flushed, shaking her head. "I—I asked him about that earlier this week when I went to pick up more of his pictures," she replied quickly. "Now that he's selling so much of his work, he—he says he has to stay home and paint more!"

"Ah. Well, give him our best," the bishop said.

Gabe sensed he should get back to his own store before he said something moronic. "See you, Red," he murmured. He waved at Lydianne, who was placing more paintings on the walls.

What was it that didn't seem right? Why did Red's responses feel half a beat off?

And why have the lights been burning in her attic every evening you've walked past her house? What's going on with her?

It was a question Gabe couldn't ask aloud, because Red would know he'd been acting like a schoolboy with a big crush on her. And if he admitted that his evening strolls had become more frequent—and that they always took him past her home on Maple Lane—she'd think he was spying on her. Or stalking her.

After he'd closed up shop and handed the day's receipts to Jo, Gabe drove Dat home. They had church the next morning, so his *mamm* and two sisters were in the kitchen preparing a couple of dishes to share at the common meal while they put the finishing touches on a supper of pork chops, fried apples, and baked potatoes.

Lorena and Kate looked up from the fresh snicker-doodles and brownies they were arranging in lidded containers. "How'd you do today? Was The Marketplace busy?" fourteen-year-old Lorena asked.

"One of these Saturdays we want to come and shop!" Kate declared, glancing at their mother. "Mamm kept us busy washing the rugs and curtains today."

Gabe chuckled, snatching a cookie from Kate's bin. At nearly thirteen, she was a younger version of their plump mother, while coltish Lorena favored their tall, slender *dat*. "We did well, and we were glad to have Harvey Shetler spelling us for a few hours this afternoon," he remarked. "Maybe come winter, when the customers thin out, you girls can be our helpers—"

"We'll *discuss* that before we get anybody's hopes up," Mamm interrupted him in a purposeful tone. "I don't like the idea of young girls working amongst so many English—at least not until they're out of school."

When his sisters' faces fell, Gabe winked at them. "Mamm's probably right about that part," he admitted. "But there's no reason you couldn't go in with Dat and me for a while some Saturday to look around, and then somebody could bring you home."

"Or we girls could *all* ride in with you men some Saturday, see the new shops, and then take the buggy into town to buy dress fabric before school starts," Mamm said as she removed the big skillet of pork chops from the stove top. "No reason for the mare to stand around all day waiting for you."

Dat took his place at the head of the table. "She won't. The shopkeepers' horses graze in the pasture under some shade trees," he explained, "and Pete's putting up a pole barn for them soon. We'll put that barn to *gut* use during our auctions—and when the scholars drive their ponies to school, too."

Mamm set the platter of sizzling chops near Dat's place

and fetched the bowl of fried apples. "Sounds like you figure to be at The Marketplace every Saturday for a long time to come," she remarked. "Do you really want to spend so much time there after you've put in a full week at the furniture factory, Martin?"

As Gabe took his seat, his parents continued their conversation. Mamm had been hinting for the past few months that Dat should retire, but his father was having none of that—because he preferred spending his time with the men in the factory to being at home, where his wife would come up with chores he didn't really want to do.

After their prayer, Gabe filled his plate and ate without saying much. Dat was regaling Mamm and the girls with gossip he'd heard at The Marketplace, so Gabe's mind wandered to what seemed to be his favorite subject of late. What would Red be eating for supper? Would she spend her Saturday evening alone—or had she taken Hartley the money he'd earned on his paintings? If Gabe stopped by her place, would she welcome him in for a glass of lemonade? Or would she beg off, finding reasons not to spend time with him after hours?

Only one way to find out.

After he'd eaten a couple of his sisters' brownies, Gabe slipped into the bathroom to check his appearance in the mirror. He doubted Red would care if he put on a clean shirt, but on the off chance that he'd see her, he did it anyway. He slipped through the front room, where Dat was absorbed in the *Budget*, and out the front door before Mamm noticed he was leaving. Living at home with his family meant he couldn't come and go in total privacy—and sooner or later, he'd have to answer some questions about his after-supper destination.

What would his parents say about his strolling past Red's place, hoping to see her? Would Dat insist it was bad business to date an employee? Would Mamm bombard him with questions about whether he was courting Red with the intention of marrying her? His mother was eager to see him hitched and starting a family—

And what would Red say to that? She doesn't seem to hanker for the traditional Amish lifestyle, or she wouldn't work in the furniture factory, right?

Gabe strolled quickly toward the county blacktop that marked the city limit of Morning Star, which bustled with car traffic and folks going out for Saturday night supper. He turned down Maple Lane and stopped when Red's house came into view. It was a red brick bungalow—a single-story home with a pillared front porch beneath what was most likely an attic.

It had been an English house in the countryside when Red's father, Fred Miller, had bought the place, and it sat on a couple of acres of land, which he'd fenced as a pasture for the horses. Because Fred didn't farm—and because the babies that had come after Regina hadn't survived long— the house and the property had been just the right size for the three of them. After Fred and Edna had died in that horrific bus accident, Red's insistence on remaining in her home alone had been yet another choice that set her apart from most young Amish women.

Gabe recalled that Preacher Clarence and Cora had made quite a fuss about their niece keeping her house, be- cause it gave her too much independence—and because living in the country alone left her vulnerable. They'd objected to her holding a job at the furniture factory, too. Preacher Clarence, as Regina's closest male relative, felt responsible for her and believed her place was with them until she married. As Gabe recalled the situation, Clarence would've *forced* Red to move to his house, had Bishop

Jeremiah—and Dat—not taken her side and agreed to assist her shortly after her parents' funeral.

Red stood her ground—has lived life her own way. Maybe she thinks you don't have much to offer, without a home of your own . . . or maybe she'd be content to remain at her place after she married—

Gabe started walking again. Where were these thoughts about marriage coming from, when he hadn't even kissed her?

Hah! She might run screaming in the other direction if you tried that. This is Red we're talking about, after all. Quiet, blend-in-with-the-furniture Regina Miller.

As he approached her house, he noticed that the lights above the porch were on again, and the attic window was open. Why would a woman alone need any more space than she had on the main floor? Surely her bedroom wasn't in the attic—the spacing of the back windows suggested two bedrooms downstairs. And in the summertime, it would be uncomfortably warm for sleeping up there. As he wondered about these things, Gabe felt compelled to call her name, to see if she'd come to the window.

But he kept quiet. He didn't knock on her door, either, which would've been the normal thing for a guy to do if he wanted to see a woman. Gabe had so many questions for Red, yet he hesitated to ask them. Was that due to the shyness and uncertainty he'd never felt around other young women—maybe because the relationship might turn out to be special?

Or are you afraid of what you'll find out about her?

After a few more moments of indecision, Gabe headed back toward town. On the chance that Red might come to the window for a breath of air, he hurried past. He didn't want her to spot him staring up at her, after all. Dusk was turning the sky to a pale, pearlescent gray as he crossed the county highway and headed into Morning Star's business district.

When he spotted a Mennonite guy he knew outside the bulk store, he called out to him. "Hey there, Nick—long time no see! How are you and the wife doing?"

Nick looked up from his cell phone. "Can't complain," he replied. "Just finished a pizza, and Mary Beth wanted to shop for a couple things before we headed home."

Gabe glanced at the screen of his friend's phone. "You're watching a baseball game—on your phone?"

"Checking to see how the Cardinals are doing. While we were in the pizza place, they had a no-hitter going."

Gabe blinked. He was way behind, tech-wise, and he marveled at how quickly Nick was flipping from one image to the next with his dexterous thumb. As faces flashed by on the screen, a thought popped into his mind. "You can look stuff up about people on that thing, *jah*?"

Nick chuckled. "It's called *googling* them, Flaud," he teased. "You want me to do a search for hot, single girls willing to date a knucklehead like you? I could sign you up for a dating service—"

"Forget that noise," Gabe interrupted playfully. "Look up a painter named Hartley Fox. He's surely got a website, and maybe a photo of himself on there."

"Hartley Fox," Nick murmured as he brought up a screen with a search line. "Does that end in *Y* or *I-E*? And is it Fox like the animal, or with an *E* on the end?"

Gabe spelled the name he'd seen in the shop at The Marketplace, watching closely as Nick typed it in and tapped the little magnifying glass beside it. Almost immediately, several lines of print and some photos popped up.

Nick slowly drew his finger upward as he scanned them. "Hmm. Stuff about Fox News . . . people with the last name of Hartley. Here's a Hartley Fox who lives in Canada. Would that be him?"

"Nope, this guy doesn't live very far from here," Gabe replied. "He paints nature scenes like you wouldn't believe—"

"No sign of anyone like that. He must not have a website—and he's never made the paper or done any local showings, apparently." Nick looked up with a shrug. "Sorry."

Gabe's brow furrowed. Before Nick quizzed him about why he wanted such information, he said, "Well, *denki* for looking. *Gut* to see you, Nick. Tell Mary Beth hi for me."

As he headed down the sidewalk, Gabe's mind clouded over with questions. Why wouldn't a painter who supported himself with his work have a website? Was Fox so reclusive that no one around the area knew who he was?

Red knew about him. But she's never mentioned how they met. Wait—check a phone book!

Gabe paused on the corner of Morning Star's main street, where a steady stream of cars was going by. With pay phones being a thing of the past, large directories weren't easy to come by around town. If Fox had a cell instead of a landline phone, a print directory wouldn't help anyway, but Gabe turned back toward the bulk store. The owner there might have a newer, more complete listing than the small one in the phone shack at home.

He walked quickly past the produce section and jars of locally made jellies, toward the deli counter in the back. "Hey there, Clem. Got a phone directory I can look at real quick?" he asked the beefy fellow behind the glass display case.

"Sure—on the desk in the office." Nodding toward the doorway, Clem kept slicing sandwich meat from a large block of ham.

"*Denki*. Won't take me but a minute."

Gabe entered the small room and sat down in the wooden swivel office chair. As he flipped through the large regional directory with white and yellow pages, he had the unsettling feeling he was on a wild goose chase. And why would that be?

Mumbling the alphabet, he finally arrived at the name *Fox*—five listings. Three of them had only initials for first names, and all of them were on the far side of North Haven, several miles away.

"No Hartleys. No *H*'s, even," he muttered.

As Gabe thought back to the questions he'd asked Red about her reclusive artist friend—and recalled the sketchy answers she'd given—he frowned.

What's going on here? What's this guy got to hide?

When he left, Gabe ambled along the crowded sidewalk, lost in thoughts that circled like suspicious dogs. The Methodist Church, with its high white steeple and its empty parking lot, beckoned him like an old friend. The back chapel door was always unlocked for those who wanted to pray, so he stepped inside the cool, unlit room to soothe his soul . . . to indulge in the comfort he could confess to no one.

Chapter Twelve

The Sunday service passed at a snail's pace as Regina struggled to stay awake. It hadn't been a good idea to slip up to the attic after she'd returned home from her busy Saturday at The Marketplace, but the sketches on her worktable had lured her to her easel for just an hour of painting to relax . . . which had become two hours, and then four. The day's sales had surpassed the previous two Saturdays', so sheer excitement—and the need to replace a lot of inventory—drove her on.

She'd gotten a good start on five new paintings, and she'd completed a few she'd begun before. Regina's brush had moved of its own accord, creating more ducks, flowery meadows, and rustic split-rail fences. The work had gone so well that she'd dared to dream about how much painting she could get done if she quit her full-time job at Flaud Furniture.

She hadn't gone to bed until well past one o'clock.

Regina's inner eyelids felt like sandpaper. As her uncle droned on—why did he always seem to preach on the parable of the prodigal son?—Regina felt her head drifting downward. She jerked awake, glancing around to see if anyone had noticed. Beside her, Jo was either intently focused on Uncle Clarence or sleeping with her eyes open, while Lydianne shifted frequently on the wooden pew bench. It was June sixteenth, and the summer humidity was making her aunt and uncle's crowded front room feel very warm and stuffy.

Regina's thoughts drifted as she went through the motions of kneeling for prayer—and then the sound of Gabe's voice leading the final hymn roused her. When she fumbled with her heavy hymnal, it fell to the wooden floor with a *smack* that surely told folks she'd been caught off guard, napping.

"Number fifty-eight," Jo whispered with a knowing smile.

Regina nodded gratefully, riffling the yellowed pages of the *Ausbund* until she reached the correct hymn. With a sigh, she saw that they had nine verses to plod through at the slow, methodical pace with which they sang most of their hymns. Just once she wished that Gabe would sing the opening line with gusto, at a snappier tempo—or surprise everyone by launching into one of the gospel songs the men often sang at their Friday night practice gatherings. She yearned for words that had more to do with praising the Lord than the weight of the sins for which they needed His pardon.

Sin was a heavy subject, of course. But Regina had noticed that her success with her NatureScapes shop made it easier to forget she was living a double life. Her lies were piling up at such a rate that she'd stopped thinking so much about them, to escape their weight on her conscience.

At long last Bishop Jeremiah gave the benediction. "No need for a meeting today!" he called out. "The Marketplace continues to attract a lot of customers, and our shopkeepers are all doing better than they'd anticipated."

As everyone stood up, Regina moved toward Aunt Cora's kitchen with the rest of the women. The men headed outside to set up the tables for the common meal under the shade trees.

"Hallelujah," Jo remarked as she fanned herself with her hand. "It's very warm today."

"*Jah*, my dress is sticking to me," Lydianne murmured. "Makes me grateful we can spend our Saturdays in an air-conditioned building—and thankful that the bishop decided we'd lose a lot of customers if we didn't cool the place down."

"It's a blessing to have ceiling fans there, too," Jo put in with a nod. "My kitchen at The Marketplace is much more bearable than the one at home. When I mentioned that last night, Mamm said I was getting spoiled by worldly conveniences."

The *maidels* chuckled together and began carrying pitchers of ice water and platters of cold sliced meats to the outdoor tables. As they usually did, Regina and her friends replenished the lemonade and water for the other folks before the five of them went through the line to fill their plates. The only place left to sit happened to be at a long table where Bishop Jeremiah, Deacon Saul, Gabe, and Martin were nearly finished with their first round of food.

Was it Regina's imagination, or did Gabe seem eager for her to join them? When he smiled at her, pulling out the folding chair beside her, she hoped no one would think he was getting *interested* in her—

Why is that? A few weeks ago you would've given your right arm to sit next to Gabe.

"*Denki*," Regina murmured as she set her plate down before taking her seat. The Helfings, Jo, and Lydianne didn't seem to think anything of it that Gabe had paid extra attention to her, so she tried to relax. She hoped he wouldn't start in about her paintings or ask more questions about Hartley Fox, because she was tired enough to slip up on the details of her story about the fictitious artist.

"Another fine day at The Marketplace yesterday," Martin remarked cheerfully. "We sold a couple of bedroom sets, and a dining room table with a hutch and twelve chairs. Looked to me like all you ladies were doing well, too."

"We were seeing lots of customers who came to the grand opening two weeks ago and wanted more of our noodles," Marietta said.

"*Jah*, we sold out and had to take some orders," her sister continued as she picked up a piece of cold fried chicken. "We'll have to spend a lot more time in the noodle shed this week if we're to keep up with our bulk store orders as well as stocking our shop."

"Maybe you should hire Pete to help you," Bishop Jeremiah teased. "But not to worry—he'll be starting on a pole barn soon."

"And we'll get him going on the schoolhouse after that," Saul put in. "We need to decide where to dig the foundation for it, so it'll be close to the road but won't interfere with parking and traffic at our auctions."

Regina focused on her ham sandwich, happy to let the conversation flow around her. Every time Gabe shifted in his chair, his knee brushed hers. Was he doing that on purpose? She should've been ecstatic, because he was such a nice guy—not to mention good-looking. Yet his nearness unnerved her.

You'd welcome his attention if you didn't have so much to hide from him.

"Your artist friend must be very excited about his success, too, Regina," Bishop Jeremiah remarked from across the table. He flashed her a teasing smile. "Do you roll his money over to him in a wheelbarrow?"

"When you do," Deacon Saul chimed in, "let him know that we're grateful for the commission money he's generating for our new school."

Regina forced a smile, chewing her mouthful of broccoli salad as an excuse not to answer.

"*Jah*, out in the commons I hear a lot of folks speculating about Hartley Fox," Martin put in as he leaned around Gabe to look at her. "They wonder why they've never heard of him, and why he doesn't sign his paintings. He's a real mystery man, it seems."

"You know, as adept as Red is with a paintbrush in the shop," Gabe said, green eyes dancing, "I'm wondering if *she* isn't our artist! But of course she's not—she'd never do that," he added quickly.

The room began to spin. Regina's cheeks blazed like hellfire, and when her food caught in her throat she began to choke and cough. She couldn't refute Gabe's joke and she couldn't stand to remain at the table one second longer, so she bolted. On her way through the kitchen, she spat her broccoli salad into the wastebasket—and kept on going. Out the back door of her aunt's kitchen she raced, wondering where she could go that folks wouldn't find her.

You can run but you can't hide. Now everyone at that table knows you've been painting those pictures and telling all those lies about it.

Gabe sat at the table, stunned. The faces around him mirrored his shock. He was appalled at himself for blurting out his suggestion in front of everyone at the table—even if he'd been joking.

But the circumstances add up, don't they? And the way Red ran off suggests that she's too guilty and upset to even set the record straight.

Still, he wished he'd handled this differently. He'd thought long and hard about why it was impossible to locate an artist named Hartley Fox, but the idea that Red might be painting those beautiful pictures—in her attic, late at night—hadn't occurred to him until moments ago when his *dat* had called Fox a mystery man.

"D-do you suppose it's *true*?" Jo whispered. "Regina's made herself pretty scarce the past few weeks—"

"She's seemed really tired at work, too," Lydianne put in, shaking her head. "And she hardly says three words to me during our breaks, like her mind is off somewhere else."

"I had no idea," Marietta said with a perplexed sigh. "We've all known Regina since we were kids—"

"Let's not jump to any conclusions," Molly insisted. "Maybe Gabe's idea startled her when she was swallowing her food, so—"

"Guilt was written all over her face," Saul stated sternly. "What we witnessed was the knee-jerk reaction of a sinner caught in a tangle of lies—a web of deceit—and we need to confront Regina immediately. She's a member of the Old Order, and her very soul is at risk, after all."

Gabe agreed, but he didn't say so out loud. He tossed his crumpled napkin onto his half-eaten meal, no longer hungry. He, too, had joined the church years ago, and he was keeping a secret every bit as pernicious as Red's. He just hadn't been caught yet.

"I need to get over to her house right now—and take Clarence and Ammon along," Saul went on in a rising voice, "because if this is true—"

"I'll go," Bishop Jeremiah said. "There's no call to accuse her of something that might indeed be a conclusion we've jumped to."

"But it's the deacon's responsibility—and the preachers'

job—to pay the first counseling call," Saul protested. "I've thought all along that there was something fishy about this Hartley Fox fellow—"

"I'll go," Jeremiah repeated. When he placed his hand on Saul's arm and looked him directly in the eye, the deacon went quiet.

"You mean well, Saul," the bishop continued, "but Regina's a quiet, sensitive young woman and she deserves a chance to explain herself without feeling she's already been condemned for sins she might not have committed."

Gabe relaxed a bit. Saul tended to be overzealous in his pursuit of Old Order truth; the bishop would give Red a chance to talk without feeling threatened. Still, he felt terrible about bringing this down on her head. If he'd watched his mouth, he could still be sitting with her—could've asked her out for a date later, when they weren't with so many people.

You blew it. Why would she want to spend time with you now?

Gabe remained at the table, listening to the conversation about whether his *dat*, Saul, and the *maidels* thought Red was talented enough to paint those nature pictures—and nervy enough to sell her work under a fake name. After several minutes, he excused himself to get some dessert, but rather than returning to the table, he tossed his silverware into a tub of sudsy water. He made conversation with other folks as he meandered away from the crowd. No one seated elsewhere seemed aware of why Red had made her sudden exit, but it was only a matter of time before everyone in the congregation would hear the story behind it.

He walked toward Maple Lane so he could give Red the apology she deserved and hear her story. As Gabe came within sight of the quaint red brick house, however, he heard the *clip-clop* of a horse's hooves.

Bishop Jeremiah was approaching from the other direction.

Gabe remained behind some lilac bushes on the opposite side of the street, not wanting to interfere with the bishop's business. When Jeremiah knocked on the front door and Red appeared a few moments later, Gabe couldn't miss her distraught expression and tear-streaked face. The bishop stepped inside.

Gabe knew he should leave. His heart went out to Red, however, and the possibility of making amends compelled him to cross the street and sit against the side of her house until the bishop left. When he heard their voices, he realized that the window was open.

Leave. It's wrong to eavesdrop.

Bishop Jeremiah cleared his throat. "Regina, you left us with some questions about whether—"

"I painted those pictures!" she blurted out miserably. "I—I'm sorry, and I know we have to talk about it. We might as well get on with it, *jah*?"

For the second time that day, Gabe sat wide-eyed. Again his conscience prodded him to give Red her privacy while she poured her heart out to the bishop. But he couldn't seem to move.

Chapter Thirteen

Regina burst into tears and couldn't stop crying. Bishop Jeremiah rose from the armchair and returned to the front room with a box of tissues. She nodded gratefully as she mopped her face, trying to pull herself together.

"I—I'm sorry," she repeated before loudly blowing her nose.

"Take your time, dear," the bishop said. "The hard part's over, now that you've admitted what you've done."

Regina wasn't so sure about that. Talking with Jeremiah Shetler, one of the most patient men she knew, would be a lot easier than explaining her secret habit to the rest of the congregation. She had visions of Uncle Clarence forcing her to sell her home and move into his so she wouldn't relapse into her deceitful ways. And her *maidel* friends would be so disappointed in her. She'd have to close NatureScapes, just when she'd been earning some serious commissions for the schoolhouse fund.

Why had she foolishly believed the truth wouldn't catch up to her?

"Do you want to tell me about how you came to be a painter?" the bishop asked. "Or would you rather I asked you specific questions?"

Regina let out a shuddering sigh. "I loved to sketch and

color as a little girl," she began. "For birthdays, I'd ask for paints and crayons and paper—and once I was in *rumspringa*, I begged my folks to let me take a painting class at Koenig's Krafts."

She blew her nose again, wistfully recalling her childhood and the parents who'd loved her so much. "I was in *rumspringa*—and I was a shy girl who didn't socialize much—so Mamm talked Dat into paying for one class, about composition and arrangement. The teacher encouraged me to try watercolors, and I was transported into another world."

Bishop Jeremiah nodded, taking in every word. "You have a lot of talent, Regina," he agreed. "When I see those— *your*—paintings, I want to touch the animals and the flowers. They look so alive."

Regina sighed sadly. "My younger siblings didn't survive, and we lived a ways from town, so my art was a substitute for the friendships most other kids formed," she explained. "I put away my paints when I joined the church. But after my parents died in that bus accident, I couldn't stop asking God why I was sitting up front with a cousin while Mamm and Dat got hit by the train after the bus stalled on the tracks. I—I got my paints out again, trying to stay sane."

"Survivor's guilt," the bishop whispered. "I recall how shattered you were those first few years, Regina. You were awfully young to lose your parents—"

"Twenty-two," she murmured. "Who can believe they've been gone ten years?"

"—but I could understand why you wanted to stay in this home, surrounded by the things your parents left behind, rather than live with your uncle and aunt," he continued. "Clarence gave me more than one earful about being too indulgent, too trusting of your ability to get by on your own. When Martin offered you a job, however, the two of us overrode your uncle's insistence that he should be responsible for you—that your welfare was his duty."

Regina grimaced. How many times had she heard that same tirade—that same talk of duty—from Uncle Clarence?

"And although we Old Order folks take our family responsibilities seriously," Bishop Jeremiah went on, "I believed Clarence was more motivated by a hidden agenda than by the love he felt for you."

Regina looked down at the soggy tissues in her lap. "He wanted to sell this place, didn't he? Figuring the money would be his as payment for taking me into his home."

Bishop Jeremiah's eyes widened. "You knew about that?"

She let out a sigh. "He also figured that when I had no further bills to pay here, I wouldn't need my job at Flaud's anymore, ain't so?" she asked softly. "*Denki* from the bottom of my heart for saving me from becoming his prisoner, Bishop—because that's how I would've felt if I'd moved into one of his rooms upstairs."

Regina felt a stray tear trickling down her cheek. "And now I've betrayed your trust in me by continuing to paint, and by lying to cover it up. I knew it was wrong all along," she admitted hoarsely, "yet the idea of earning money for the new schoolhouse convinced me to open my shop. And once customers complimented my work so lavishly, well— that *pride* I felt, and all the money I was making, blinded me to the sin I was committing every time I picked up a paintbrush. Saying I'm sorry isn't enough, is it?"

Bishop Jeremiah sat quietly, taking in her furniture— probably noting that she hadn't dusted for a while, and that her decor was more decorative than that of most Amish folks. "Saul and the preachers—especially your uncle—won't be satisfied if I tell them you've confessed to me today."

She felt a brief glimmer of hope, yet Regina knew the bishop expected her to face the reality of her Amish faith. "I have to go before the congregation for a kneeling confession now, ain't so?"

Bishop Jeremiah nodded. "*Jah*, you do, Regina. Had you come to me on your own and confessed before this blew up, I would've considered pardoning you, and the matter would've remained between us and God," he murmured. "When you got so flustered at the common meal, however, Saul knew immediately that you'd pretended to be Hartley Fox so you could sell your paintings."

Regina looked down at her lap miserably. "I suppose Jo and my other friends were appalled at the way I deceived them."

"They were surprised—but Molly insisted no one should jump to conclusions just because you left the table," he said. "I sense that your friends will remain very supportive. And they'll miss your company out at The Marketplace."

With a sigh, she blinked back fresh tears. "I'll be shunned, won't I? Cast out for six weeks—or worse."

"I suspect so. We won't know that until the preachers and I decide on the action we'll recommend and the congregation votes on it."

Regina knew, however. Deacon Saul would leave no stone unturned when it came to her paying full penance. Uncle Clarence would feel that every picture she'd ever painted and sold, and her fake identity— along with her other lies—were embedded like sharp, pointed rocks in the road to her salvation. Only a full shunning would satisfy them.

"I guess I have two weeks to prepare myself," she said with a hitch in her voice.

"It'll be painful, but it's for the best, Regina. Shall we pray about it?"

Regina bowed her head and squeezed her eyes shut. God had known all along about her painting and her lies, of course, but that didn't make it any easier to face up to them as the bishop prayed.

"Lord and Father of us all, we come before you as errant children needing your love and forgiveness—every one of us," Bishop Jeremiah added emphatically. "Guide us toward Regina's confession and reconciliation, that in these acts of contrition we may carry out Your will for us in a manner that's right and pleasing in Your eyes. Forgive us our debts, Lord. For if You were to judge us for all we've done wrong, who amongst us could stand? Amen."

Regina remained seated with her head bowed, awaiting what the bishop would say next. He'd been more than generous with his compassion. Some of the other members of their church wouldn't be nearly so gracious . . . including her uncle and aunt.

"I'll report to the preachers and Deacon Saul that you've confessed to me and that you've offered to give a kneeling confession two weeks from today," he said as he rose from the armchair. "The fact that you initiated your confession is much better than if I had to convince you to see the light."

Bishop Jeremiah's remark didn't make her feel better, however, nor did it solve all her problems. "What about the rest of the paintings I have? Shall I sell them—or close the shop immediately?"

Bishop Jeremiah held out his hand to her. "Do what you believe God would have you do. Fair enough?"

"Oh, you've been more than fair," she replied as she

grasped his strong hand to stand up. "From what you saw of Martin's reaction, do—do you think he'll fire me for this? Without my job, well . . ."

The bishop squeezed her hand. "I trust you two to consider all the angles and make the decision that's best. You'll be in my prayers."

After he left, Regina dropped back down on the couch. A sense of deep shame and desolation enveloped her until she couldn't sit still, so she climbed to her attic studio. As she lovingly flipped through the finished pictures in her bins and glanced at the dozen or so paintings hanging on her strings, she counted about fifty finished paintings and a couple dozen sketches.

She could easily sell out on the upcoming Saturday, or by the next one, for sure, before her confession at church.

But if you're put under the bann, *and if you lose your job, what will you live on? Will you become dependent upon Uncle Clarence's charity?*

The thought petrified her. If the Flauds fired her—if she was forced to sell her home—what sort of life would she have, living in a small upstairs bedroom? She was grateful to her uncle and aunt for their concern, but the prospect of spending the rest of her life under their roof and her uncle's watchful eye made her panic.

A sob escaped her. As a show of true repentance, the folks at church would expect her to give up her painting immediately, but she'd been self-supporting for too long to accept the idea of rolling over and playing dead, as it were.

Regina told herself that the proper response to this crisis would be to hand her future over to God, to give up her artwork right this minute as a display of her sincere devotion to the Old Order faith. She had to trust that God would take care of her.

In her heart of hearts, however, Regina knew she'd be painting until all hours of the night right up to the morning of her confession. It was the best way she knew to deal with the stress of this situation—the possibility of running out of money, and the heartache of facing the end of her independence.

A pity party wouldn't solve anything, would it? Didn't God help those who helped themselves?

That was faulty reasoning—succumbing to her sinful nature, the way the Old Order would see it—but Regina wiped away the fresh tears forming in her eyes and sat down at her easel. She'd never worked on the Sabbath, but considering all the sins she had to confess in two weeks, what was one more?

Chapter Fourteen

Gabe wasn't surprised when Red asked for a few minutes of his and Dat's time Monday morning. As he followed the two of them into the office, Lydianne looked up from the front desk, where she was recording their receipts and orders from Saturday's sales at The Marketplace. Her expression was somber as she watched him and Dat enter the back office with Red.

Gabe closed the door. After eavesdropping on Red's chat with Bishop Jeremiah, he knew what she was going to ask—not that he could admit he'd been listening beneath her window. Her faded kerchief and the stained gray dress she wore accentuated the shadows beneath her red-rimmed eyes, and he suspected she hadn't gotten any sleep the previous evening.

He hadn't slept much, either.

"I—I've come to apologize for my deception," Red began in a small voice. "And because I'll be confessing in church in a couple of weeks, probably going under the *bann*, I—I also need to know if I'm going to lose my job."

Gabe let his father answer Red's question. If he let on how he admired her for coming in to state her case, the emotions her story had stirred within him on the previous afternoon would make her and Dat wonder how he knew so much—or why he suddenly *cared* so much.

His father gazed steadily at Red from the old wooden chair behind his desk. "So what are you apologizing for, exactly?"

Gabe recognized this tactic. Whenever Dat disciplined his children, he made the guilty party spell out the incriminating evidence of his or her wrongdoing.

Red looked at her lap with a sigh. "Yesterday, when Gabe guessed I was the artist who'd painted those pictures, he was right," she replied without looking up. "I'm sorry I've deceived everyone and told so many lies to cover it, Martin. While talking with Bishop Jeremiah yesterday, I agreed to a kneeling confession next time we have church, and I expect I'll be shunned."

She paused, licking her lips nervously. "But meanwhile, I—I need to know if you'll be kind enough to keep me on here at your factory, or if I need to figure out another way to support myself."

Gabe's heart throbbed painfully. Red had placed herself at his father's mercy without tears or drama or excuses. He wanted to blurt out that she had a job at the factory for as long as she needed one—that he considered her one of their most valuable employees, no matter what sins she'd committed with a paintbrush after hours. But it wasn't his place to say such things.

"So it's true." Dat tented his fingers beneath his chin. "You gave folks a lot to speculate about when you rushed from the room yesterday, Regina."

She nodded meekly.

"Your uncle was mighty upset when the story made it around to where he and Cora were sitting," Dat continued. "He feels you've set a bad example, shown how too much independence—separating yourself from your family by living alone—can lead to temptation and worldly ways. Unfortunately, the ones watching you most closely are our young girls, like my Lorena and Kate and your cousins, Emma, Lucy, and Linda."

"*Jah*, I'm sure my uncle will remind me of that," Red mumbled wearily.

In the silence that followed, Gabe again wanted to extend his support instead of making her wait for a response, the way his father was doing. He could understand why she'd balk at living with the Millers, where she'd be under her strict, authoritarian uncle's constant scrutiny— until she married, anyway.

You could save her from such a fate.

Where had that thought come from? He was no more ready to marry than Red was.

As the silence stretched on, Gabe looked away from Red's increasingly desperate expression. This was no time to let his emotions drive him to say things he might regret. He couldn't deny how much better he understood Red— and how much more intrigued he was by her—because he'd overheard her chat with the bishop, however.

Red understood, as well, that it was best to let Dat have his say in his own *gut* time rather than to wheedle or plead with him.

Finally Dat cleared his throat. "You can keep your job until the congregation votes on your penance," he said. "You've always done *gut* work for us, and we've gotten several orders from The Marketplace. I hope our new business venture won't prove to be a mistake—an opportunity for Amish folks to succumb to the lure of success and greed."

Gabe bit back a retort. How many times had his father expressed delight at the increase in sales Flaud Furniture had seen because they'd expanded into The Marketplace?

Did Dat think he was above the potential pitfalls he'd just mentioned, immune to the temptation to work an extra day each week so they made more profit?

"*Denki*," Red whispered. "I really appreciate your keeping me on. I'll do my best to restore your faith in my—"

"It'll be a while before folks will trust you again, Regina," Dat interrupted brusquely. "Even after you've served out your *bann*, the memory of all those paintings and the lies you told us will linger in our minds. For now, be satisfied that you're employed for two more weeks."

Gabe's brow furrowed. What had happened to the concept of *forgive and forget*—the idea that once a penitent soul had been forgiven, the slate was wiped clean? When Red retreated to the staining room, Gabe remained seated. No sense in making his *dat* think he was eager to show her his support—although he was.

"What do you make of this business, Gabe? I never had an inkling about Regina's artistic bent," his father said with a shake of his head. "And I certainly never figured her for such a liar that she'd make up a fake name to cover her identity."

Gabe shrugged, answering carefully. "Me, neither. She's always been more thorough with stain and varnish than any of our men, but I had no idea she could sketch and paint such amazing pictures. She's got a real talent for it."

Dat's eyes flashed with disapproval. "And she knew she was to put all that away when she joined the church, too," he said tersely. "She's painted herself into a proverbial corner, because she's past due for finding a husband to support her—and what man will have her now? If Regina's made up a fake name and life story to sell her paintings, what else will she lie about?"

Gabe let his father leave the office first, to give himself time to cool down. Why was his *dat* so certain nobody would want to marry Red? Sure, she was thirtysomething and she'd told a few whoppers, but he'd always sensed that Regina Miller had remained a *maidel* so she could live life on her own terms.

Would God consider that such a sin, the way Dat seemed to?

"Regina, are you okay?" Lydianne asked softly. She closed the door of the staining room behind her, shutting out the whine of saws and the rumble of generators. "When the bishop headed over to your place yesterday, we *maidels* didn't want to barge in. We were worried about you, but we—we didn't know what to say."

"*Jah*, I can imagine." Regina looked up from the oak bench she was staining, which fit alongside a dining room table in place of chairs. "Why did I tell so many lies so I could sell my work? If I'd kept my mouth shut—just kept painting in my attic—"

"We would've missed your wonderful pictures," Lydianne pointed out as she squeezed Regina's shoulder. "Now we know why you've spent so much time by yourself lately. Even though your art's not considered acceptable, we're *amazed* at your paintings."

Regina gazed into Lydianne's eyes, grateful to hear no sign of rebuke in her voice. "*Denki,*" she murmured. "But I should've known to leave it alone."

Lydianne leaned closer, to be sure no one outside the door could hear them. "One look at your paintings reveals how much love you put into them, Regina. You must feel such a sense of accomplishment every time you finish one."

Regina blinked and kept on applying stain. Lydianne had moved to Morning Star just a few years ago, and she'd never guessed that this organized, analytical member of their *maidel* circle had such an appreciation for art.

"When I'm painting, I'm in another world," Regina admitted. "I don't think a lot about what I'm doing, or how I'm combining the colors and shaping the elements of the scene. It just happens."

Lydianne nodded and poured some of Regina's oak stain into a separate container. "Jo says it's that way when she's up to her butt in cooking, too. She gets lost in the *joy* of it." She sighed wistfully as she chose a clean paintbrush. "I don't have any sort of talent or activity that I get totally lost in. I'm a little envious—which is a sin in itself."

"*Ach*, but look at the way you total up numbers in your head!" Regina protested. "Nobody else has a mind as tidy and organized as yours! You reason things through, while I go with my gut feelings—which is why I'm in trouble," she added ruefully. "If I'd considered the consequences of opening a shop under a fake name, I wouldn't be in a world of hurt right now."

Lydianne crouched beneath the table that went with Regina's bench, brushing stain on its trestle. "Did Martin let you keep your job?" she asked in a tight voice. "If you have to leave, I'm not sure I want to be the only female—"

"He's letting me stay until we see what folks decide on for my penance. If he fires me after that, I—I don't know what I'll do." To keep from bursting into tears, Regina refocused on her work, brushing oak stain onto the rest of the perfectly sanded seat.

Lydianne worked silently for several minutes before clearing her throat. "No matter what happens at church, Regina, I'm sticking by you—and so are the Helfings and Jo," Lydianne insisted softly. "After you left yesterday, we agreed that we *maidels* need to stick together. That's what friends are for."

Startled by the thrum of emotion in her friend's voice, Regina looked up from her work. "If I get shunned, we can't eat at the same table—"

"So we'll all sit in chairs on the porch."

"—and you won't be able to accept anything I hand you—"

"It's easy enough to pick it up from a tabletop, ain't so?" Lydianne insisted with a shrug.

Regina blinked, deeply moved by such loyalty. "You're forbidden to even *talk* to me while I'm under the *bann*," she whispered hoarsely.

Lydianne stopped staining to gaze at Regina straight on. "We'll figure it out," she stated simply. "Maybe Bishop Jeremiah will convince the preachers that because you've already confessed to him, shunning won't be necessary."

"I have no doubt that Ammon, and Uncle Clarence, and Saul will push for the full six-week—"

"What if we *maidels* vote against shunning you?" Lydianne interrupted with a twinkle in her blue eyes. "The *ayes* have to be unanimous, after all."

Regina smiled sadly. "*Denki* for the thought, but after what the bishop—and Martin—have said, I expect the preachers to hold me up as an example of what happens when members get too independent. So the unbaptized girls won't be tempted to follow in my footsteps, you know."

"We *maidels* still intend to stick with you. None of us wants to forfeit the control we have over our lives." With a sigh, she added, "If you have to leave the factory and your home, Regina, I suspect the preachers will be watching me next, because I also live alone and support myself."

Regina felt gratified by her friends' support, but she knew better than to get her hopes up. After years of re-maining a *maidel* so she could paint in secret, she fully expected the congregation—especially the men—to rein her back into ways that were more submissive to God's will.

And what exactly is God's will? How does anyone— even Bishop Jeremiah—know they're following God rather than their own inclinations?

Regina didn't have long to ponder this question, because a few moments later the door opened and Uncle Clarence and Aunt Cora came in from the main workroom. Gabe's expression was apologetic when he met her gaze.

"This is our staining room," he explained to their visitors. "Lydianne and Re—Regina—work in here to keep the sawdust and other impurities from the factory from drifting onto the wet pieces they're finishing."

It sounded odd to have Gabe call her by her full name, but he was keeping everything proper, because her uncle and aunt weren't here for a social call. When Uncle Clarence dismissed Gabe with a wave, Lydianne knew to cover her stain and brush and leave the room, as well.

After the door closed, the work space suddenly felt claustrophobic. There was no getting away from her aunt and uncle's presence until they chose to leave. The hum of the exhaust fan in the ceiling seemed strangely loud, but it didn't block out the thud of her accelerating pulse.

"*Gut* morning," Regina said as she continued to brush stain onto the bench's seat. "I can't stop staining until I've finished this flat surface. I didn't expect to see you here—"

"We felt it urgent to express our shock and displeasure this morning," Uncle Clarence said bluntly. "The bishop has told me what he learned at your place, after you *ran* from the common meal. We need to protect your young, impressionable cousins from the details of your *unthinkable* situation while we speak with you, Regina. So here we are."

She fought fresh tears, slowing her brush strokes. It

seemed easier to focus on her work rather than to face her uncle directly. Because both the benches were wet and her aunt and uncle had no place to sit down, Regina hoped they would leave sooner. Aunt Cora fanned the air to disperse the odor of the stain—or perhaps because she was too nervous to speak while Uncle Clarence was chastising her niece.

"I confessed to Bishop Jeremiah yesterday," Regina pointed out in the calmest voice she could muster. "I'm sorry I've hidden my artwork, and that I deceived folks—"

"*Sorry?*" Uncle Clarence demanded. He snatched the brush from her hand and threw it at the opposite wall. "You've lived a lie ever since your parents passed, haven't you? Did they know you painted, Regina, or did you lie to them, too?"

Stunned by his vehemence, Regina clasped her hands to keep them from shaking. "Mamm and Dat allowed me to take a painting class at the craft shop," she replied in a quavering voice. "I was still in my *rumspringa*—"

"Well, that ended more than a decade ago! Did you intend to remain single all your life rather than giving up your odious habit—your *art*?" he continued angrily. "That's wrong, and you know it!"

"Clarence," Aunt Cora whispered nervously. "Everyone out in the factory can hear you—"

"And they *should* hear me!" he retorted. "There should be no secrets, because we can see exactly how keeping secrets has eroded our niece's soul. I told Jeremiah long ago that Regina should live with us, but *no*—he allowed her to have her way. What a mistake that was!"

Regina prayed for the floor to open up and swallow her. She'd figured her uncle would come to the house to confront her—

But it's more his style to humiliate you in public, ain't so? Just one of the reasons you don't want to live with him.

"You will make a full kneeling confession, Regina," her uncle stated sternly. "And you'll pay a long and heavy penance for all the ways in which you've broken your vows and slapped God—and your aunt and me!—in the face with your *lies* and your flagrant disregard for faithful behavior."

Regina knew not to point out that the congregation hadn't yet voted on her fate. For lesser transgressions, folks could simply sit on the pew bench in the front as the bishop discussed what they'd done wrong, and the public recognition of their wrongdoing was considered sufficient punishment. Preacher Clarence, however, was inclined to prescribe harsher disciplinary action—to be sure the guilty party fully recognized their wrongdoing and renounced it.

"I'm sorry," she repeated. "Until the meeting, I've said and done all I can to—"

"*Sorry?* You think it's enough to be sorry?" Uncle Clarence demanded, staring her down with his icy blue eyes. "Why would we believe you, after what we've learned?"

"Clarence, really. That's enough," Aunt Cora whimpered.

"No, it's not," he retorted. "We're putting her house up for sale. We'll need to prepare her room for when she moves in with us—and we'll need to find her a husband. Be thinking of single men who live a ways from Morning Star, because any fellow who knows about the tales she's told won't marry her."

Regina blinked repeatedly, refusing to cry. She found an odd comfort in hearing Uncle Clarence imply that although he felt obligated to take her in, he didn't want her in his home for the long haul. Scowling at her one last time, he turned toward the door.

Before they left, Aunt Cora gazed sadly at her. *I'm sorry*, she mouthed.

Regina gave a single, silent nod. Aunt Cora was always apologizing, and it was their way to silently acknowledge the pain Uncle Clarence caused them during his rants.

I'm sorry, too, Aunt Cora—sorry that your marriage is one of the reasons I've never looked for a husband.

At the click of the doorknob, Gabe stepped away from the exterior shop wall where a screened, louvered window allowed fresh air into the staining room. He didn't want the Millers to know he'd been listening to their conversation—and he was so upset, he didn't dare meet up with them as they left the building.

Gabe knew Preacher Clarence had expressed the traditional, conservative viewpoint of many Old Order church leaders. But he'd set himself up as Red's judge and jury before the congregation had had its say about her fate. And, without even discussing it, Clarence had declared he'd be selling Red's property! He'd also threatened to marry Red off as the antidote to her transgressions, and as a way to remove her from his household—as though he wanted no further connection to her.

That attitude was just *wrong*. And it was another reason that Gabe's dissatisfaction with the Amish faith was churning inside him of late. Where was the spirit of forgiveness that Jesus had taught His followers? Was Red expected to endure the censure of her family and friends for two weeks before confessing in church—only to face another six weeks of separation before folks voted on whether to take her back?

Sure, she'd made some mistakes. Didn't everyone sin and fall short?

He stepped back into the factory through the back door, unobserved. Eventually the whine of the saws and the thrum of the generators settled his rankled emotions. As Gabe watched his father walk the Millers to the front door, however, he sensed he'd be doing a lot of soul searching about Red's predicament—and about the direction his own future would take, as well.

Friday afternoon Gabe volunteered to deliver a wagon-load of furniture to a customer who lived beyond New Haven. He hated to miss the weekly hymn singing—but he didn't want to listen to the men rehash Red's situation, either.

As he returned to Morning Star that evening, he almost stopped to see Red, but he didn't want the rumor mill to rev up if anyone passed by and saw the Flaud Furniture wagon parked at her place.

Feeling extremely limited by his religion, Gabe parked the wagon at the factory, walked the three blocks home, and hitched up his rig. He drove to the secluded spot in the countryside where he often went to soothe his soul, craving the release of his pent-up, jangling emotions. When he'd leaned against the back wall of a deteriorating barn, away from curious eyes and ears, he sang his heart out—sang to Red, mostly. As daylight softened into dusk, he prayed that someday he could share his music with her in this spot that felt sacred to him.

Would she understand why he came to this place in secret?

Of course she will, came the reply from deep within him. *Who knew the two of you had so much in common?*

Chapter Fifteen

When Regina entered The Marketplace through the back entrance on Saturday morning, she was greeted by the cinnamon-sweet aroma of Jo's rolls, as well as the fresh scent of coffee perking in the commons area.

"*Gut* morning, Jo," she said, peeking into the kitchen adjacent to her NatureScapes shop.

Jo's face lit up and she stepped out to give Regina a hug. "It's *gut* to see you, girl. I wondered if you'd come in today."

Regina smiled tiredly. Jo had introduced the topic she'd be dealing with all day, and she hoped she'd concocted some convincing responses. "Just between us *maidels*, I want to put the next two Saturdays to *gut* use, because I might not have my job after I confess at church," she admitted.

"I can understand that," Jo replied softly. "If Mamm and I were unable to bake, we'd have a tough time getting by on our egg money and the rent from our *dawdi haus*. When you don't have a man's income to fall back on, you have to be more aware of where your money comes from."

The Helfing twins called out their greetings as they each carried a large box of bagged noodles past the shop. When Lydianne showed up a few moments later, Regina began filling the blank spaces on her walls with paintings, gratified by her friends' support.

"You look awfully tired," Lydianne remarked with a note of concern.

Regina sighed. "I've been torn between painting as much as I can before church meets again and giving it up altogether as a sign of my recommitment to Old Order ways," she murmured. "Painting won out. I couldn't stand sitting around worrying about what's going to happen to me after my confession."

Lydianne nodded sympathetically as she began setting up the cash box. "I'd be in a bad way if Martin let me go," she admitted. "I'll do everything I can to persuade him what a valuable employee you are—because without you there, *I* would have to take on all the staining, in addition to keeping the books."

When they heard voices in the adjacent shop, they saw Gabe and his father wheeling in a large glass-front china hutch. Was it her imagination, or did Gabe briefly seek her out by looking between the slats that separated their shops? He hadn't said much to her during the past week, as though Uncle Clarence might've turned him against her—yet his expression suggested thoughts and emotions he hadn't expressed in words.

As exhausted as she was, Regina knew better than to read too much into the way Gabe looked at her.

"I hope to stay on everyone's *gut* side today, minding my business while they mind theirs," Regina remarked to Lydianne as she continued hanging pictures. "After the earful Uncle Clarence gave me on Monday, I can't handle any more confrontations."

A few minutes before The Marketplace's doors were to open for business, however, Deacon Saul walked past Regina's shop carrying one end of a large quilting frame toward his wife's shop; Preacher Ammon was hefting the other end of it. Following like ducks in a row came Ammon's middle-aged, unmarried sisters, Esther and Naomi. Their curiosity immediately soured to disapproval when they saw Regina standing behind the counter.

"I feel a storm blowing in," Regina whispered as her stomach tightened into a knot. "You can bet they'll be in here as soon as they've positioned that quilting frame for Martha Maude."

"I'll handle the customers so you can steer Saul and the Slabaughs out into the back hallway," Lydianne suggested. "This isn't the time or the place for hashing out church business, after all."

When Preacher Ammon and his sisters entered the shop ten minutes later, however, Regina knew he didn't share Lydianne's opinion.

"What's this?" he demanded, gesturing at her art-covered walls. "Bishop Jeremiah made it clear that you were to conduct no more of this sinful art business, didn't he?"

Regina swallowed hard, heat rising into her cheeks. Her seven or eight customers turned to watch the discussion between her and the man in the black straw hat. "He left it up to me whether I'd sell the rest of my paintings or—"

"And given the choice between right and wrong, you chose *wrong*!" Ammon interrupted. "How are your neighbors to take your confession seriously if you continue to sin up to the very last minute?"

As if the preacher weren't attracting enough attention, Deacon Saul stepped into the shop to have his say as well. "I was hoping not to see you here this morning, Regina," he said brusquely. "What were you thinking, returning to your store after both the bishop and your uncle spoke with you about this matter?"

Regina felt trapped. The two church leaders stood in front of the doorway with their legs slightly apart, their arms crossed over their chests, frowning sternly, so stepping into the hallway wasn't an option. The only way to move this disastrous conversation along was to give her best answers, hoping the men would be satisfied by her reasoning—or become disgusted enough to leave.

"Martin will decide about keeping me on at the furniture factory after my confession," she murmured. "Meanwhile, I have bills to pay. I need to support myself—"

"Yet another sign of your pride and arrogance—not believing that God will take care of you!" Preacher Ammon interrupted.

"The way I see it," Saul put in, "Martin will let you go because your artwork has set such a harmful example for his daughters and the rest of our young people. If we mention to Martin that he's enabling your sinful behavior by keeping you on his payroll, he'll fire you first thing Monday morning."

"And besides," the preacher put in with a wry smile, "once your house has sold and you're living with Clarence, what need will you have for an income?"

Regina choked on a sob. She felt the foundation of her life crumbling away much faster than she'd anticipated, so she grasped at another straw. "I'm selling off my inventory so—so the church will earn its commission for the schoolhouse fund," she said, gesturing at the paintings on her walls. "Otherwise, what will I do with all these pictures? Back when you were telling the congregation about The Marketplace's potential income, you were counting on the commission—and rent—from this shop—"

Saul waved her off. "The other stores are bringing in more than enough to compensate for the closing of yours, Regina. It's your soul—your salvation—we're concerned about."

"Seems to me you've forgotten all about being Amish," Naomi muttered as she came in to stand beside the men.

"Had I not seen these paintings with my own eyes,"

Esther chimed in from the doorway, "I would never have believed how you've *deceived* us for all these years, Regina. This is no mere whim we're talking about. It's obviously a deeply ingrained habit—like an *addiction*."

As the Slabaugh sisters left the shop, Regina struggled to keep her composure. Why try to further defend herself? No matter what she said at this point, the deacon and the preacher would twist it to their advantage, wouldn't they? She bowed her head and remained silent, figuring the men would have the last word anyway.

"We've stated our case," Preacher Ammon said after several moments of disapproving silence. "You may show your repentance by immediately leaving your store, or you may continue down your wayward path. Your decision will affect the discipline you'll receive after you confess in church. What would God have you do, Regina?"

With that searing question hanging in the air, the two men left. Regina stood in place, clenching and unclenching her hands as she willed herself not to burst into tears with so many customers present.

What *would* God have her do? She'd talked with Him ceaselessly as she'd painted this past week, believing that the swift, effortless way her brush created new paintings— income to sustain her during her uncertain future—was a sign of His presence and approval. God helped those who helped themselves, didn't He?

But you knew, deep down, that the church leaders wouldn't see it that way.

Regina sighed and opened her eyes. If she left the shop this morning, should she close it up and send her customers away? Or should she ask Lydianne to manage it in her absence? She didn't want to get her good friend in hot water by asking her to stay in a place the deacon and the preacher considered a pit of sin.

When she turned to step behind the counter, however, the line of customers—and the number of paintings they held in their hands—took her completely by surprise. Rather than leaving the store during the confrontation they'd witnessed, folks appeared even more eager to purchase her work.

"I—I guess I'd better help ring up these sales," Regina said with a quiver in her voice. "Thank you all for your patience—"

"Do you think this'll be your last day here?" one lady asked with a sympathetic smile. "I *love* your work, and I was looking forward to buying gifts here for a long time to come—"

"What a bummer, the way those guys got on your case," a young man in line remarked. "I didn't realize *you* painted these awesome pictures—"

"We don't mean to get you in more trouble, miss," another woman began, "but if you won't be open after today, I'd like to see the rest of your paintings *now*—"

"Me, too!" the fellow behind her blurted. "I want to stock up!"

Regina gaped at Lydianne. Never had she imagined such an outpouring of support for her artwork. "I brought along everything I've completed," she said as she reached behind her. "While I fill in the wall display, you can thumb through these bins to see the rest."

As she attached more of her watercolors to the planks, Regina felt a secret thrill about the way folks were snapping them up. New customers coming in had apparently heard the reason folks were choosing so many of her pictures, and they, too, decided to buy something while they still had the chance.

By twelve fifteen, all her paintings were gone.

As the final customer left, Lydianne scribbled a

SOLD OUT sign and posted it on the shop's closed wooden gate. "Can you believe what happened this morning?" she whispered as she joined Regina beside the checkout counter. "*Now* what'll you do?"

Regina shook her head. "I don't know. From the church's point of view, I should stop painting—dispose of my brushes and sketch pads and pack it in. And yet," she added wistfully, "what'll I do with my evenings if I give it up before I absolutely have to? In a sense, Esther has it right. Painting *is* an addiction—"

"Puh!" Lydianne blurted. "Far as I can see, she and Naomi have always had their noses in the air, acting superior to us younger *maidels*—but it's because they envy us for having so much fun. They wish we'd include them in our activities, but . . . well, they're just different."

"Who's different?" Jo asked as she peered between the slats separating the stores. "So it's true. You've sold *all* your paintings! I've been having a rush myself or I'd have come over after Saul and the Slabaughs left."

"You'd have thought Esther and Naomi were seated on either side of God Himself, the way they were passing judgment on Regina," Lydianne remarked as she walked closer to Jo. "Oh, but I wanted to smack them! And their brother, too."

Jo sighed. "I couldn't hear all the words, but Saul and Preacher Ammon sounded really harsh," she said. "I'm sorry you had to endure that with customers in your store, Regina. I was so humiliated for you, I thought about spilling a cup of hot coffee on Saul out in the commons— *accidentally*, you know."

Regina shrugged as she joined her friends. The elation of watching her paintings being bought in such a frenzy was wearing off, and she would soon have to face whatever came next. "I appreciate you girls standing by me," she murmured. "Guess I'll head home—although I suppose I could help at the Flauds' shop, the way I originally intended."

"Phooey on that," Lydianne said, slinging her arm around Regina's shoulders. "I'll go over there—and you can bet I'll give Martin a piece of my mind if he starts in about how *sinful* you are. Men that age are worse than biddy hens when they huddle together. If one fellow gets his feathers ruffled, they all cluck up a storm, but they rarely *do* anything except point their fingers—usually at some poor gal who's trying to get by the best she can. I get mighty tired of that, you know?"

As Regina gathered her empty bins, she was surprised at the vehement remarks her two friends had made. But she'd need a lot more than the support of four *maidels* if she was to get through six weeks of being under the *bann*. She'd deposited enough cash in the bank to last awhile—but what would she do with herself in the evenings?

And how would she survive life with Uncle Clarence?

Chapter Sixteen

As Gabe sat on the pew bench on the Sunday of Red's confession, the tension in the Slabaugh sisters' farmhouse hung like storm clouds. Because Esther and Naomi set up for church in their basement, the gray concrete walls and floors added to the bleak, claustrophobic atmosphere as they sang a slow hymn about the wages of sin being death—which made Gabe even more antsy. All the chatter the past week had been about Red's amazing sales—and about her decision to keep the business open until her formal confession, despite the church leaders' warnings.

Her future seemed even drearier than the morning's first sermon. Preacher Ammon was lecturing about those who heard the call of Christ yet ignored it.

"We are to spend our time honoring God," he exhorted the congregation. "When we pursue worldly pastimes that set us apart—that lead us into the temptations of individualism and independence—we can only diminish the unity the Old Order way of life promotes. These pastimes can force us to hide behind secrets and to weave webs of deception so dense we can lose our souls and not even know it."

As Ammon continued his stern warnings to those who would stray, Gabe peered between the heads of the older men who sat in front of him, to see how Red was holding up. The preacher hadn't mentioned her by name, but as he spoke further about the evils of pride, fame, and ill-gotten profits that come from engaging in art for art's sake, everyone knew he was talking about her.

Poor Red. Her complexion was washed out and her eyes were rimmed in a sorrowful shade of pink that stabbed at Gabe's heart. As the sermon continued, she slumped lower, holding her head in her hand.

Gabe longed to tell Slabaugh to move on, to speak of encouragement and forgiveness, but he kept his mouth shut. At least he'd stopped his father from firing Red this past Monday. Dat had been ready to hand Red her pink slip, after Saul and Ammon had convinced him that he was enabling her to keep painting her pictures at her house rather than to trust in God for her survival.

This reasoning made no sense to Gabe. Why did the deacon, the preacher, and Dat feel Red needed to live at the Miller place, totally dependent upon Clarence's charity? Why couldn't they trust her to put away her art now that she'd been called out for it and was ready to confess?

What penance would they prescribe if they found out about your *worldly pastime?*

The thought made Gabe even more agitated. Only a financial argument had kept Dat from firing Red, because their orders from The Marketplace were putting them behind schedule—and they would fall further behind because one of their men was off work for a while with a painful case of shingles.

When Bishop Jeremiah delivered the main sermon, the tension eased a bit. Rather than inciting anxiety and guilt, the bishop's words focused on Jesus' teachings about judgment and forgiveness.

"Let's not forget that our Lord was a peacemaker—a

man who countered the religious leaders of his day by telling them not to judge, or they would be judged," he reminded those seated on both sides of him. "Jesus told his disciples to remove the log in their own eyes before they remarked on the mote in their brothers' eyes. *Hypocrites*, he called them, as he warned them to first relinquish their own sins so they could see clearly to help those around them who floundered."

Gabe felt the focus in the room shift away from Red— if only for a moment. Folks were looking at their laps, wondering if Bishop Jeremiah knew of secret habits they hadn't told anyone about.

"I've heard voices raised in outrage and accusation this week, concerning one of our members," Bishop Jeremiah continued softly. "Let us not forget that we all fall short of the glory God would have us attain. We all disappoint Him on a regular basis—even if our particular shortcomings might not be known to the folks around us.

"As we approach today's Members Meeting, let us put the words of the prophet Micah into everyday language and write them across our hearts," their dark-haired leader continued as he gazed at his congregation. "What does the Lord require of us but to do justice, to love mercy, and to walk humbly with our God? For when we raise ourselves in self-righteousness above another, we become prideful and blind to our own human failings."

Gabe's heart thudded in gratitude. They were truly blessed to have such a compassionate man as Jeremiah Shetler for their bishop.

Even so, as the Members Meeting began, Gabe felt twitchy. Without any prompting, Red went to her knees in front of the bishop as the two preachers remained seated alongside Saul on their bench.

"Regina, you confessed to me two weeks ago that you painted the wildlife scenes you were selling at The Marketplacc and that you'd made up a name to cover your identity," Bishop Jeremiah said. "Is this correct?"

"*Jah*, it is," Red replied softly. "I should've put away my painting when I joined the church, but I didn't. I'm sorry for the lies I've told, and for the way I've hidden my artwork these past several years, and for opening the shop at The Marketplace under a fake name and false pretenses. I'm willing to accept whatever discipline and penance the congregation feels is appropriate."

As folks shifted on the hard wooden benches, Preacher Ammon rose to stand beside the bishop. The expression on his bearded face was stern.

"That's all well and *gut*," he said, "but when Deacon Saul and I saw that you were still open for business on Saturday after you'd confessed to the bishop, we felt you were being less than sincere about giving up your artwork."

"And you said you were selling those paintings to support yourself, in the event you lost your job at the furniture factory," Deacon Saul put in from the bench. "Have you thought any more about what we said, about depending upon the Lord to provide for your future?"

"Matter of fact," Bishop Jeremiah said in quick defense, "before the service this morning, Regina handed me all the money she took in that Saturday—not just the commission for the schoolhouse fund. It was a voluntary act, an act of faith on her part."

"Probably trying to buy her way out of the *bann*," one of the women muttered.

Gabe peered across the room to see who'd made that remark. Bishop Jeremiah looked up as well, appearing none too pleased.

"That was inappropriate," the bishop stated. "This is precisely the attitude I've become concerned about. Malicious opinions are so unlike this congregation—and they undermine the Old Order's emphasis upon unity and peace as well."

After a few moments of heavy silence, Bishop Jeremiah continued with Red's confession. "Let's recall the vows you took when you were baptized, Regina," he suggested gently. "You promised to renounce the devil and even your own flesh and blood. You agreed to commit yourself to Christ and His church. And you said you would be obedient and submissive to the word of the Lord and to the *Ordnung*."

Red nodded, swiping at tears. "I've failed miserably, ain't so?" she asked in a tremulous voice. "But I'll do better now. I hope folks will help me along—will forgive me for being so wrapped up in my painting, and for all the ways I've deceived them."

As she headed outside to await the congregation's verdict, Gabe felt fiercely proud of Red for giving all that money to the church. Considering the buying frenzy on that Saturday, it must've been thousands of dollars.

It would've paid her bills for months, even if Dat fired her. Would've kept her from becoming her uncle's charity case.

Yet to show her faith, Red had given away a large chunk of her financial security. In her place, Gabe wasn't sure he could've done that.

Maybe you should show your *faith—come clean and live like an honest man.*

Gabe blinked. Such thoughts had occurred to him all week, but he didn't think he'd be helping Red's case if he—

This isn't about her. She's already confessed, but you have not.

Gabe refocused, listening to the usual procedure during which the bishop called for questions and any further details from the congregation. He groaned inwardly when Preacher Ammon insisted that, despite Red's show of remorse, the congregation should vote for the full six-week shunning. After Bishop Jeremiah suggested that four weeks was probably enough, considering Red's voluntary confession and donation, Preacher Clarence shook his head.

"We're talking about *years* of Regina's defying the Old Order to keep painting," her uncle pointed out. "She stayed in her parents' house—and has remained a *maidel*—because she couldn't give up her art. What's six weeks, when you consider how long she's indulged in such wayward, dishonest behavior? I also insist that she sell that house and move in with us, where she'll be less likely to fall into temptation's trap again!"

The bishop smiled. "Matter of fact, Regina put her house up for sale yesterday," he said. "She didn't want to mention it before she'd told you and Cora, but there it is. Another sign of her sincerity, as I see it."

Gabe almost laughed when Preacher Clarence's eyes widened to the size of saucers, as though he'd assumed Regina would never initiate such a drastic step. Once again Gabe was impressed with all Red had done to renounce her former independence. He already felt sorry that she'd have to endure Clarence's humorless personality as she toed his line and became a flawless example of Amish womanhood for her younger cousins.

"Well! Will wonders never cease?" Preacher Clarence blustered as he shot his wife a startled look. "But I don't see how this changes Regina's need for the customary six weeks under the *bann*."

Bishop Jeremiah appeared sadder and older as he

gauged the feelings of those present. "We'll vote on the six-week option," he said with a sigh. "If, however, the vote is not unanimous, we'll consider the lesser penance of four weeks. Shall we proceed?"

Gabe wasn't surprised that the *ayes* bounced like a rubber ball along the rows on the men's side—until it came to his turn. "No," he stated.

Folks murmured, wondering if his defense of Red implied a *relationship*, but Gabe suddenly didn't care what they thought. As the vote continued along the women's side, he noticed his father looking at him with a speculative expression.

"No," said Jo Fussner emphatically, and Gabe wasn't surprised when the Helfing twins and Lydianne echoed her negative vote.

When the last vote had been voiced, the bishop said, "Five folks believe a six-week *bann* is too long. Do any of you five wish to give us your reasons for—"

"Puh! Those *maidels* and Gabe—her close friends— want to let her off easy!" one of the women muttered.

Once again Bishop Jeremiah scowled as he tried to figure out who'd made the remark. "And who among us doesn't pray that our friends will stand with us in times of trial?" he asked softly. "That settles it. Because some of you are unable to release your negativity—and because Regina has voluntarily turned over more than four thousand dollars and put her home on the market—her *bann* will be reduced to four weeks. Lydianne, will you bring Regina back to the meeting, please?"

"While it's admirable of Regina to hand over the money she made her last day in business," Deacon Saul put in from the preachers' bench, "wouldn't it be a stronger show of faith if she forfeited *all* the profits she's earned on her paintings? The Old Order doesn't condone any of her artwork, after all."

Something inside Gabe snapped. Ordinarily when a member was shunned, the proceedings were orderly and low-key, without the nit-picking he'd witnessed this morning—and without the stories that had flown around town since he'd accidentally guessed that Red had painted those beautiful wildlife pictures.

"Something's been bothering me for the past couple weeks," Gabe said as he rose from his seat. "I need some clarification about *artwork*. Why is it perfectly acceptable for us at Flaud Furniture to create beautiful, outrageously expensive furniture, yet it's not all right for Regina to paint her pictures? Isn't fine furniture a form of art?"

Gabe's heart thudded hard as he spoke. He was vaguely aware that Red was slipping back onto the bench beside her friends, but the stunned expressions on everyone else's faces convinced him to continue. "And let's not forget that the bedroom and dining room sets we produce are custom-made and usually sold to English customers for thousands more than the average Amish family could afford. Red has to paint dozens of pictures to earn what one piece of our furniture costs."

A movement caught Gabe's eye. His *dat* was glaring, motioning for him to sit down—but his father's disapproval only goaded him to go on.

"Along that same line, why is it acceptable for Saul to create elaborate fairy-tale buggies in his carriage factory, which he sells to theme parks for thousands of dollars?" he demanded earnestly. "Regina's being shunned for painting scenes from God's own wondrous creation—and she's not painting human faces, so she's not creating those graven images the Old Order objects to. *And* she's sold her work to generate money for the new schoolhouse," he added ardently. "Had The Marketplace not opened, no one would be the wiser about her paintings, and we'd be funding the building another way."

Hissing whispers filled the concrete room as Deacon Saul glared at Gabe even more vehemently than his father.

"Sit *down*," Dat ordered tersely. "This is not the time or the place for such harebrained opinions about what puts food on your table!"

Red's wide-eyed gaze from across the room stilled Gabe's heart, and he knew he wasn't nearly finished with what he needed to say. "We at Flaud Furniture and the folks at Hartzler Carriage Company—create items of beauty partly because it brings us joy, and because God has given us the talent to do what we do," he pointed out fervently. "So why do we Old Order Amish consider Red's God-given talent with a paintbrush a *sin*?"

Chapter Seventeen

Regina's mouth dropped open. Never had she imagined that Gabe had such impassioned ideas about art bringing joy; nor had she ever heard anyone challenge a leader of the church about his livelihood. She'd often wondered why art was condemned by the Old Order, but Gabe had just nailed it: the fine furniture she finished at Flaud's never raised an eyebrow, yet the pictures she produced with her smaller brushes had set her apart as a sinner in need of serious repentance.

"We *maidels*—and Gabe—voted *no* on a six-week shunning," Lydianne whispered as she grasped Regina's arm.

As the older women in front of them murmured in shocked disbelief at Gabe's impassioned speech, Jo also leaned close to Regina. "We got your time reduced to four weeks, thanks to the bishop's levelheaded way of handling *some* people's bad attitudes."

Regina didn't have a chance to thank her friends, because Deacon Saul was rising from the preachers' bench with an expression that would scald water.

"I suggest you sit down, Gabe, rather than question Old Order ways that have been in place for centuries," Saul said tersely. "Have you forgotten that furniture and buggies have a *function*, and that they serve a *purpose*? Seems to me you're a lot more concerned about Miss Miller and *joy* than you are about the business your *dat* has established as much for *you* as to support his family."

"*Jah*, since when are you so concerned about talent and art?" Martin challenged with a scowl. "You have a factory to oversee!"

When Gabe met her gaze again, Regina's entire being thrummed. The emotions on his handsome face spoke of a conflict raging within him—and possibly of a decision he'd just reached. He appeared to be composing a response to his *dat* and Saul as he remained standing.

Meanwhile, Bishop Jeremiah was holding up his hands for silence as the chatter in the room got louder. "Folks, we have business left to finish," he reminded them.

"*Jah*, I need to speak about some unfinished business, too," Gabe blurted before the bishop could continue. "You folks seem fine with me being your song leader for our hymns—and you fellows who sing with me on Friday nights love it as much as I do—but you have no idea that music goes much deeper for me. I—when I was in my *rumspringa*, I bought a guitar and took some lessons—without telling anybody," he went on in a rush.

The room fell silent as folks considered this. On the women's side, Delores Flaud's face tightened with shock—and apprehension.

Gabe nervously raked his hair back. "I learned to play pretty well, and after I joined the church I didn't give it up," he confessed as he gazed around the crowded room. "Music comes easy for me, and sometimes I slip into the Methodist church and play their piano—they leave their back chapel unlocked for folks who want to pray, you see. Their hymns are about God's love and Jesus forgiving our sins, and when I play them I feel centered and—and closer to God."

"Have you lost your mind?" Martin demanded under his breath. "Why are you—"

"No, I've found my soul," Gabe shot back without missing a beat. "And now that Red's situation has come out, I can't remain quiet and be one of the hypocrites Bishop Jeremiah preached about today.

"And just for the record," he went on in a coiled voice, "I'm *appalled* at the way Saul and Ammon confronted Red in her shop—in front of her customers—and at the way her uncle belittled her at work after she'd confessed her wrongdoing. These leaders of our church were not the least bit uplifting or encouraging as they spoke with her—as they humiliated her in public. If that's what the Old Order faith is about, why does anyone want to belong to it?"

Gabe released a loud, shuddering sigh. "That said, I'll make my confession."

As Gabe went to kneel in front of a stunned Bishop Jeremiah, Regina couldn't believe what she was seeing, or what he'd said about playing the guitar—not to mention the way he'd so staunchly defended her and rebuked their leaders. Did she dare believe that Gabe had feelings for her? Or was he simply being driven by guilt to come clean?

"Son, think about what you're doing," Martin protested. "If you're shunned, no one will be able to speak to you, or to give or receive anything from you—"

"That's an Amish thing," Gabe pointed out with a shrug. "English customers will have no qualms about handing me their credit cards at the factory or at The Marketplace, as they've always done. My sins are comparable to Red's— they concern an art form, and my need to keep it secret. So it seems reasonable that I confess the way she has, ain't so?"

Bishop Jeremiah appeared flummoxed for a moment, but then he motioned for Martin to take his seat. "Whenever a member confesses, it behooves us to take him seriously," he said after the undercurrent of chatter stopped. He gazed at Gabe, who knelt before him with his head bowed. "Let's be clear about what you're confessing, Gabe. You bought a guitar and took lessons during your *rumspringa*, and when you joined the Old Order you continued to play it— and to play the piano at the Methodist church, as well. And you've kept this a secret because, although you know we consider musical instruments worldly, you didn't want to give up playing them. Do I have that right?"

"I *love* playing them," Gabe corrected him softly. "I've always wondered why talent that comes from God and has brought me such joy would be considered a sin."

"Sin's the most natural condition of all," Preacher Ammon put in with a curt laugh.

A few rows in front of Regina, Gabe's *mamm* shook her head in disbelief. "How can this have been going on since—and we've had no idea?"

"It's like I told Regina," Esther Slabaugh remarked archly. "It's an *addiction*."

"So are gossip and negative thinking, and I've had enough of them," Bishop Jeremiah snapped. He gazed at the Slabaugh sisters until they lowered their eyes. "I believe we need to pray for God's wisdom and guidance before we proceed. And we need to pray for one another as well."

The room rang with an uneasy silence. Folks bowed their heads. A dehumidifier kicked on and filled the basement with its noisy rumble. As the minutes ticked by, Regina wondered what folks would decide about Gabe— and what other surprises this fateful day might reveal. When Bishop Jeremiah spoke again, even the three men on the preachers' bench appeared more contrite and mindful of their attitudes than before.

"Now that we've heard your confession, Gabe, we'll take the vote," he said. "We've lowered the customary six-week *bann* to four weeks for Regina. Because you've come forward so willingly, that's my recommendation for you as well."

Gabe exited through the door at the far end of the basement as Regina had. She hadn't enjoyed feeling the gazes of the entire congregation as she'd left, yet once she'd stepped outside into the open air, she'd felt freer and greatly relieved.

The worst was over. She'd faced the congregation, and she knew what they expected of her. She'd forfeited the most recent money she'd made from her paintings and put her beloved home on the market, despite the overwhelming sense of loss she felt . . . the claustrophobic numbness that loomed at the thought of spending the rest of her life in a guest room, with Uncle Clarence and Aunt Cora being constantly present and holding her accountable.

The vote went quickly. Because Regina had been shunned, she wasn't eligible to vote—not that she would've disrupted the process by saying *no*. She believed Gabe was sincerely trying to face the music, so to speak, and she was pleased that a unanimous decision settled the matter quickly. After Bishop Jeremiah informed Gabe of his four-week *bann*, folks rose from their seats, eager to be out of the Slabaugh sisters' gray basement. The women went upstairs to set out the common meal, but because Regina was to be excluded from the time of fellowship, she slipped out the basement door to walk home.

Home, she thought with a deep sigh. How much longer would she be able to remain in the house where she'd grown up and been so happy? She had a lot of belongings to get rid of before she took up residence in her uncle's house. Because it was Sunday, she wouldn't begin packing, but to keep from sinking helplessly into depression, she could make lists of all the tasks before her. She could decide where to donate her furniture, her kitchen utensils, her art supplies, and—

"Red! Wait up!"

Gabe's voice made her turn around. Regina had been concentrating so intently, she'd almost reached Maple Lane without realizing it. Rather than appearing downtrodden or distressed, Gabe flashed her a smile that made her pulse beat in triple time as he jogged toward her.

"Now that the church has banned us from the common meal, why don't you and I go into town for a pizza?" he asked. "We have some catching up to do!"

Gabe knew he'd never forget the happy shine of Red's hazel eyes as she watched him approach. They'd been employer and employee for years, knowing better than to forge any other sort of connection, yet the possibility now intrigued him. Dressed in her Sunday cape dress of dark brown, with her auburn hair coiled into a bun and tucked neatly into her pleated *kapp*, Regina Miller held an unexpected appeal for him—and his new awareness of her took him by surprise. He had the urge to frame her dear, freckled face in his hands and kiss her, even though it was way too soon for that—and way too dangerous to think about.

When they'd slid into opposite sides of a booth and had ordered a large sausage and mushroom pizza, Gabe gazed across the table at her. "I feel this enormous sense of freedom now," he murmured. "Even though Dat has

told me not to return to work until my attitude improves—
until I appreciate all he's done to establish my future—I've
finally expressed my real feelings about how the Old Order
exasperates me."

Red's eyes widened. "He told you to stay away from the
shop? Who's going to oversee the building of all that furniture we've taken orders for?"

Gabe shrugged. "I guess it's not my problem for a
while. I'm not ready to go crawling back just yet."

She took a long sip of her cola. "Now that I've been
shunned, he'll probably fire me," she murmured. "I—I'll
have real estate expenses and final utility bills to pay
and—"

"Red, I'm sorry you've given up your home," he said as
he reached for her hand. "I really admire you for turning
over that money and for doing as your uncle expects you
to, but I can't imagine how painful this must feel. You've
had your own life for so long, and soon that'll be gone."

Gabe was immediately sorry he'd expressed his condolences, because he'd made Red cry. She blinked furiously,
releasing his hand to wipe away her tears so the folks
around them wouldn't see how upset she'd become.

"I really, *really* don't want to live at Uncle Clarence's,"
she admitted, "but selling my house seemed like the only
way to convince the church leaders I'm serious about
repentance."

He took her hand again, savoring the feel of her sturdy,
stained fingers linked between his. "If it's any consolation,
when Jeremiah informed us you'd already put your house
up for sale your uncle's stunned expression was priceless."

"Well, it was nothing compared to the look on your
dat's face—and your *mamm*'s—when you confessed to

playing the guitar," she shot back. "You might as well have announced you were a space alien from Mars."

When his own emotions welled up unexpectedly, Gabe had to look away. "I did the right thing by confessing about my music, yet I feel like my family and my faith have turned me away—so I might as well go live on Mars," he added with a sigh. "I knew they'd be disappointed, but I— I didn't expect Dat to cast me out of the factory, or to accuse me of being ungrateful. I didn't realize that following the *Ordnung* would feel so harsh."

Red squeezed his hand. "It's the separation part of shunning that's meant to bring us sinners to our senses," she pointed out. "Although, truth be told, it's the opportunity for solitude I'll miss the most when I leave my house. I'm not used to following somebody else's schedule or spending my days in compliance with a man's expectations."

Gabe blinked. Unlike Red, he took for granted that he'd be making his own decisions about how he spent his time—and without a job, he'd need to find something else to *do*. It also occurred to him that he'd never held a deep conversation like this with anyone—certainly not with the girls he'd dated previously, or even with the one he'd been courting years ago.

He sensed he was just scratching the surface of the quiet little mouse who so meticulously finished furniture. He felt as though he could tell Red anything and she wouldn't get upset with him or feel offended. Gabe brightened at the idea of getting better acquainted with her, now that their relationship was taking place outside the factory.

"An English gal I know thinks that shunning is a man-made rule the Amish have concocted—that it has nothing to do with God's will or what He really wants of us," Gabe said softly. "She believes God and Jesus forgive us when we ask—that we don't need the church telling us we have to suffer for weeks on end because we've sinned. And some of the things we've done—like painting pictures and playing instruments—aren't even sins for most Christians," he added with a shake of his head.

Gabe's spirits rose. Red was following his every word, not glaring at him as though his ideas contradicted the Amish principles they'd grown up with. So he dared to take his line of thought one step further.

"Seems to me we've done our part by confessing," he said. "And for all we know, God has already forgiven us, so maybe we should *enjoy* this next month of being outcasts! What do you say, Red? What do we have to lose?"

Chapter Eighteen

Regina gaped at the handsome young man across the table from her. Gabe's playful question made her heart race, because no one had ever gazed at her so intently, with such obvious interest in her.

What if we began dating? What if we fell in love? I wouldn't have to live forever with my aunt and uncle—

The squeeze of Gabe's hand brought her back to reality, however. What did they have to lose? It was a dangerous question. If he'd been discussing such things as sin and forgiveness with an English girl—and if he fell under the influence of such worldly ideas and left the Old Order—the Amish believed he had *everything* to lose, including his salvation in the Lord. Not to mention his family.

"Who would've guessed that you and I were kindred spirits?" he asked softly. "You could've knocked me over with a feather when I realized you'd painted those fabulous wildlife pictures, Red. I admire you for having the guts to come clean—but I'm even *more* amazed that you had the nerve to concoct a fake name so you could open a shop and sell them!"

Regina's cheeks burned at his praise, at the attention he was paying her.

"Your name's not Hartley, but you're indeed a fox, Red!"

Gabe went on before she could formulate a response. "And it's worth considering that you've quietly pursued your God-given talent rather then pretending it doesn't exist—trying to banish it from your life. If I got rid of my guitar, I might just cease to breathe."

The sudden seriousness of his words strummed a chord deep inside her. Regina gazed into Gabe's eyes again, deeply grateful that at long last someone else understood what drove her to paint and create.

"I'd love to hear you play sometime, Gabe," she whispered.

His face lit up. "That can be arranged." He released her hand when the waiter placed their pizza in the center of the table.

Regina inhaled the aromas of sausage and cheese as the steam from the pizza warmed her face. When had a simple meal ever seemed so inviting—so exciting? She always enjoyed her meals in town with her *maidel* friends, but this was so different. She was on a *date*, with Gabe, not to mention indulging in talk about forbidden pastimes while everyone else was at the Slabaugh sisters' farmhouse.

"Do you suppose they're talking about us at the common meal?" she asked.

Gabe placed two pieces of pizza on a plate and handed it to her. "Between the two of us, we've given them plenty to say, ain't so?" he replied lightly. "I wonder if they're also asking if maybe we've got it right—if maybe God intended for us to *use* the gifts He gave us rather than hide them away. If we've made them think about that, it's worth being cast out for a while."

Regina shook her head. "I can't see Uncle Clarence—or Deacon Saul or Ammon Slabaugh—ever considering our artistic inclinations acceptable."

Gabe took a big bite of pizza, thinking as he chewed.

"So then what does it mean that God created us in His image? What if God paints pictures and plays musical instruments, and the Amish have had it wrong for all these centuries?"

Her eyes widened. She'd never thought about that, nor had she ever considered Gabe the sort of fellow who pondered religious matters enough to ask such startling questions. "If you really want to ask those questions, you'd better be talking to Bishop Jeremiah rather than those other church leaders."

"*Jah*, the answer to any such question generally depends upon whom you ask, ain't so?" He flashed her a smile. "I've had all the soul baring I can handle for one day, though. Let's talk about something else—like your painting, Red. I'm guessing you paint up in your attic and, well—could I see your studio, while it's still intact?"

Regina nearly choked on her pizza. How on earth did Gabe know she painted in the attic? Was it even proper for her to take him up there—and did she want to show her inner sanctum to anyone? "I—how did you figure out—?"

Gabe smiled sheepishly. "Okay, just one more confession today," he replied. "I got curious about Hartley Fox, because you opened a store for him, yet he wasn't willing to help you. I had a friend check online and I couldn't find him in the phone book, either—and I'd been walking past your place, noticing how your attic lights were on nearly every evening—"

He exhaled loudly. "Well, there it is. I was sort of spying on you, Red. Wondering if you were dating this Fox guy, and—and trying to solve the mystery of the woman I've been working with for years yet didn't know at all. But I really want to know you, honey-girl," he added softly. "Please don't be mad at me."

Gabe had been walking past her house? And he'd figured

out that she worked late into the night, in her attic? Regina set her half-eaten piece of pizza on her plate, suddenly not hungry anymore.

"I'm sorry, Red," he whispered. "I invaded your privacy, didn't I?"

Regina blinked, meeting his earnest gaze. "Truth be told, if *you* figured out what I was doing, and you discovered Hartley Fox didn't exist, other folks would eventually have done that, too," she replied softly. "I opened my shop on the spur of the moment, without considering how many holes my story would have in it. I had so many paintings stashed away, and I saw a shop at The Marketplace as a worthwhile way to donate part of my profits to the church—"

"Your heart was in the right place," Gabe insisted. "Your wildlife paintings are so realistic they could be used in the classroom, so our scholars could see God's creation more clearly. But our preachers would never look at them that way," he added with a sad sigh.

"My paintings are all gone," she pointed out. "All that's left is for me to box up my paints, brushes, and sketch pads and dispose of them . . . before I backslide into my old ways again. I was figuring to do that when I got home from church today."

Gabe relaxed against the back of the padded booth, fighting a smile. "Ah, but wouldn't that be considered *work* on the Sabbath?" he pointed out. "How about if I stop by tomorrow after you get home from work, and we'll figure out what to do with my guitar and your paint-ing supplies?"

Regina blinked. "I was thinking I'd donate them to the thrift shop—"

"But if we use the buddy system, I can be your witness and you can be mine," he suggested. "If we take our stuff to the thrift shop together, we'll keep each other honest, ain't so?"

Regina laughed so loudly that folks at the nearest tables looked over to see what was so funny—not that Gabe's suggestion was outlandish. She just suspected he had something totally different in mind from what he'd put into words.

But he wanted them to do this *together*. He wanted to spend more time with her.

"All right," she agreed, trying to decipher the meaning behind the shine in his deep green eyes. "We can be accountable to each other. Is that what you mean?"

"That's my story, and I'm stickin' to it."

Gabe whistled all the way home. Spending time with Red had put a shine on his whole world and had taken some of the sting out of his *dat*'s tongue-lashing. He'd discussed issues with her that he didn't dare broach with anyone else of the Amish faith, and his soul felt freer for it. Maybe, with Red's help, he could come to terms with the restrictions their faith imposed upon folks who'd been born with an artistic bent.

Or maybe he'd realize he'd been living a lie, and that it was time to break away.

It was a startling thought. Gabe had never seriously considered living any other life than the Old Order one in which he'd grown up—and it would break his mother's heart if he left it.

When he arrived home and saw Dat placing a card table in the corner of the kitchen farthest from the main table, however, Gabe stopped in the doorway.

"Martin, you're taking this too far," Mamm was saying in a tremulous voice.

"He's to eat at a separate table," Dat insisted sternly. "Those have always been the rules of the *bann*. We're not to speak to him, either—but I have a few things to say before I stop talking to him."

"But some families put the separate table at the end of the kitchen table," she pointed out, "and some families skip the separation part altogether at home, so why not—"

"We need to make our point crystal clear, Delores," he shot back. "In this house, we honor God and we abide by the *Ordnung*. At twenty-seven, Gabe's old enough to understand our ways—and to face the consequences of his behavior at church this morning."

Gabe's insides tightened. For a fleeting moment he was tempted to leave this unpleasant conversation before his parents realized he'd overheard it. But it was time to face the music.

"I confessed, *jah*?" he asked softly. "Are you saying I didn't do the right thing?"

When Mamm turned, Gabe saw her red-rimmed eyes and immediately regretted the pain he'd caused her. Dat, however, focused on arranging the card table just so in the corner—as though there was any way to place it other than with two sides against the walls.

"You could have gone to one of the preachers, or to Bishop Jeremiah, and made your confession in private instead of throwing it—and your criticism of Saul and me—in our faces," his father said stiffly.

"But I didn't say a word that's not true." It was exactly the wrong thing to say, because his father would interpret his remark as back talk. But he couldn't unsay it—and he wouldn't apologize.

His father slowly straightened to his full height. He was a couple of inches shorter than Gabe, but there would never be any denying which man was the head of the Flaud family.

"If we charged less for our *outrageously expensive* furniture," Dat began, "we would have to let some of our employees go. And if Saul—or we—went out of business, several men in our congregation would be hard-pressed to find other work that paid a living wage. Their families would probably have to leave Morning Star in search of a steady income."

His father held his gaze unflinchingly. "After all your years as the shop foreman, Gabriel, I'd think you'd be aware of the responsibility that comes with running a business as large and as successful as ours," he continued. "And I thought you had the sense not to humiliate the goose that's laid your golden egg. That's why I don't want you back in the shop until you've seen the error of your ways—and that's why you'll not eat at my table until I'm convinced you've learned from the mistakes you made today."

The silence became deafening. Mamm was clasping her hands so hard, her knuckles turned white as she looked from him to Dat. Gabe felt chastised—and perhaps his father had made some valid points—but he was far from ready to beg for forgiveness. His *dat* was presently in no mood to accept an apology anyway.

"I doubt anyone's shocked or offended that you play the guitar, but *plenty* of folks believe you crossed the wrong line with your criticism this morning—including your *mamm* and me." With a final glare, his father headed through the front room. The screen door banged shut behind him.

When Gabe could breathe again, he let out an impatient

sigh. "Was I really so wrong to confess, or to stick up for Red?" he asked under his breath. "I was only—"

"Give your *dat* time to cool off," Mamm suggested in a shaky voice. "You took him by surprise—well, you took everyone by surprise, son. In all my years, I don't recall ever seeing anyone go down on his knees spontaneously."

"I didn't intend to cause so much trouble," he said ruefully. "Maybe I should leave, so your kitchen won't become a battleground at every meal—"

"Don't go," Mamm pleaded. She looked older as she blinked back fresh tears. "If you leave home, your *dat* will assume you want no part of belonging to our family— which will only make the situation worse. Not to mention that your sisters and I would miss you terribly."

She approached him with her hands extended, and when Gabe clasped them he could feel how she was trembling—how she was struggling with her emotions so she could say what needed saying. It was a balm to his soul that she was willing to touch him despite the rules of the *bann* that forbade such contact.

"Give God time to work out His plan, Gabe," Mamm continued softly. "We have to believe He can use this unfortunate situation to create something *gut*—because all the things He created, He declared *gut*."

Gabe swallowed hard. His mother's simple faith, her way of looking beyond Dat's black-and-white mind-set, had always made him grateful to be her son.

"Maybe God will even bring about something positive with your music," she murmured with a shy smile. "You've been blessed with a beautiful, clear voice—and although I'm not supposed to say this, I'm not surprised you have a talent for the guitar."

Gabe remained still. What could possibly follow his mother's unexpected statement?

Mamm smiled at their clasped hands. "My *dat* didn't realize I overheard him, but he used to go to the loft in the old barn and play a guitar he kept hidden up there," she admitted. "When our family walked past the appliance store in town, he'd stop to listen if there was a musical show playing on a TV in the window. Then he'd go home and pick out the tunes he'd heard. You come by it honestly, dear."

Gabe hugged her close, grateful for what she'd shared about his grandfather—and fascinated by it. He and his *dawdi* had shared a special bond—and they'd always sung together, no matter what they'd been doing. "Did he ever confess to it?"

Mamm shook her head. "He was such a kind and generous soul—such a special, patient man—I can't believe God condemned him to eternal punishment for playing an instrument, either. But we can't tell your father what I've just told you."

"I won't say a word," Gabe whispered. He glanced at the card table in the corner, already feeling the vast chasm in the kitchen, though the distance between the tables was only about ten feet. "And I'll do my best to make peace with Dat, in time. Right now I'm feeling a little raw."

Mamm nodded sadly. "Your intentions were *gut*. Sometimes we have no idea how our words will be heard, or what will change because we said them. It'll all work out, Gabe, and peace will fill our home again. We have to believe that."

Chapter Nineteen

On Monday morning, Regina slipped directly into the staining room, relieved that Martin hadn't seen her. Her first priority was to keep her job. She prayed that doing her best work and staying out of the break room—maintaining the separation from other employees that the *bann* required—would convince him she was sincere about her confession.

What if Martin hears you're seeing Gabe—and what if he thinks that's improper?

As she applied the first coat of maple stain to a lovely chest of drawers, Regina decided that total silence about Gabe—not even telling Lydianne about their date on Sunday afternoon—was best. Gabe's absence would create tension in the shop, and she didn't want to invite Martin's resentment by mentioning his son in any way.

Regina leaned into her work, brushing stain over turnings that adorned the front edges of the chest. The turnings ran diagonally within their recessed areas, like the strands of a rope, and it required her utmost concentration to keep the stain from running in stray rivulets while she carefully coated the grooves and spaces.

Someone opened the door, but she remained focused

on her work. If Martin had come to talk to her, she needed to remain calm.

"Hey there, Regina. How's it going?"

Regina relaxed at the sympathetic ring of Lydianne's voice. "I'm okay. Staying out of trouble," she added with a chuckle. "How was the temperature out in the shop when you came through?"

"Chilly." Lydianne came close to where Regina stood, keeping her voice low. "The men are saying it was a mistake for Martin to order Gabe off the job, because they need guidance deciphering the orders he took at The Marketplace on Saturday—and Martin didn't hear the details. You know how Gabe uses his own shorthand writing when he's jotting a customer's ideas."

"*Jah*, you have to be able to read between his lines." Regina smiled, because she could usually interpret Gabe's scribbles. It was just one of the ways they communicated without having to spell out every little detail.

"Martin's still so upset that he's not seeing straight," Lydianne continued with a sigh. "I came in here to work where it's quiet. The bookkeeping can wait awhile."

Regina straightened to stretch her back muscles. She was grateful that Lydianne wasn't giving her the silent treatment because she'd been shunned, as most folks would. "How was the common meal yesterday? Were folks wound up about Gabe's confession?"

Lydianne laughed softly. She dipped her brush into a bucket of maple stain, to work on the cheval mirror that went with the bedroom set Regina was working on. "There was plenty of talk—and not just about Gabe's guitar playing and visits to the Methodist church," she replied. "Saul and Martin had a lively discussion about the way Gabe criticized them, but other folks—the women mostly—were considering what Gabe had said about God-given talent . . . about when it crosses that invisible line and becomes a sin."

Regina sighed and resumed her staining. "I've had that conversation with myself—and God—for most of my adult life."

"Anyone who looks at your paintings knows you've got a gift," Lydianne said earnestly. "And we can't miss that joy Gabe talked about when we see your texturing and shadings of color, Regina. It's a shame you have to put it all away. I'm really sorry."

Regina blinked hard to keep from crying. "But I knew I was breaking the rules—my church vows—every time I picked up a sketch pad or sat down at my easel," she pointed out. "And then, when I opened my shop, I burned with every lie I told you and our friends and Bishop Jeremiah. It was a stupid thing to do, and it was the wrong thing to do. But I jumped in feet-first anyway."

They worked in companionable silence for a few minutes. Regina wanted so badly to tell Lydianne about her pizza date with Gabe—except someone passing by the staining room might hear them. For all she knew, Martin was standing outside the ventilation window listening to them.

"We *maidels* are having a little potluck supper in the office at The Marketplace this evening," Lydianne said softly, "and we want you to join us, Regina. We've been *gut* friends too long to let a shunning come between us."

A warm glow filled Regina's heart—and then she panicked. How could she tell Lydianne she had plans with Gabe? It wouldn't take long to drive to the thrift shop and donate his guitar and her art supplies, but she'd been hoping they'd find other things to—

"You can't come?" Lydianne interrupted her racing

thoughts. "Or you feel you shouldn't be associated with us—or the shops?"

"I'd love to come!" Regina blurted. "But I—I plan to take my paints and easel and other supplies to the thrift store this afternoon, and I won't be very *gut* company after that. Might need to hold a pity party and get it out of my system, you know?"

Lydianne's eyes widened. "*Jah*, I guess an artist would have a tough time saying *gut*-bye to her paints," she murmured.

Regina burned with telling yet another lie. When had she gotten so good at fabricating fibs on the spur of the moment? Was she sincere about her confession if she kept concocting such blatant stories—even if she told them with the best of intentions?

"How about if we meet tomorrow evening, then? We want to discuss how things are going overall with the shops, and we want to keep you company during your *bann*," her friend put in pensively. "What with putting your house up for sale and getting ready to move in with Preacher Clarence, we figure you can use a little girlfriend support."

"I'll be there. *Denki* for thinking of me, Lydianne," she whispered. "What would I do without friends like you?"

Regina rode her bike home faster than usual—not only because she'd gotten through a day at work unscathed by Martin's foul mood, but because she was excited about seeing Gabe. Somehow, knowing she'd be going to the thrift shop with him to donate her beloved art supplies made the trip easier to think about. He was as emotionally invested in their errand as she was, and he'd been right: without a witness, it would be tempting to pack her brushes and paints into a box and merely hide them away, as she'd heard folks did with their cigarettes when they tried to stop smoking.

They almost always start up again in a weak, stressful moment. And so would you.

Regina forgot all thoughts of sacrificing her art, however, when she spotted a horse and buggy in front of her house. Gabe sat waiting in a wicker chair on her front porch. What an unanticipated thrill it was to see such a handsome man rising to meet her with an eager smile. Maybe with Gabe for company, she could navigate the difficult road that lay ahead, away from her artwork and into a life of more honest, transparent devotion to God and the Amish faith.

"You're already here!" Regina exclaimed as she approached the porch steps. It was a silly, obvious thing to say, and her grin probably tipped Gabe off about how nervous she was. She felt as excited—and jittery—as a girl going on her very first date.

Yet when he brushed back his brown hair, he appeared as young and inexperienced as she felt. "I wanted to be here before you got home so—so I wouldn't chicken out and leave my guitar stashed in its hiding place," he admitted. "A dozen times I've caught myself rethinking our trip to the thrift store—"

"Been there, done that," Regina put in as she parked her bike beside the porch. "We'd better gather my stuff from the attic *now,* before I take a notion to backslide. It's a *gut* thing we're doing this together, *jah*?"

His smile sent a telltale tingle up her spine as she ascended the porch stairs to stand alongside him. "So I get my wish? I get to see your studio, before—"

"We'd better do more packing and less talking about it," Regina interrupted, opening the front door. If Gabe could tell how worked up she was getting at the thought of dismantling her painting haven, he was kind enough not to mention it.

She preceded him through the front room, wishing she'd taken time to tidy up. But what did it matter? When she'd ridden past his rig, she'd tried not to focus on the FOR SALE sign the Realtor had posted during the day. Regina led Gabe quickly into her bedroom, praying she'd get up to the attic without tripping on the stairs because she couldn't see them through her tears.

"What a great place," Gabe remarked as he followed her. "I've always loved Craftsman-style architecture. Plenty of practical built-ins and just enough rooms to make life comfortable without much space to accumulate extra junk."

Regina laughed in spite of the heartrending task that awaited her upstairs. "Oh, I've acquired my share of stuff," she said as she opened the trap door in the wall. "Now I have to figure out what to do with it. Clearing out the attic is just the tip of the iceberg."

Once she stepped up off the trunk and started up the stairs, she was aware of Gabe following behind her—his eyes level with her backside. Regina kept moving so she wouldn't worry about whether she'd gotten even more stain on her old, threadbare dress at work—or if he'd spotted the gap in the seam she kept forgetting to mend. The comforting aromas of watercolor paints and her warm, stuffy studio enveloped her as she reached the landing and turned toward the front of the house.

After today, you'll have no need to come up here—

Regina stifled a sob as she entered her studio, wishing Gabe wasn't around to witness her meltdown. He was directly behind her, however, and she found herself stepping into his embrace as he caught up to her.

"Red, I'm sorry, honey-girl," he murmured as he held her close. "This has to be so hard for you."

Regina pressed her face against his purple shirt, clinging to his warm shoulder as her emotions got the best of her. She couldn't form words, and bless him, Gabe simply let her cry it out. For several minutes they stood together in the airless attic, surrounded by her empty easel, the worktable where she'd left her paints and sketch pad, and the strings stretched across the attic's width—now empty, because she'd sold the last of her paintings on Saturday.

As she regained control of her emotions, Regina became aware of the way she fit so perfectly against Gabe, and the muscular strength of his warm body, as well as the clean scent of him and the way his breathing was synchronized with hers. She eased away, conscious of how plain and dowdy she was compared to him. So often she'd daydreamed about Gabe holding her close, and yet she'd ruined these precious moments by bawling like a baby.

"I'm sorry I'm being so—"

"Don't apologize," he put in quickly. "This is a big part of your life you're about to surrender, Red. Anybody would be upset."

Regina glanced at her familiar, beloved equipment—the props of the secret play she'd been performing since her parents' deaths. When she dragged her sleeve across her eyes, Gabe gently took her hand.

"How can I help?" His words hung suspended in the warm, motionless air as he awaited her answer.

She sighed forlornly. "We should find a box for this stuff. I suppose that one in the corner will get us started."

"Want me to pack it all up for you? You can wait downstairs, if that'll make it easier."

Regina held his gaze as he gently thumbed a tear from her cheek. "That's a very nice thing for you to—"

"See? I may be a sinner, but I have *gut* intentions," Gabe said with a chuckle. "You're one of the few who seems to realize that right now."

Regina looked sadly at her easel and the stool in front of it. "If we wait for me to feel ready to box it up, we might never get out of here," she mumbled. "I feel like such a sissy saying that, but I'd be grateful for your help, Gabe. *Denki* for understanding."

Before she started crying again, she left the dear little room where she'd spent many an evening totally engrossed in the details of her paintings. Maybe the Slabaugh sisters had it right—maybe she was so addicted, she'd have more trouble giving up her art than she'd anticipated. Once downstairs, she entered the kitchen to make some iced tea. If Gabe was going to rescue her from her desperation, the least she could do was offer him something for his trouble.

She was pouring freshly brewed tea over the ice cubes in two glasses when she heard Gabe's footsteps on the hardwood floor. He went straight out to the buggy with the box, which gave her time to wipe her face again and put on a weak smile.

"How about some tea? And I have a few cookies," Regina offered when he came inside again.

Gabe's fingers covered hers as he took the glass. His gaze lingered on their hands for a moment before they broke contact.

Regina closed her eyes wearily. "I forgot I wasn't sup-posed to directly hand you anything."

"And I chose to overlook it," he said before taking a long sip of the tea. "Or maybe, since we've both been cast out, that rule about the *bann* doesn't apply to us. I've never understood what it accomplishes anyway, except to further humiliate a person—like kicking a man when he's down." His face clouded over. "I endured enough of that watching

Dat put a card table on the far side of the kitchen yesterday. At every meal, I'll be like a misbehaving scholar the teacher has placed in the corner."

Regina watched the way his Adam's apple bobbed in his clean-shaven neck each time he swallowed more tea. Why did such an ordinary motion hold so much allure? Why were his dimples suddenly the cutest things she'd ever seen? And why was the image of Gabe eating apart from his family so difficult to think about?

"I'm sorry," she whispered. "That part's easier for me, living here by myself."

Gabe shrugged, placing his empty glass on the counter. "Speaking of Dat, what'd he say to you today? Any more warnings? Or rules you have to follow?"

"I didn't see him all day, because I stayed in the staining room. Hiding out," she admitted. "Lydianne came in to work with me, because he was apparently in a *mood*. And from what I overheard when he lectured the men in the shop, it had become a rampage by quitting time."

Gabe frowned, glancing toward the front door. "Shall we get going, in case Dat comes over here to talk to you? I suspect it won't help your case if he learns I've been here."

A few minutes later they were rolling down Maple Lane, taking the long way around town toward the thrift shop, as though Gabe thought his father wouldn't be as likely to spot them on that route. The *clip-clop* of his mare's hooves lulled her into a comforting sense of familiarity. When Gabe took her hand, she found a smile.

"It's a pretty day," she remarked as they passed the city park and the local car dealership. She stopped herself before she mentioned that she used to spend sunny afternoons like this one making sketches for future paintings.

"It is," Gabe agreed. "We'll have to find other ways to fill afternoons like this, when we used to slip away and enjoy our forbidden pursuits. Or *not*," he added in a defiant whisper.

Had she heard him correctly? When Regina glanced at his face, Gabe remained focused on the street up ahead where the thrift shop was, his jaw tensed. As they reached the intersection where they should turn, however, Gabe clucked for his mare to go faster.

"Didn't you mean to take that street?" she asked quickly. "Or do you know a different way—or a different shop where—"

Gabe steered to the shoulder of the road and stopped. His green-eyed gaze silenced her. "Why ruin a perfect afternoon by disposing of our most precious belongings as though they're *junk*?" he asked raggedly. "I want to sit at that spot by the river where you composed your pictures of the Kraybills' old barn. And I want to play my guitar for you while you sketch whatever strikes your fancy today. Just one last time, why don't we enjoy doing what we most love to do—together?"

Regina sucked in her breath. "Won't that make it harder to go to the thrift store next time? If we lose our resolve— if we backslide today—"

"Who's to know, except God? And who's to say He'll really find fault with us?" Gabe pleaded softly. "I won't tell if you won't, Red."

In that fateful moment, Gabe Flaud became more than a fun-loving, good-looking carpenter trying hard to accept the punishment the church had prescribed for him. He was a child of God desperately awash in need and indecision, just as Regina was.

And she loved him for it.

"Well, I *would* love to hear you play—just once," she whispered. "Then we really do have to give it all up,

Gabe, or God will know we're not sincere about keeping our promises."

Gabe grinned. "That's all I'm asking for, Red. One last time—like a going-away party for my guitar and your paints. Let's go!"

Regina sensed they were sliding down a slippery slope, yet she was so tickled by Gabe's suggestion—and caught up in the joy of sharing their art with one another—that she didn't protest. As he urged his horse down the road at a faster clip, she tied the strings of her *kapp* to keep it from flying off.

She didn't dare think about the possibility of someone from church spotting them. She just rode the wave of exhilaration that made her pulse race with each *clip-clop* of the mare's quickening hoofbeats.

Chapter 20

As Gabe plucked out the melody of "You Are My Sunshine," filling in between the beats with quick running notes, his fingers flew effortlessly, driven by the delighted awe on Red's face. Her sketch pad rested forgotten in her lap as she watched his hands. When he finished with a flourish, she applauded exuberantly.

"My word, Gabe, could you have possibly squeezed in any more extra notes?" she teased. "You sounded like you were playing with twenty fingers instead of ten!"

When Red met his gaze, Gabe's heart stood still. He'd always played in secret, so Red's praise sounded particularly sweet. "Well, now you know how often I've practiced over the years," he admitted softly.

"And I know why you didn't want to stop." She relaxed against the old boards of the Kraybills' barn with a sigh. "So where have you been playing that nobody's caught you in all that time? Surely not at home."

"Oh, no," he replied quickly. "With two little sisters, I would've been caught long ago. I, um, designed the wooden tool chest in the back of my rig so my guitar is hidden in a compartment under my equipment. Whenever I take a notion to play, nobody thinks anything of it as I drive off— as though I'm running an errand, or doing whatever single guys do in their spare time," he added with a chuckle. "My parents like to assume I've been seeing somebody. They don't press for details, and I don't volunteer any, either."

"A hidden compartment in your tool chest," she murmured. "That's pretty clever."

"*Sneaky* is more like it. Devious," he added, none too proud of his admission.

"It's a lot less expensive than keeping a house, the way I did," Red pointed out. As her pencil began to move again, a dilapidated split-rail fence appeared on her sketch pad. Tall stalks appeared in the foreground, dotted with wildflowers. "Dismantling the deception I've built around my painting will take a lot of time and willpower. It's much more than giving up my easel and paints."

She let out a heavy sigh, even as she continued to sketch. "I never dreamed I'd be dismantling the very satisfying life I've made for myself over the years," she murmured sadly. "Every time I think about how much stuff I have to get rid of, I feel totally overwhelmed."

"So don't think about it," Gabe whispered. The pained expression on her flawless face was more than he could bear. "For these couple of hours we've carved out for ourselves, let's just enjoy what we do—and who we've become. After all, God didn't create the world in one session," he pointed out. "How can He expect us to make all of our changes in a single day?"

When Red's hazel eyes widened, Gabe felt himself falling headlong into their depths . . . into the soul of this woman who'd so effortlessly captured his admiration and imagination. Her lips parted as if she were ready to speak, yet no words came out. It was an opportunity he couldn't pass up.

He cradled her face in his hand, leaning closer until her breath fanned his cheek—until he was gently brushing her lips with his. Red's soft moan coaxed him to deepen the kiss. Gabe was vaguely aware that his guitar had slipped off his lap, and when Red wove her fingers through his hair he thought he'd died and gone to heaven. Their kiss lasted for several long, sweet moments, yet it ended too soon.

Red eased away first, gasping softly. "*Gut* thing we're sitting behind the barn instead of on the riverbank where somebody might spot us," she remarked in a breathy voice.

"*Jah*, folks at church would probably say we're leading each other astray, talking and kissing when we're supposed to maintain separation during our *bann*," Gabe muttered as he shifted away from her. "If you were any other girl—"

"I am who I am," she put in. "And I'll probably be unemployed if your *dat* gets the least inkling about our being together, if only because you defended my art."

"Why is our relationship yet another thing we have to hide—especially when we've been friends for years?" he retorted vehemently. "If it weren't for the Old Order's archaic, stupid rules—"

He stopped there, sensing he might say something that would further upset her. Regina Miller was indeed who she was—and he respected her immensely for realigning herself with a faith he was rapidly losing patience with. "*Denki* for going along with this wild idea about indulging our talents just one more time," he whispered. "It wasn't the right thing to do—"

"It was exactly what I needed today," she put in with a rueful laugh. "Let's don't spoil it by acting all sanctimonious or beating ourselves up. How about if you play me another song while I finish this sketch? I have no idea what I'll do with it, but for now I want your music to inspire my drawing."

Gabe blinked. She'd suggested the perfect antidote to his qualms. Hadn't Red always been a calm, levelheaded problem solver—even before he'd known about her artistic abilities?

He picked up his guitar again and began to strum slowly, playing through a chord progression in six-eight time as he worked up the courage to sing the words. Why should he feel self-conscious about singing to Red? She heard him every Sunday at church.

Yet it was different as they sat behind the Kraybills' barn, still thrumming with their first kiss. Maybe she wouldn't even like the song, but Gabe drew in a breath anyway. "'O the deep, deep love of Jesus,'" he began softly. He'd played it so many times, he closed his eyes and let the melody carry him along. "'Vast, unmeasured, boundless, free . . . rolling as a mighty ocean in its fullness over me.'"

As she listened, Red relaxed against the barn with her eyes closed. The dreamlike expression on her face made Gabe long to kiss her again—yet it seemed a sacrilege to begin a song about the love of Christ and then interrupt it to indulge an affection that had blossomed as quickly as the wildflowers she'd sketched on her pad.

When he finished the hymn, he sighed. "That wasn't exactly the most romantic song a guy could sing to impress a gal he likes," he murmured apologetically.

Red's eyes fluttered opened, clear and shining. "Ah, but even if it was about Jesus, it was a love song. And it's a beautiful tune," she added.

Gabe smiled. "Something about the minor key speaks to me when I'm feeling troubled. The Methodist hymnal listing said it was composed in the late eighteen hundreds, but it feels a lot more . . . relevant than the hymns we sing in our church." He gazed into the distance, not sure he should voice any more of his doubts. Yet he sensed Red would listen objectively even if she found his ideas unsettling.

"Sometimes, on the Sundays when we don't have a service, I think about going to the Methodist church—to sit way in the back and take it all in—but in my Plain clothes, I'd look pretty odd to them," he added solemnly. "I've made it as far as sitting outside the back exit of the sanctuary, where I can hear the congregation singing as the pipe organ plays. It's so magnificent I can hardly breathe, Red."

He looked at her, grateful that her expression registered interest rather than shock or revulsion. "Is it wrong to want to worship God with glorious music?" he whispered. "Will the Lord condemn me to eternal damnation because I want to join a different faith? I—I'm facing a lot of attitude adjustments if I'm ever to feel totally positive about remaining in the Old Order."

Red's hazel eyes widened briefly at the way he ended his sentence, yet she took her time to consider what he'd said. "I don't know the answer to that," she admitted. "But Gabe, if you left our church, I'd really miss you. Everyone would."

His heart swelled at her admission. "*Jah*, and my leaving would throw a wrench into the furniture factory, and Mamm's life, as well—which is the main reason I've kept my secrets to myself for so long. I could start up my own furniture shop somewhere else to support myself, but I'd be creating a permanent wound in my family that would never heal."

She was nodding, her pencil lying loose on her sketch pad as she clasped her hands prayerfully in her lap. "We have a lot of thinking to do, you and I. At least we can discuss these matters without getting as upset as our families—

and other church members—do. If any of the preachers—
especially Uncle Clarence and Ammon—had overheard
this conversation, I suspect we'd be expelled before we
even completed our shunning."

"Doesn't sound like a very forgiving, Christian way to
handle us, does it?"

His question hung in the air unanswered for several
moments.

"How about if we get a sandwich at the diner in Higher
Ground?" Gabe suggested. "It's a pretty sure bet we won't
see folks we know there."

Nodding, Red gathered up her materials. He felt a pang
of regret that after years of knowing each other, they were
skulking around, avoiding their church friends—and their
families—when they should be celebrating the discovery
of their kindred spirits.

If push came to shove—if the Old Order church leaders expelled him for continuing to follow his musical
yearnings—would Red go with him?

Chapter Twenty-One

Regina hurried along the shoulder of the county highway Tuesday afternoon, a white sack in her hand as she headed to The Marketplace. She'd had no time to cook anything for the *maidels'* potluck, so she'd chosen an assortment of candies and cookies at the bulk store after work. Her hands and dress were messier than usual because Martin had startled her by coming into the staining room when she'd been carrying an open container of walnut stain—which had splattered all over her. She hoped her friends wouldn't be too put off by the fumes.

"Regina, wait up! Come ride with me!" a familiar voice called from behind her.

Lydianne was waving from her open rig. A few moments later, Regina climbed in on the passenger side and the two of them continued along the county highway, which was busy with what counted as rush hour traffic in Morning Star. Whatever Lydianne was bringing to their supper smelled heavenly, but Regina didn't get a chance to ask about it.

"I looked all over for you after work, but you'd disappeared," Lydianne remarked.

Regina nodded. "I'd hoped to be out the door right at quitting time, but Martin came in for a little *chat*," she said. "Seems he was making sure I'd actually been at the factory working these past couple of days, because he hadn't seen me—"

"Because you were trying to maintain the necessary separation," Lydianne put in with an exasperated sigh. "If I've told him that once, I've said it at least three times since yesterday. So . . . hopefully he wasn't hinting at firing you?"

Regina shook her head, but she felt none too confident about the real motive behind her boss's appearance. "When I assured him I wasn't the sort to miss work without telling him, he went off onto a tangent about Gabe being gone and how many orders were piling up in his absence," she replied. "I wasn't sure what to say about that, considering Martin was the one who ordered Gabe not to come to the factory until his attitude improved."

"*Jah*, I'm guessing things at the Flaud house are tense," Lydianne murmured. "Doesn't help that Delbert Plank had to go to the clinic for ten stitches today, so he can't use his right hand for a long while." She let out a humorless laugh. "Martin might be asking us girls to operate some of the shop machinery if we lose any more of the men."

"Maybe he should reconsider what he said to Gabe," Regina said softly. "I-if I were in Gabe's shoes, I'd feel like I'd been cast out by my family as surely as by the congregation."

Lydianne looked speculatively at Regina. "Martin expected his son would come around immediately to apologize. The way you're telling it, I'm wondering if you know more than the rest of us about Gabe's feelings."

Regina nipped her lip. She'd already said too much to the astute young woman beside her.

Checking the traffic in both directions, Lydianne steered her mare into a left turn to approach the white plank fence surrounding The Marketplace. "All right, I'll come clean," she said with a chuckle. "I spotted you and Gabe in his buggy yesterday afternoon. And I'm happy for you both, Regina."

Lydianne might as well have punched her in the stomach. "Oh my," Regina gasped. "Please don't let on about—"

"I won't say a word, Regina."

"—especially to Martin, because—"

"Especially not to Martin," Lydianne assured her, "and not to our friends this evening, either, unless you say something first. They'd be delighted to hear about you two being together, though. Gabe's such a nice guy—and he did rise to your defense on Sunday."

"Why are you already making us out to be a couple, Lydianne?" Regina demanded, more stridently than she had intended.

Shrugging playfully, Lydianne hopped down to open the gate, which had been left unchained by the *maidels* who'd already arrived. After Regina clucked for the mare to pull the rig through the opening, Lydianne closed the gate again and hooked the padlock on the chain without snapping it shut. She was still chuckling as she clambered back into the driver's side.

"Deny it if you want to, girlfriend, but you two were coming back into Morning Star from wherever you'd been, looking like you'd had a fine time," she said. "And I think it's wonderful, Regina. Your secret's safe with me."

Regina's cheeks went hot. She chuckled nervously, hoping she could indeed trust her longtime friend. "Okay, so I couldn't come to a Marketplace meeting last night because I *did* load up my painting supplies, like I told you," she said in a rush. "Gabe suggested that we should take his guitar and my art things to the thrift store together—to hold each other accountable, you know—so we were on our way to do that. But he drove past the turnoff."

She exhaled with a mixture of frustration and exhilaration. "I spent the afternoon sketching down by the river, while he played his guitar and sang. We really *are* going to get rid of our stuff, Lydianne, but it didn't happen yesterday as intended."

Her friend's expression softened. "That sounds so romantic," she whispered. "But be careful, Regina. If *I* spotted you together, other folks could, too."

As they pulled around behind the large red stable that housed The Marketplace, Regina wondered if anyone else had seen her and Gabe. When Jo and the Helfing twins called out their greetings, however, she composed her face so she'd give nothing else away. She loved all these young women dearly, but if they *all* found out she'd spent time with Gabe, the news was bound to spread.

"*Gut* to see you two!" Molly called out.

"My, but that's an attractive dress you're wearing, Regina!" Marietta teased.

Regina couldn't help laughing. "Thanks to Martin, I sloshed stain all over myself today," she said as she hopped to the ground with her white sack. "When you see what I brought for our meal, you'll know I cook every bit as well as I mind my appearance, too. Grabbed some candy and cookies at the bulk store."

"I didn't cook, either," Lydianne put in as she reached behind the seat. "I called ahead for pizza and picked it up on my way out of town."

The twins clapped their hands, laughing. "We love pizza!" Marietta crowed.

"Mostly because it's not made from the broken noodles left after we bagged them up today," Molly remarked as she held up a casserole covered in foil. "You know how we always bring a noodle-and-cheese dish, *jah*?"

Jo was at the back door, chuckling as she held it open for them. "Mamm and I have zucchini coming out our ears already, and some green beans left from canning yesterday," she said. "So I sautéed them together with oil and seasonings. Seems we've covered all the main food groups—and we're all here together, which is the most important ingredient for a *gut* potluck."

As Regina followed her friends up to the loft, she felt a twinge of sadness when she spotted the empty shop area where NatureScapes had been. She was grateful that the other *maidels* still wanted her to participate in their meeting despite her *bann*, however. As the five of them gathered around the old table in the office, Regina realized she was hungry for more than the assortment of food they were setting out.

"How did things go last Saturday? There was a big produce auction, *jah*?" she asked as she popped open her clamshell containers of chocolate chip cookies, brownies, and fudge. "After the talking-to I got from Saul and the Slabaughs on the previous Saturday, I didn't think I'd better show my face."

Molly put out a stack of paper plates. "It was our busiest day yet," she replied. "We need to seriously increase our noodle production to keep up with the demand here."

"The Wengerds brought a couple of wagons loaded with baskets of beautiful veggies from their fields and greenhouses," Jo said enthusiastically. "Several folks from church had big baskets of produce, as well as people from as far away as Cedar Creek and Clearwater. Jude was our auctioneer, of course."

"Customers were already asking when the next produce

auction will be," Lydianne said with a nod. "I think we should allow Nelson and Michael to set dates that will work well for them."

"But we missed *you*, Regina," Marietta said with a sad smile. She opened a bag of disposable forks and spoons. "Lots of folks were asking what had happened to the wonderful paintings in your store—"

"And that brings us to our first order of business tonight," Jo said as she removed the foil from her casserole. "We'd dearly love it if you could come help us on Saturdays, Regina—act as a floater, perhaps, when some of us could use an extra pair of hands. The preachers surely couldn't object to that, because you'd no longer be painting your pictures."

Regina was so hungry she'd snatched a slice of pizza from the box, but she paused before taking her first bite. "I'm not supposed to speak with anyone or hand them anything, or—"

"It's like Gabe said on Sunday," Jo interrupted with a smile. "You can certainly handle transactions with English customers, ain't so?"

"But won't church members realize you've been *communicating* with me, if I'm working with you?" Regina asked pensively. "I don't want to get you in trouble. I really appreciate it that you've invited me tonight, and that you're not . . . shutting me out."

Molly grasped Regina's wrist, her expression earnest. "We just can't do that, Regina," she insisted. "Who will stand up for us *maidels* if we don't stand together?"

Everyone around the table nodded as they began to eat.

"I think we can agree to not talk to you while you're helping us—at least in public, while anyone's looking," Lydianne suggested after thinking about it.

"But that won't stop us from winking or making faces

or sticking our tongues out at you!" Molly teased. "What're friends for?"

Laughter filled the room and lifted Regina's spirits. Where would she be without these loyal friends? They ate in silence for a few minutes before the conversation continued.

"I can understand that you might not want to come since you wouldn't be earning any income, though," Lydianne said pensively. She pulled steaming slices of pizza from the box and positioned one of them on Regina's plate.

"*Jah*, there's that," Regina agreed as she spooned up some zucchini casserole. "But as I recall, Lydianne, you're not making any money here, either, because you volunteered to do the bookkeeping and to help the Flauds—or whoever needs you."

"We might have a solution to that," Jo said with a cat-like smile.

Everyone watched Jo fill her plate again, sensing she enjoyed making them wait for the explanation that had put a lilt in her voice. When Jo glanced up at them over a fresh slice of pizza, she began chuckling so hard she could barely chew.

"All right, so we have some *gut* news!" she announced. "First, the owners of the bulk store and Koenig's Krafts want to open stalls here at The Marketplace, starting this Saturday—"

"Oh, that's fabulous!" Lydianne said as the others nodded.

"—and second, Margaret Shetler and Delores Flaud have asked to hold their annual family reunions here this summer," Jo continued happily. "So we'll be needing someone to manage these events, and we'll need to set the fees for using the facility. It seems only right that the person who becomes our event manager should be paid for her time, from those fees."

Everyone began talking at once, filling the office with happy chatter. Regina was pleased about this news, even if the prospect of managing family events didn't particularly appeal to her. Once she was stuck in her uncle's guest room, however, it would get her out of the house more often.

"And our other topic for discussion tonight involves helping our Regina," Jo put in with a kind smile. "Seems to me that if we'd like her to help us in our shops, we *maidels* should throw a packing frolic before she moves. Packing is a huge job, and I couldn't imagine having to do it all by myself."

Regina's eyes widened as the office got quiet. "Oh my," she whispered. "That would be such a help. Jessica—the real estate agent—hinted that the place would sell faster if it didn't look so, um, cluttered."

Lydianne laughed softly, squeezing her shoulder.

"But she also warned me to be patient, because it might take weeks or even months for someone to buy it," Regina continued with a sigh. "Morning Star's a small town. People need a compelling reason to move here."

"Maybe if you keep your clutter, the house won't sell— so you won't have to move in with Clarence and Cora!" Marietta teased.

Regina laughed along with her friends. It was good to feel their support, to know their friendship hadn't been affected by her *bann*. "I've thought of that," she admitted, "but I doubt Uncle Clarence would allow it."

"I don't see why you should have to get rid of your house—especially because it belonged to your parents," Molly said in a protective tone. "Nobody seems to care that Marietta and I have a house, or that Lydianne rents a place on the edge of town."

"Single Amish gals have houses in other church districts, too," Jo pointed out. "I'm thinking this is mostly Preacher Clarence trying to control his niece. We're such a wayward, independent bunch, we *maidels*. We need constant guidance, you know."

Regina smiled sadly. "*Jah*, you've pegged it right. I *really* don't want to live with my aunt and uncle," she said with a sigh. "I—I only put my house up for sale because Uncle Clarence said I had to . . . and because if Martin fires me, I can't afford to keep it anyway."

"Why would he fire you?" Lydianne shot back. "I've reminded him time and again that we can't lose any more employees if we're to keep up with all our orders."

"*Jah*, but the way most men see it, we women shouldn't be living on our own," Jo reminded them. "Who's to say that Martin and Clarence won't put their heads together and decide that if Regina moves back into the Miller place, she won't need an income anyway? So Martin might feasibly let her go because Preacher Clarence thinks it's his responsibility to support Regina while he keeps her on the straight and narrow. From a male viewpoint, that would fit the Old Order's way, ain't so?"

Regina sighed glumly. She could certainly imagine that scenario happening. The way her friends were nodding, they understood the possibility of it, too.

Marietta finished her slice of pizza and eyed the desserts. "Regina, we'll help you box up your stuff, but maybe you could keep your things around—"

"In case your house doesn't sell—or in case your situation changes somehow," Molly continued in a hopeful tone. "After you're voted back into the congregation's *gut* graces, maybe your uncle will decide you should stay in your house instead of being one more female at his place."

Shaking her head, Regina reached for another slice of pizza. "I can't see him changing his mind because of *that*," she murmured. "Lots of men don't have any sons or sons-in-law in the house."

Once again Lydianne squeezed Regina's shoulder. "We'll pray that things work out so you'll be happy, Regina. Maybe that's God's will," she added emphatically. "Who's to say Clarence Miller has a corner on knowing what God wants, just because he's a preacher?"

Jo's eyes widened. "I wouldn't go spouting off on that topic in front of Clarence if I were you!"

"*Jah*, he'll think Regina put us *maidels* up to saying that, and then he'll be keeping an even closer eye on all of us," Molly said. She flashed Regina an encouraging smile. "No matter what, we all want the best for you, and we'll help you however we can."

Regina was grateful when their discussion turned back to the more cheerful topics of the two new stores that would open on Saturday and the two upcoming family reunions. After they'd finished their meal and cleaned up, she and her friends went out the back way and headed home. Lydianne offered her a ride, so they left together.

"Do you want to be the events manager?" her friend asked after the mare was clip-clopping down the road. Without much car traffic, they moved along freely as dusk was falling.

Regina shrugged. "Hostessing isn't really my cup of tea," she replied, "but maybe it would give me something to do—get me out of the house once I'm living with Aunt Cora and Uncle Clarence. Unless *you* want that job, Lydianne."

"I suppose if no one else jumps on it, it'll fall to me as

the business manager," she replied, watching for traffic. "We've got some time to decide on that, though. The reunions aren't scheduled until September."

As they turned off the blacktop and approached Maple Lane, Regina wondered what she might be doing by September . . . after she and Gabe had completed their four-week shunning and their lives had settled into place again. It would be nice to know that at the end of the rocky path her life had recently taken, better times awaited her.

But life wasn't a fairy tale. There was no way to predict a happy ending.

After Lydianne dropped her off, Regina hurried past the FOR SALE sign and entered the house. She'd always loved the way evening's light softened her rooms, and she hoped to savor several more days surrounded by the eclectic furnishings she'd found at flea markets and antique stores. Everything was arranged just the way she wanted it—and once she moved in with her uncle and aunt, she'd have to be satisfied with the furnishings that were already in their guest room.

That's so depressing. Don't think about it until you absolutely have to.

Regina entered the kitchen to brew a cup of tea—and spotted a sheet of paper on the kitchen table.

Regina, we got an offer on your house today! It would be a perfect starter home for this young couple and they're so excited! Once everything's been approved and signed—probably within the next month—they'll be able to move in. They love your furniture and would like to buy most of it. We'll talk soon. Jessica

Regina sniffled as she reread the note. She'd be leaving by the end of July?

As this painful reality slammed into her, Regina left the kitchen, stifling a sob. She dropped down onto the couch and buried her face in one of the soft cushions— which would soon belong to someone else.

It was going to be a long, lonely night.

Chapter Twenty-Two

By Friday evening's meal the tension at home was so stressful, Gabe wondered who would feel compelled to leave the kitchen first. At the table across the room, his father's demeanor was so icy that frost could've formed on the walls.

Glancing fearfully at Dat's stormy expression, Kate and Lorena shared none of the usual stories about their day after the silent grace. Mamm fidgeted with the food bowls, making sure Dat could reach everything to serve himself first—and she'd prepared his favorite meals the last few nights—as though these efforts might put him in a better mood. When Gabe had tried to apologize on the previous two evenings, his father had silenced him.

He inhaled deeply before making another attempt. What else could he do? The tension had become more than anyone could bear. He wasn't supposed to initiate conversation, but how else could he apologize? "Dat, I'm sorry about the things I said at church—"

"Not sorry enough!" his father blurted. "Why should I take your apology seriously? You've *claimed* you regret what you said about our business—and Saul's—yet you still defend Regina's sins, and you show no remorse for indulging in your own! You *say* you've gotten rid of your

guitar and stopped playing that Methodist piano, but I
don't believe you!"

Gabe clenched his jaw to keep from lashing out in
frustration . . . and guilt. His guitar was still hidden in the
tool chest on his rig. And with so many hours in his work-
less days to fill, he had indeed played and prayed in the
Methodist church's hushed sanctuary. After Pastor Mike
had come to see who was playing the piano, Gabe had even
chatted with him a few times. The more Dat railed at him,
the less he felt like giving up either instrument.

"I'm not sorry I asked those questions about why the
Old Order considers Red's artistic ability a sin, because I
need an answer," he murmured. "I didn't want to lie about
that, because bearing false witness only adds to the sins that
seem to be piling up higher every time I try to talk to you
about—"

"This is pathetic! Thomas and Mose would never lower
themselves to doubting our faith, much less stand up for
a member whose shunning was justified," Dat retorted.
"I should have brought one of them into the business instead of—"

"Martin, think about what you're saying," Mamm
pleaded. She glanced sadly at her two teenaged daughters,
seated across the table from her. "Girls, please take your
plates up to your rooms to finish your dinner."

Lorena and Kate quickly left the kitchen. Gabe envied
their escape—and he resented the way Dat had thrown his
two older brothers' names into the fray. Mose had appren-
ticed with a farrier when he'd turned fourteen—and later
married the man's daughter—while Thomas had relocated
to Indiana after answering an ad in the *Budget* calling for
workers in an RV factory. Neither of them had shown any
inclination toward furniture making—or for working with

their *dat*—so for better or worse, the foreman's position had fallen to Gabe.

Dat saw things differently, however. "I'm saying what needs to be said," he retorted, glaring at Mamm. "I'm trying to bring Gabe back into the fold with a clean heart and pure intent, but his half-baked apologies—and the rumor that he's been dating Regina—aren't helping his case."

Heat flared beneath Gabe's shirt collar. Had someone spotted them together? Should he rise to Dat's bait or play dumb? The last thing he wanted was to put Red's job in jeopardy.

Mamm sat up straighter, struggling to settle her emotions. "Gabe has repeatedly apologized and attempted to bring peace back into this family," she whispered hoarsely, "yet you *judge* his apologies as insufficient because they're not worded just the way you would—"

"His apologies are lame and insincere, Delores," Dat stated bluntly. "I've seen no signs of remorse or—"

"And your attitude has become even more high-toned and inexcusable than you claimed Gabe's was in church," Mamm protested more loudly. She swallowed hard, struggling to remain strong in the face of Dat's rancor. "The finger-pointing must end before the forgiveness can begin, Martin."

"It's not your place to tell me how to conduct myself, Delores."

Gabe's anger flared. "Despite my apologies, you've forbidden me to return to work, and I seem to be a source of constant tension every time you and I are in the same room. I give up," he added as he rose from his chair. "I don't know what else I can do to—"

"*Jah*, that's it! Run off with your tail between your legs—"

"Gabe, please don't go!"

As the screen door banged shut behind him, Gabe felt torn between staying at home—mostly because Mamm had stood up so staunchly for him—and leaving town altogether . . . making a clean break with the Old Order.

Gabe instinctively knew Red would understand his dilemma and perhaps shed some light on a solution. As he walked toward Maple Lane, however, he cut across some pastures in case someone from church was watching him. Approaching her house from a different direction, he noticed that the attic windows were dark. His breath caught when he saw the UNDER CONTRACT banner attached to the agency's sign in her front yard.

Gabe hurried up to Red's porch and knocked loudly on the screen door. Lamps were lit and the front room was in disarray, but he saw no sign of her. "Red, can we talk?" he called into the house. "It's me—Gabe."

A few moments later, she came down the back hallway. Still wearing her stained old dress and kerchief from her day at the furniture factory, Red was a welcome sight, but she appeared pinched and pale. "Hey there, Gabe, come on in. I was, um, packing up the spare bedroom."

His problems suddenly seemed like molehills, compared to the emotional mountains she was facing. "So your house has already sold?" he asked as he stepped inside. "When do you have to be out, honey-girl?"

She shrugged forlornly. "The real estate agent thinks all the paperwork might be done within a month," she replied. "Apparently a young couple are buying it as their first home. They want to buy most of the furniture, so I suppose it's a blessing that I don't have to figure out where to take it all."

When Gabe saw the telltale shine of tears in her hazel

eyes, he opened his arms. "You're not sounding like you feel very blessed right now," he whispered.

As Red rushed into his arms, his heart lurched. She felt thinner, and she was trembling with the effort it took not to cry. Gabe had the overwhelming urge to kiss her—but what would that solve? Instead, he held her close, rocking her gently.

"*Denki* for understanding," Red said in a halting voice. "I don't mean to be such a wet blanket—"

"That makes us two of a kind," he remarked with a sad laugh. "I left the house under a dark cloud—but I can't imagine what it must be like to know that in a few weeks, somebody else will own your home. I'm sorry this has happened so fast, Red."

For several moments they simply stood in one another's embrace, savoring the warmth that kept each of them from feeling totally alone. Red sighed and eased away. "Jo and the girls are having a packing frolic for me someday soon, but since I'm not painting anymore I had to have *something* to do tonight." She looked at him with red-rimmed eyes. "I'm in such a state, I guess I haven't even had any supper."

"I walked away from mine," Gabe muttered. "Shall we go into town and get something?"

With a disparaging glance at her stained, careworn dress, Red grimaced. "Let's stay here. I suspect peanut butter and jelly might be the best I can do—"

"But PB and J with you sounds like a *feast*, considering how everyone at the Flaud house is strung too tight to eat anything," he remarked under his breath. "Three times I've apologized from my separate table in the corner, but—well, I don't know what else to do. I feel bad grousing about it, considering *your* situation."

It was such a simple thing, sitting down across the table

from Red, yet Gabe felt so at home. Her oak cabinets glowed in the last rays of sunlight that streamed between the forest green panel curtains. Her walls were painted a bold shade of Granny Smith apple green, and the counter-tops were covered with cranberry red ceramic tile. She'd painted her table and chairs royal blue, and other details around the room matched them. It was a Plain kitchen, yet it reflected Red's artistic inclinations.

Red set out two ivory plates with blue borders. When she brought a half loaf of store-bought sandwich bread, a large jar of peanut butter, and two jars of jelly to the table, Gabe felt oddly contented.

Is this how it would feel if you and Red got hitched and lived in this quaint little place?

Gabe banished the thought from his mind immediately. A different family would soon be living in this house, so it was useless to fantasize along that line.

"Penny for your thoughts," Red teased. "An interesting grin just lit up your face."

He nipped his lip and reached for the bread bag. "I was just thinking how *homey* your kitchen feels," he hedged as he helped himself.

Red's eyebrow arched slightly as she accepted the bread bag and removed a couple of slices. "So have you ever been serious about making a home with somebody, Gabe? I can't imagine you've come this far without, um, breaking a heart or two."

He blinked. Why would Red be thinking *that*?

As he removed a large blob of peanut butter from the jar with his knife, Gabe decided to tell her about his past, be-cause it put his present predicament into perspective. "Matter of fact, I was courting a gal a few years older than me several years ago—which was the main reason I joined the church," he admitted.

"*Jah*, that happens a lot in our faith," she murmured as she, too, began making a sandwich.

Sensing nothing critical in her tone, he smeared strawberry jam on his other slice of bread and put his sandwich together. "Louisa was everything I thought I wanted," he began in a faraway voice. "I was only eighteen, but her *dat* invited me to work on his construction crew, and we got on well from the start. I knew we newlyweds would have to live with her folks until I could afford to build us a house—"

The heartbreak came back in such a rush, Gabe slashed through his sandwich with his knife and tore it into two very jagged halves.

"My word, what happened?" Red whispered, quickly grasping his wrist. "Don't hurt yourself!"

Gabe released the knife, embarrassed yet comforted by her gesture. "Louisa decided another fellow suited her better. A guy who already had a house on a big farm."

"Ouch," Red muttered. "I'm really sorry."

He sighed. It felt good to share the painful story, even if it was the least romantic thing he could possibly talk about. "About that time, my two older brothers were finding reasons to leave town—and I could hardly keep working for Louisa's father—so when Dat asked me to manage the furniture factory, it seemed like a *gut* plan for the future," he explained in a rising voice. "Now that my shunning's making him show other colors, I'm not so sure—but enough about that. You're being very generous, sharing your food and listening to my tale of woe, Red."

She took a big, hungry bite of her sandwich. A dab of apricot jam lingered alongside her mouth as she chewed, enticing Gabe to kiss her. Refocusing, he asked a question of his own.

"So what about you, Red? Have you left a special guy behind?"

Her hazel eyes widened suddenly and she appeared too startled to answer. Red hastily took another bite of her sandwich. Something in her wistful expression warned him that her reply might cut closer to home than he'd expected.

"Well, I kept this house so I could paint, you know," Red reminded him softly. "I couldn't pursue my art and marry anyone—"

"Surely there's been somebody," he pressed. "You're a pretty girl, Red, so I can't believe the guys have kept their distance."

When her gaze locked into his, Gabe's heart fluttered like a frightened bird.

"*Jah*, I fell for a guy a while back," she whispered, "but he didn't have a clue that I existed, so—"

A loud knock interrupted them before he could ask who would be so stupid as to ignore a sweet young woman like Red. Startled, she rose to look toward the front door. "*Jah*, who's there?" she called out.

"It's your friendly neighborhood bishop, come to see how you're doing, Regina," a familiar male voice replied.

Red's eyes widened into hazel plates before she went to answer the front door. Gabe had no way to escape; even if he tried to go out the back exit, he'd have to pass through Red's front room first.

And then Jeremiah Shetler was filling the arched kitchen entryway with his tall frame. A knowing smile lit his face when he spotted Gabe. "I had some time before our Friday night men's singing session, so I stopped by to see how Regina's doing. I'm glad she's not handling the sale of her home alone," he added. "Or maybe, for two folks under the *bann*, it's a case of 'misery loves company,' eh?"

"*Jah*, there's that," Red put in as she gestured for the bishop to take the other chair at the table. "We're both in such a low mood, peanut butter and jelly's all the effort we've put toward supper. I was in *gut* company by myself before Gabe showed up, though," she added quickly. "Sounds like things aren't any too warm and fuzzy at the Flaud place."

Gabe immediately wished she hadn't mentioned his predicament at home, yet an expression of concern replaced the bishop's previous teasing grin.

"What's happening with your family, Gabe?" Bishop Jeremiah asked.

He sighed. There was no use in dodging the bishop's question—and maybe he was exactly the person who needed to hear what was going on. "I've done everything Dat has asked," he replied softly. "I'm eating at a card table in the far corner of the kitchen. Three times I've apologized, but Dat doesn't think I'm sincere—or sorry enough. I walked out a little while ago because things got so tense I couldn't stay any longer. Mamm tried reasoning with him," Gabe added sadly, "but Dat told her to butt out. I've never known him to be so rude and nasty."

The bishop's eyes widened. He glanced at Red's wall calendar. "You've got more than three weeks of your *bann* ahead of you," he said. "That's a long time for tensions to escalate within a family. I'll see what I can do—and if it seems best, you're welcome to bunk at my place for a while."

Gabe sat up straighter. "That's a very generous offer. I appreciate whatever help you can give us, because it's really tearing Mamm apart that we men aren't getting along."

The bishop nodded and then focused on Red. "How are you doing, Regina? Your house sold mighty fast, ain't so?"

Her smile slipped. "The other *maidels* are going to help me pack," she said with a sigh. "I—I really don't want to leave, but Uncle Clarence won't believe I've truly given up my painting unless I do that. It's going to pinch, moving into the spare bedroom at their place."

Jeremiah considered this. "I personally have no problem with you or Lydianne living independently, but Clarence is the man of your family—and he and Preacher Ammon agree it's best for him to be responsible for you now."

Regina's expression was glum. "If Martin fires me because the men don't believe I need an income, I'm going to go stark, raving crazy," she muttered. "Aunt Cora runs her household a certain way, and I'm not used to spending my days at home anymore. It's going to be a major adjustment for both of us. But I guess I have to start following the rules again. *All* the rules."

The hitch in her voice alerted Gabe to the depth of Red's distress, which she'd been covering with a cheerful front. As always, Bishop Jeremiah listened carefully to her concerns—but after he prayed with them and went on his way, Gabe felt even more aware of the dark, oppressive cloud hanging over him and Red because they were trying to obey the *Ordnung*.

"What if we just *left*, Red?" Gabe blurted. "I could make furniture and you could sell your paintings! We'd get by just fine living English."

Red's horrified scowl told him he'd gone too far—but he couldn't take back his words, and he didn't feel like apologizing yet again for speaking his mind.

"Could you *really* leave your family behind?" she whispered. She rose from her chair, looking away from him.

"I don't have many relatives left, but if I had to go the rest of my life without speaking to my friends again—knowing *I* had ripped apart those relationships—I can't imagine how lonely I'd be, Gabe. And how guilty I'd feel for breaking my vows."

Gabe sensed he was heading down the wrong road, but something inside him snapped. Escaping the Old Order straitjacket suddenly seemed like the only sane way to live, and he had to do some tall talking to convince Red he was right.

"What sort of religion decrees that your family and friends are no longer allowed to speak to you, simply because you regret a decision you made when you were too young to know what you were getting yourself into?" he demanded. "That's how it happened with me—and you were awfully young when you got baptized, too. If Christ died to save us from our sins, why would God snatch away our salvation just because we want to consider a different lifestyle?"

Red's hand fluttered to her heart as she stared at him with a proverbial deer-in-the-headlights expression. It was too late to change course or back down, so Gabe kept talking, hoping to convince her.

"What other options do you see, honey-girl?" he asked in a gentler tone. "I'm fed up with all these rules, but—but for *you*, I think I could stay Amish if I could keep my guitar and you kept your paints. If we got married and kept each other's secrets, who'd be the wiser? And you wouldn't have to live with Clarence that way, either."

Red staggered backward. The emotions warring on her flushed face told him he'd said all the wrong things yet again. He'd known for a long time that he wanted to marry her, but what respectable girl would accept such a bungled, back-door suggestion of a proposal? "Okay, so I shouldn't have said—"

She held up her hand to silence him. "We can't let on as though we've given up our artistic pursuits if we really haven't," she stated with an unwavering gaze. "We're either *in* or we're *out*—we're faithful, or we're not. And if you think for one minute that I'd consider a marriage built on continuing our longtime lies, Gabriel Flaud, you've got me figured all wrong."

Her words scared all remaining rational thought from him. "Why do you always have to follow the *Ordnung*?" he fired back. "Old Order rules drive me nuts because they seem so arbitrary—and they have *nothing* to do with my faith in God! It's a *gut* thing we figured out we have such a major difference in mind-set before we tied the knot, ain't so?"

Regina's heart shattered as she watched Gabe walk out—forever. His stride was stiff and quick, and he didn't once look back as he headed away from the house. After all the years she'd known him, she'd never dreamed that irreconcilable differences would explode in their faces and send them on separate paths.

But she'd stood her ground. She hadn't allowed Gabe's hints at marriage or the prospect of avoiding her uncle's spare bedroom to sway her. Gabe's persuasive voice and winsome smile hadn't led her back to the artistic primrose path she'd promised to leave behind.

She was Old Order Amish. She'd confessed, she was serving out her penance, and when she was voted back into the fold, she would stay where she belonged. Without Gabe.

We're either in *or we're* out—*we're faithful, or we're not.*

That was the black and white of it . . . even if Regina suspected her words would come back to taunt her in the coming months. With a parting glance at their two plates, which looked so cozy together on her kitchen table, she plopped down on her sofa. All she could do was stare into space, feeling hopelessly empty.

As it sank in that she and Gabe wouldn't be friends any longer, Regina's fingertips burned with the need to paint. She curled in against her knees, willing herself to stay away from the old trunk in the back bedroom where she'd stashed her art supplies. Every fiber of her being regretted the fact that Gabe had driven past the turnoff to the thrift store the other day, and that they'd instead indulged in an idyllic afternoon of her painting and his guitar playing.

The memory of their time together would torment her forever—and the knowledge that her paints were still in the house made Regina's sandwich lurch in her stomach. She rushed to the bathroom and vomited. In a trance of regret and weakness, Regina opened the old trunk and grabbed her sketch pad. Within moments she was propped against the head of her bed with her knees bent slightly, lost in a hopeless haze of wretched need.

As her pencil flew feverishly over the page, the image of Gabe that materialized appalled her—because it was so perfect and so wrong. She'd always avoided drawing human faces, believing that God would condemn her far more harshly for producing such graven images than He would for painting wildlife and nature scenes. But it seemed her imagination wasn't ready to give Gabe up completely, because she'd drawn him effortlessly with only a few erasures.

Regina finished the sketch quickly, complete with Gabe's strong jawline, soulful eyes, and dimples. To avoid meeting his gaze, she'd drawn him looking off into the distance over her shoulder. With a will of its own, however, her pencil made a few more strokes and then Gabe was looking right at her, his face alight with the love she'd seen blossoming in his soul.

Regina burst into tears. Would this be the *only* way she would again behold his affection for her?

Maybe artistic talent isn't such a blessing, if I use it to torment myself.

When her inner voice came at her from a different place, however, Regina felt terribly unsettled. *Maybe Gabe had a point—what if God isn't the least bit offended by our talents? What if it really is just the age-old beliefs of Amish church leaders that condemn us?*

"Put it all away," she muttered as she rose from her bed. "If your faith is truly strong, you can forget your *gut* times with Gabe ever happened. With any luck, you can go back to being the finisher at his factory—the mousy one who's invisible to him."

As she dropped her sketch pad and pencil back into the old trunk, however, Regina knew she'd just told the most despicable lie of all: she'd lied to herself.

After jogging along Maple Lane at record speed, Gabe finally had to slow down at the intersection to catch his breath. He was a mental mess—an emotional wreck. Deep down, he knew he should return to Red's and beg her forgiveness for the hurtful words he'd flung at her. His frustration with Old Order ways had gotten him so cranked up, he wasn't even sure of everything he'd said.

But he'd broken her heart—that much he knew.

His own heart wasn't in such good shape, either. And

why would it be? Red had merely been standing by the beliefs they'd been taught all their lives, and he'd implied that they could be perfectly happy living English—and that she'd surely want to marry him rather than follow through with the promises she'd made to the church.

It was a stroke of genius to suggest that if you married her, you could continue hiding your guitar playing and painting, too, idiot, Gabe chided himself. Escaping the Amish way was *not* the solution to all his problems. But he sure wanted it to be.

He turned left on the county road that ran past the Shetler place. It would soothe his soul to sing with the other men who'd gathered for the Friday night singing—

But Dat will be there. And the bishop will wonder why you left Red by herself. A man who loved her would've stayed with her this evening.

With a sigh, Gabe continued down the road. He'd had no real intention of joining the group anyway, because he wasn't supposed to socialize with his friends. And even if he were allowed to join the group, he didn't want to inspire the counseling session that would surely come about when Bishop Jeremiah had him and his father together, along with Saul, Glenn, and Matthias—and other fellows who'd offer advice about how to live peaceably during a family member's *bann.*

Gabe stopped just as he came within sight of Bishop Jeremiah's tall white farmhouse, because voices were wafting on the evening breeze. From behind a tree, he spotted several men from the congregation on the Shetler porch—some of them were seated on the steps, while those who'd arrived early, his *dat* among them, had claimed one of the porch chairs or the swing. They were singing "It Is Well with My Soul," and their flowing four-part harmony made

Gabe itch to join them—because Matthias sounded a little lonely on the top descant notes, which the two of them usually handled together.

Closing his eyes, he allowed the serenity of the tune to wash over him, even though the words about being at peace didn't describe him at the moment. It was such a blessing to sing with his friends, such an effortless joy to share songs they'd been singing together for as long as Gabe could recall. When the upper voices sang "It is well" and then the lower voices echoed the words, Dat's rock-solid bass had the power to realign all that was out of kilter in Gabe's heart. He and his father had sung together since Gabe was old enough to mimic the lyrics, even if he hadn't yet known the meaning of them.

He let out the breath he didn't realize he'd been holding. *You could go up to that porch and make peace with Dat right this minute—apologize and ask his forgiveness yet again. With Bishop Jeremiah and all the other men there, he wouldn't dream of berating you. And then you could sing with them and feel so much better.*

Reality punched him in the gut, however. Under the circumstances, Bishop Jeremiah might allow him to reconcile with Dat, but then Saul and the others would silently stare him down—deny him permission to join their social gathering. When he'd broken his baptismal vow and the rules that went with it, he'd forfeited the right to participate in the fellowship he needed so badly at the moment—and those men wouldn't let him forget it.

Gabe leaned his head wearily against the tree trunk. Once again he considered leaving to live English—who needed those ancient ways that made a man feel despised and so desperately alone, just because he'd made a mistake?

But Red had a point. If he left the Amish faith, he'd lose his family and his singing friends forever.

Sighing wearily, Gabe turned away as the men struck up a lively version of "Do Lord." Deep down, he knew he wouldn't be at peace again until he reconciled with Red—but the chances of that happening were slim to none, unless one of them had a radical change of heart.

Should he go, or should he stay?

Chapter Twenty-Three

On Saturday morning, Regina quickly tucked her art supplies into the baskets on the back of her bike. As she pedaled, she clenched her jaw against another crying jag—because she was *tired* of crying, and because she was on her way to The Marketplace. She didn't want to explain her blotchy face to her friends, and she hoped Lydianne wouldn't ask how she and Gabe were getting on.

Regina told herself she was doing the right thing by ridding herself of her temptation to paint. She was fulfilling the promise of her confession, and that was a positive step toward her reinstatement as a faithful church member.

If I'm doing the right thing, why do I feel so low?

Regina forced herself to focus on the traffic. When she turned onto the street where the thrift store was, she recalled the day when Gabe had kept on driving . . .

The joy you shared with Gabe that day is just a memory—and maybe you should forget about it. You should throw away that sketch of him, too.

When she'd gathered her paints, brushes, and sketchbook this morning, however, she couldn't bring herself to destroy her drawing. The Old Order considered it a graven image—forbidden—yet Regina clung to the pencil portrait as her last memento of a love that had budded and then withered before it could bloom. Maybe someday she could free herself of the handsome face she'd rendered so perfectly on paper, but she'd tucked it into her dresser drawer, beneath her spare *kapps* and black stockings.

As she entered the thrift store's parking lot, she headed for the donation box—an enclosed structure with a metal flap to cover its opening. Steeling herself, Regina lifted the flap and dropped her two bags of art supplies inside.

As she pedaled away, a little voice cajoled her. *You can buy watercolors, brushes, and another sketchbook at the discount store in New Haven. Who would know?*

Regina shook her head to rid herself of that dangerous thought. The Slabaugh sisters had it right: painting was her addiction. It would take all her strength to kick the habit that had gotten her into such trouble with the church.

She arrived at The Marketplace just before Jo opened the doors to customers. Heavy, dark clouds hovered in the sky, matching her mood. How would church folks react to her presence, considering she was under the *bann* and no longer a shop owner?

After a restless night punctuated by dreams of Gabe living English with someone far prettier than she, Regina inhaled the welcome aromas of Jo's brownies, cinnamon rolls, and fresh coffee as she entered the building. Lydianne and the Helfings waved cheerfully at her. Their eagerness to be with her eased the sting of Gabe's harsh words and the way he'd walked out on her.

Jo beckoned the four of them into her shop. "We're glad you've come, Regina!" she said in a low voice. Her expression saddened quickly. "Bishop Jeremiah stopped by to say Glenn's wife died in the night, so he won't be here today—or maybe for a while."

Regina immediately forgot her own troubles. "Oh my.

I haven't seen Dorcas at church for a while, but I had no idea she was at death's door."

Jo shook her head. "Apparently the vitamins weren't improving her anemia, and she had other ailments she didn't look after, either. You'd think a mother with young children would've taken better care of herself."

"Poor Glenn," Regina murmured, glancing toward his store. "Should we open his shop?"

"Seems a pretty small favor," Marietta put in. "We *maidels* would do that for one another, ain't so?"

"I'll do it," Regina said. "And if I see any of you girls swamped with customers, I can help you, too. That's the nice part of having partitions we can see through, ain't so?"

Regina felt better having a purpose for her day. Spending her time in Glenn's wood shop also made it easier to accept that Koenig's Krafts now occupied the space where NatureScapes had been—and it moved her farther away from the Flaud shop. She wasn't eager to face Gabe yet.

What if we just left, Red? I could make furniture and you could sell your paintings! We'd get by just fine living English.

The atmosphere at the Flaud house must've gotten more stifling than she'd realized if Gabe was so ready to leave his family forever. A part of her was thrilled that he'd hinted at marriage, yet his abrupt exit had shown her a side of him she wasn't comfortable with.

It's best you saw his true colors—his lack of commitment to the faith—before you fell in love with him.

Regina sighed as she walked along Glenn's shelves of small wooden toys, familiarizing herself with their prices. Truth be told, she'd fallen for Gabe long ago. Since her shunning she'd hoped, deep down, that he'd rescue her from her aunt and uncle's spare room, but that bubble had burst once he'd expected her to jump the fence. She didn't want to live with Clarence and Cora Miller—but she didn't want to live without them and the girls in her life, either. If Regina left the Old Order, the preacher would make no allowances because she was their niece: if she broke her vow to the church, she would be dead to him and his family.

Regina eased into one of Glenn's rustic rocking chairs. Fashioned from flat slats of varnished birch embellished on either side with birch branches that still had the bark attached, the chair made a comforting noise as she rocked on the plank floor. When four customers entered, Regina rose and invited them to browse—

"Did my son sleep at your place, Regina?" a familiar voice demanded. "Delores is worried *sick*. And if you're letting Gabe hide at your house—"

Regina turned toward the doorway, her cheeks burning as Gabe's irate father entered the shop. "My stars, Martin," she protested softly. "Why would *I* have anything to do with Gabe not coming home?"

"And why would you ask such a question in front of Glenn's customers?" Bishop Jeremiah asked as he entered behind Martin. He placed his hand on the older man's shoulder. "Gabe stayed at my place last night. Let's get some coffee, Martin. Seems we need to continue our chat from last night."

Martin shrugged out from under the bishop's grasp, his scowl deepening. "Why are you chatting with *me*, Bishop?" he challenged. "None of this would've happened if my son had made his confession in private."

"Let's go," Jeremiah insisted, gesturing for Martin to precede him. "Delores *is* worried. And when I stopped by your place a while ago, it wasn't Gabe who'd upset her."

As Bishop Jeremiah escorted Martin to a table in the commons, Regina relaxed. If anyone could set the Flauds' situation straight, it was their district's compassionate bishop—but that didn't stop the customers in Glenn's shop from stealing secretive glances at her. No doubt they questioned her morals, after Martin's outburst about Gabe staying at her place—

And what must Gabe think of my morals, if he's invited me to leave the Old Order? Why would he believe I'd forsake everyone I've ever loved?

It was a baffling dilemma. For years, Regina had dreamed of marrying Gabe—and perhaps because he hadn't noticed her, she'd continued painting to console herself. She prayed that Bishop Jeremiah could unruffle Martin's feathers—and that he would give Gabe the encouragement he needed before he got desperate enough to leave the church.

As the rain began to beat down on the building's roof, Nelson and Michael Wengerd carried their hanging baskets, flats of flowers, and vegetables into the building and set them in the commons area in front of their interior shop. After about an hour of thunder and lightning, a lull in the customer traffic gave Regina a chance to walk around inside The Marketplace. A glance toward Flaud Furniture told her that Gabe hadn't come to work. Despite Bishop Jeremiah's continued company and the presence of customers in his store, Martin looked no more cheerful than he had earlier in the day. In fact, her boss's florid face and scowl accentuated a demeanor that seemed uncharacteristically crabby and erratic.

When she spotted Rose Wagler in the Quilts and More shop, focused on an embroidery project, she couldn't resist walking in that direction. Outside the store, Martha Maude and Anne Hartzler sat at a quilting frame stitching on a star-pattern quilt, greeting the customers who'd braved the rain. When they saw Regina, however, both women focused intently on their work, as though she weren't standing a few feet away from them.

It was the hardest part of being shunned, that strict, silent separation church members insisted upon.

Regina lingered for a moment anyway, inhaling the rich scents of the vanilla and cinnamon candles that burned in displays near the doorway. Next to Rose, six-year-old Gracie sat in a small chair, intently poking her needle into a large cross-stitch design on a flour sack towel. When the little girl spotted Regina, her face lit up.

"Hey there, Regina! Look at this!" she exclaimed as she hurried toward the doorway. "My towel has a bunny sittin' in a tulip patch! Mamma says we can use it at home when I finish it, coz it'll make dryin' the dishes really fun!"

Fond memories made Regina's breath catch in her throat. "Oh, it's been years since I embroidered—and just like you, Gracie, I used to sit stitching with my *mamm*," she whispered wistfully. "It was our favorite way to spend Sunday afternoons and long winter evenings."

The little blonde nodded, happily waving a clear plastic bag stuffed with skeins of embroidery floss. "I like pickin' out the colors, coz colors make me *happy*! Mamma let me get a big ole bag of floss at the craft store—fifty skeins!— so we can share!"

"*Jah*, you won't need to buy any more for a *gut* long while," Regina said with a chuckle.

As Rose approached the doorway to corral her little girl, who was too young to understand the harsh rules of shunning, Regina took her cue to leave—but her heart was racing.

I like pickin' out the colors, coz colors make me happy!

Gracie's bagful of floss—brilliant blues, deep greens, sunny yellows, vibrant reds and purples and pinks—had

made Regina *immediately* happy. She yearned to reclaim
her paints from the thrift store—

*If you stitched your wildlife pictures on towels, you'd be
creating something practical! No one could fault you for
artwork that women could use every day.*

She blinked. Her mother's dear voice had come out
of nowhere. A solution to her soul's deepest hunger had
just dropped from heaven like the manna that had fed the
Israelites in the wilderness.

Regina returned to Glenn's shop to help a couple of
ladies who'd gone inside, but her mind was racing ahead
to formulate a plan for her sanity's salvation. *Embroidery!*
How could she have forgotten the hours of pleasure she
and her mother had shared while stitching colorful designs
on tea towels?

*Oh, Mamm, this might be the idea that makes living
with Uncle Clarence and Aunt Cora bearable. Well—
almost bearable.*

During the next lull in business, Regina made a beeline
to Koenig's Krafts. She felt so full of hope and anticipation, she could forget that her watercolors had once sold
for such princely sums in the shop she was entering. Spotting the needlework section near the back, she was barely
aware that Martin was ranting about something in the adjacent furniture shop. His voice was growing louder and
more insistent until—

"Martin?" Bishop Jeremiah interrupted. "Martin, you'd
better sit down before—"

Regina reached eagerly for a package that contained
thirty skeins of bold, bright floss colors—and instinct
compelled her to choose the bag of variegated colors hanging beside it as well. She could already imagine using the
deep green for a mallard's head and then stitching its feathers
with the blended shades of browns and tans in one of the

variegated skeins. When she spotted flour sack towels in packages of three, she picked one up, figuring she should try her new pastime before committing to any further expense. Then impulsively she added a second package to the growing stack of items in the crook of her arm.

"Could I interest you in a shopping basket?"

Regina turned with a start, laughing when a bespectacled young Mennonite clerk offered her a blue milk crate. "*Gut* idea!" she said, dropping her selections into the crate. "When the crafting bug bites, you can't get out of a store with just one or two things."

"*Jah*, those crafting bugs keep us in business," the clerk said with a laugh. "If your eyesight's better than mine, maybe you won't need a high-intensity lamp or a needle threader or—"

"Somebody got a phone? Call nine-one-one for an ambulance!" Bishop Jeremiah called out from the Flauds' shop. "Martin's passed out and I can't rouse him."

Alarmed, Regina peered between the slats of the shop divider. Martin had apparently collapsed onto the dining room table where he'd been sitting.

"I'm on it!" the clerk said as she grabbed her cell phone from her apron pocket.

From the central commons where she'd been refilling the coffee maker, Jo rushed toward the furniture shop, followed by the Helfing twins, Lydianne, and the Hartzler women. Everyone was talking in low, urgent voices, speculating about why Martin's behavior had become increasingly troublesome of late and what had made him pass out.

"Do you have any idea where Gabe is today?" Regina asked as the bishop massaged Martin's shoulders. "I'll go get him. Or I can fetch Delores—"

"Gabe's delivering furniture over past Cedar Creek,"

Bishop Jeremiah replied. "All things considered, it might be best if I accompany Martin in the ambulance and get him settled before we drive Delores to the hospital."

"I'll go to the house and stay with her," Martha Maude said. "She and the girls need to know about Martin."

The wail of an approaching siren told them of the ambulance's arrival. Shoppers and the other folks in The Marketplace had gone quiet, remaining a respectful distance from the emergency workers who hurried through the front doors.

At the sight of their gurney, Regina turned, stabbed by the painful memory of her parents' covered bodies being wheeled from the crushed remains of the bus they'd been riding in on the way home from a wedding out east. Dozens of times over the past ten years she'd wondered why God had allowed the bus to stall just before its rear tires cleared the railroad tracks. The racket of the train speeding toward them—the wail of its horn as it warned them of its approach—would be forever etched in her memory.

Why had she been seated in the front, where she and her cousin had clambered out after the collision, when her parents in the back hadn't even known what hit them? Counselors had assured her there'd been nothing she could've done to save them, yet questions and guilt still plagued her at times. At twenty-two, she hadn't been ready to deal with her parents' deaths—or the possibility that it had been God's will for them to die while she'd survived.

"Martin, thank God you've opened your eyes!" Bishop Jeremiah said. "No fussing, now. We're taking you to the hospital to get you checked out."

Regina waited until she heard the men's footsteps leaving the furniture store before she drew a deep breath and let go of her memories. The clerk relaxed as well. They made light conversation as she scanned the items Regina had chosen.

As she left Koenig's, Regina didn't even care that she only had a couple of dollars left in her wallet. She'd found an acceptable way to play with color and to use her sketching skills again.

More importantly, she'd provided herself with a survival tactic for when her *maidel* life was confined to a spare bedroom.

Chapter Twenty-Four

The tiny hospital room closed in on Gabe as he stood a few feet from his father's bedside. He'd never been in a hospital before—and Dat *never* got sick. The sight of so many clicking mechanical monitors and the tubes snaking away from his father's arm and chest spooked him so badly that he almost bolted. Dat was supposedly resting comfortably after they'd stabilized him, following what had apparently been a heart attack, but the man in the bed appeared too old and frail to be his father. He could've been a stranger's corpse laid out for burial.

Gabe had never been so frightened in his life.

"Hospitals aren't my favorite place either, Gabe," Bishop Jeremiah remarked softly as he entered the room. "It's normal to feel like you're suspended in a state of unreality—especially because we're so used to seeing your *dat* hale and hearty—"

"Taking charge of everything, and telling us what to do," Gabe put in hesitantly. "Are we sure he's going to—to wake up?"

The bishop gently grasped Gabe's shoulder. "They've sedated him, but believe it or not, he's much better than he was earlier today. When he collapsed at The Marketplace—"

"I should've been there helping him," Gabe blurted out.

"If I hadn't been so set on staying away from him, this wouldn't have happened."

The bishop focused on the slender figure in the bed. "We don't know that, Gabe. You were doing your best to lessen the confrontational atmosphere at home—and it was your *dat* keeping things stirred up."

Gabe looked away. He appreciated Jeremiah's support—especially because, despite Gabe's being under the *bann*, the bishop was kind enough to speak to him, to explain what had happened to his *dat*. Deep down, however, he still believed his father would be fine today if he hadn't made such a scene during his confession at church a couple of weeks ago.

"The doctors have told me that Martin's erratic behavior and moodiness of late could've been caused by limited blood circulation and the blockage they've located in the passageways around his heart," the bishop continued. "After his surgery on Monday—and after his pacemaker settles in—he should feel a lot better. His condition has been a long time in the making, Gabe, so he didn't even notice that he was getting slower and crankier, or that he wasn't feeling very *gut*."

"Or he was just too stubborn to admit to it," Gabe said with a sad laugh.

"*Jah*, that too." At the sound of voices in the hallway, the bishop turned toward the door. "Ah—*gut* afternoon, Saul. And Matthias, it's nice of you to visit, as well. Martin's under heavy sedation, but I bet his soul knows we're all here with him so he's not facing this ordeal alone."

Gabe nodded at the deacon, and he found a tentative smile for Matthias, who lowered his eyes because of the shunning situation. He feared the men would leave—or would expect *him* to leave—but Bishop Jeremiah's

presence apparently convinced the deacon to keep his
lectures to himself. Bishops and other church leaders were
allowed to counsel folks who'd been shunned, so Saul
wouldn't likely call Jeremiah out for being here.

Removing his black straw hat, Saul approached the bedside, gazing steadily at the man connected to the monitors
and tubes. "I hear you were with him when he collapsed,
Jeremiah. Probably a *gut* thing the ambulance got to The
Marketplace in a hurry, ain't so?"

"It's all *gut*, and God has it all under control," the bishop
replied solemnly.

"I was glad to see Martha Maude and Anne out in the
waiting area with Delores and the girls," Matthias said. "I
suspect she'll want to come in again soon. We shouldn't
overstay our welcome."

"All things considered, I think we have time for a verse
or two of a song," the bishop suggested. "It can be our
prayer for Martin while he's not able to join the singing."

Gabe's throat suddenly got so tight that any sort of
vocalizing felt impossible. Once again he wanted to leave
the room, but Jeremiah's hand remained on his shoulder.
After a moment, the bishop began "His Eye Is on the Spar-
row," his mellow baritone easing away the harshness of the
clinical, claustrophobic room. Saul and Matthias hummed
in two-part harmony until they reached the refrain. Then
they, too, sang the lyrics that were as familiar to Gabe as
the feel of his guitar's frets beneath his fingertips.

But he couldn't join them. The part about singing because he was happy—and free—made his eyes widen with
irony. This was a familiar song about how God watched
over every one of His children, yet since two weeks ago
when he'd been shunned, Gabe had felt anything but
happy or free. As the words and his friends' voices continued, however, he became very aware of the music's power

over him—its rhythmic way of seeping into his soul to soothe him.

Gabe also heard the silent spaces where Dat's voice should've been, resonating on the bass line. The song was still an ode to quiet faith, but it lacked the rock-solid foundational quality his father's harmony provided.

After the men had sung two verses and eased into a soft closing, Gabe mumbled his thanks for their music— but he felt compelled to leave. In the waiting area he smiled nervously at his worried sisters. After he spoke with his *mamm* and the Hartzler women, who focused on their laps, he went home to do the livestock chores.

Gabe felt as unsettled as a box of loose rocks mixed with shards of glass. As he pulled his buggy into the stable, the building felt empty and haunted. His *dat*'s buggy horses nickered as he fed and watered them. He went to Mamm's chicken house and filled the feeders. Even as eager birds surrounded him to peck their grain, he couldn't shake the lonely, terrifying sensation that his father was *gone*.

What if Dat passes in the night—or during his surgery? What if he doesn't come home and you never reconcile with him?

Gabe stumbled out of the stable, his vision blurred with hot tears. As he shut the door behind him, he knew he couldn't go into the house alone. It was the irrational fear of a small boy who imagined the worst-case scenario, but at that moment Gabe felt very young and vulnerable. He was too stunned by the possibility of his father's death to drive the sight of that too-thin body surrounded by clicking, blinking monitors and tubes from his mind.

He needed to find some company before the mental images overwhelmed him. His heart leaped at the thought of going to Red's house—

But you burned your bridges with her. Why would she care how upset and scared you feel?

Raking his hand through his hair, Gabe returned to the stable and hitched his horse to his buggy again. As he steered toward the gravel road that led to the river, his heart thudded in anticipation of sitting behind the Kraybills' barn to play his guitar. The craving to press his fingers into the strings nearly drove him crazy until he arrived and hurriedly removed the instrument from beneath his toolbox.

When he sat against the barn and began to play, however, his hands felt oddly disconnected from the music. The notes were disjointed and the guitar sounded tinny. Even after he tuned it and began again, it was as though he'd never before played "O the Deep, Deep Love of Jesus."

Gabe stared at the river as reality sank in. The last time he'd sat in this spot, Red had been with him, sketching. She'd listened to him as though he were the greatest virtuoso guitarist on the face of the earth. They'd talked about matters of the Amish faith sensibly, without their discussion flaring out of control—

You fell in love with her right here in this spot, dummy. You kissed her and your life felt like it was finally falling into place.

Gabe exhaled raggedly, his mind filled with the sensations—the hopes and dreams—she'd inspired in him. Her hazel eyes had shone with a love he'd seen nowhere else—

And then you got mad at her last night for behaving with far more integrity than you did. You offended her. You expected her to leave the faith she respects—for the sake of you and your music. Is it any wonder she shut you down, Flaud?

Swearing under his breath, Gabe rose from the grass. When he shoved his guitar into its hiding place with more force than he should have, the loud *whack* of wood against

wood—the echo of the strings' hollow tones—reflected his
dark desperation. As he urged his horse back onto the
gravel road, he headed toward Red's house despite the inner
lights and sirens that warned him not to visit her when he
was an emotional train wreck waiting to happen.

*Glutton for punishment, aren't you? She has every
reason not to open her door when she sees your face. Can
you survive Red's rejection a second time?*

Regina sat on her sofa, so engrossed in her embroidery
that she could ignore the heat of a humid, breezeless July
evening. The mallard drake amid cattails, which she'd
sketched on the first flour sack towel, was taking shape
so beautifully and so effortlessly that she hadn't stopped to
eat any supper.

Her needle seemed to have the same instinctive way of
rendering objects as her paintbrush: the drake's head was
filled in with stitches that alternated between long and
short, deep green and a slightly lighter shade, which gave
a realistic sense of depth and sheen. After she followed
the outline of his wing with variegated shades of brown,
she instinctively satin-stitched at an angle in one direction
and then turned to follow the line she'd just completed with
another line going the opposite way. The herringbone
effect might not be entirely natural—but the texture was
eye-catching enough that no one would criticize it.

Clip-clop, clip-clop . . .

Regina's head shot up. Whose horse-drawn rig was
passing her house—the bishop's? Or did she dare believe
that Gabe had come to repair their damaged relationship?
Her stomach rumbled, but hunger was the furthest thing

from her mind. She listened, holding her breath when she didn't hear any more hoofbeats.

If he comes to the door, let him in—allow him to apologize. It's the first step toward forgiveness, after all.

Regina's throat was so dry it clicked when she swallowed, waiting for his knock. Seconds ticked into minutes. Her heart fluttered in hopeful anticipation, daring to believe that all wasn't lost between her and Gabe.

Maybe if you step out onto the porch—invite him inside—

But then the horse moved on. The *clip-clop* of its shoes against the pavement beat a sad tattoo on Regina's heart as it faded into the distance.

She was alone again. Her heart had convinced her it was Gabe, even though she might never find out if he'd really come.

With a sad sigh, she embroidered to the tip of the duck's wing. After she knotted the floss off on the design's underside, she rethreaded her needle so she'd be ready to embroider the next time she picked up her hoop.

It was only eight thirty, but Regina turned off her lamp and headed for bed. What else was there to do? Supper seemed out of the question, for she'd lost her appetite when Gabe had stormed off, taking her only opportunity for love along with him. Apparently she'd given up her chance for happiness in favor of remaining steadfast in her Amish faith . . . and she felt deeply sorry about it.

Why did she have to choose between loving Gabe and salvation in Jesus? Why wasn't her world big enough to embrace them both?

Chapter Twenty-Five

All thoughts of love evaporated like steam from a teakettle as Regina spent the visiting Sunday at the Miller place. On the surface, the mood at the dinner table was pleasant enough, punctuated by the remarks that Emma, Lucy, and Linda made—even though Regina sat at a TV table five inches away from the main table. Because she was a guest, Aunt Cora had insisted that the ban on talking to her be lifted for the day. The meal's emotional undercurrent, however, was at a low boil.

"Regina, that mallard you're embroidering is so awesome!" fifteen-year-old Emma said as she passed a bowl of wilted lettuce. Her eyes were alight with rare interest, probably because she'd been bored since the end of school. "If you'd draw some designs on towels for me, I could stitch them and sell them at The Marketplace, too!"

"Puh! You'd have to learn those fancy filling-in stitches first," Linda put in bluntly. She wasn't particularly interested in embroidery, but at thirteen she was quick to point out where her two elder sisters fell short. "Lucky for you, Regina will soon be here to teach you."

Lucy, the middle daughter, focused large brown eyes on Regina after she'd glanced into the lettuce bowl and decided against taking any. "It's too bad you had to stop painting, Regina," she said sadly. "Gabe got it right when he asked why the men making fancy carriages and furniture weren't being punished for creating beautiful things when you were—"

"Enough of this talk about artwork!" Uncle Clarence declared sternly. He frowned at his daughters and then at Regina. "You see how it's been around here, niece? Your *secrets* have inspired a lot of dangerously wayward discussions amongst the girls—and their impressionable friends. I certainly hope you'll steer these three toward more proper thoughts and pastimes once you're living here."

Regina sighed inwardly. Because of her separated position, she was the last to receive the bowl of wilted lettuce—leaf lettuce from the garden, with chunks of bacon and green onion, dressed in bacon grease that had been boiled with vinegar and sugar. The lettuce that remained had drowned in a pool of dressing, appearing as limp and soggy as she felt.

How could she respond to her uncle's remark? It seemed anything she said provoked Preacher Clarence to spout criticism and warnings about setting a faultless example for her young cousins.

The girls and Aunt Cora knew better than to test Clarence's mood any further, so the meal was fraught with tension. Regina gazed longingly at the window above the kitchen sink, but she knew better than to ask if she could open it. Uncle Clarence was a hog farmer, and on this humid July day—or any day, for that matter—Aunt Cora kept all the windows closed so the odor from the hog lot didn't permeate the house.

It was one more reason Regina didn't want to move into this home. Her little house, with windows to open on both levels, usually had a nice breeze passing through it. She willed herself to tolerate the rest of her visit, holding her emotions in check until she'd be able to step out into the open air—even if it did smell like hog manure.

After she and her aunt and the girls had washed the dishes, Cora said, "Come into your room, Regina. Tell me what I can do to make your stay more comfortable."

It was a nice idea, but when her aunt led her into the room near the back stairs, Regina felt hopelessly over-whelmed. *Make this sad little room twice as big and paint the walls something other than pale gray* weren't requests she could make. Why wouldn't she be staying in the guest room upstairs, as she'd anticipated?

"It'll be cramped quarters compared to what you're used to," her aunt remarked as they stood between the twin bed and the small dresser that nearly filled the space. "But on the bright side, you won't need anything other than what you can carry in a suitcase."

Regina wanted to scream. She understood why Emma had a small room to herself and Linda and Lucy shared a larger one—and there was nothing wrong with Aunt Cora converting the spare bedroom into a sewing room. Regina knew better than to ask if the sewing machine deserved a more desirable space than she did, however.

"When do you think you'll be moving in, Regina?"

Regina heard an undertone of anxiety in Aunt Cora's question. Neither of them was looking forward to the change in their living situation that Uncle Clarence was forcing upon them, but what could she say? *If I promise I've given away all of my paints and supplies forever—if I sincerely apologize for the lies I told—can we call off this horrible relocation?*

Uncle Clarence would hear her lament through the thin walls, however. He would consider her ungrateful if she said a word against the space he was providing her.

"I don't know," Regina replied. "I still have a lot of

packing to do, and I haven't heard when the couple who've bought my house will move in."

Somehow she survived until two o'clock, when she excused herself to visit Martin in the hospital. As Regina drove her buggy along the county highway, she fought tears. If a passerby asked, she would claim it was the stench from the hogs rather than self-pity making her eyes water. It was senseless to cry, because she had no control over the situation.

But how could she find any sort of silver lining to this dark cloud? It was a bitter pill to swallow, knowing her only remaining family in Morning Star was taking her in as their duty rather than because they loved her.

The hands of the waiting room clock were stuck in place—or so it seemed as Gabe sat with his mother and sisters while Dat was in the operating room on Monday. He couldn't focus on yet another old magazine, and he couldn't drink any more of the coffee that reminded him of weak motor oil, so he headed down the hall to the restroom. After a sleepless night plagued by worries, he felt keyed-up and frayed around the edges.

Again and again, it came back to him: *If you'd talked to Bishop Jeremiah first instead of spouting off your spur-of-the-moment confession, none of this would've happened. If you'd kept your guitar and piano playing to yourself, the church leaders would be none the wiser and Dat would be happy and healthy.*

After he used the toilet, Gabe splashed water on his face at the sink. He'd tried praying while staring at his ceiling in the night, and while looking at a magazine and not really seeing it, but God had given him no peace or reassurance. He'd promised God that if Dat came through his heart surgery alive, he'd take his guitar to the thrift shop on the way home from the hospital, so Mamm and his sisters could witness his repentance—even though he sensed the Lord didn't play such petty games.

How do you know God's even listening, or that He cares what happens to you? What if you give up the music you love and Dat dies anyway? Then where will you be?

As Gabe blotted his face with a paper towel, his hands stilled. The man in the mirror appeared agitated and at his wit's end, not at peace with a Jesus who'd promised to be with him always.

If God allowed Jesus to die, why would He keep your dat *alive? Why would He listen to the pleas of a sinner like you, Gabriel Flaud?*

The breath he'd been holding left him in a rush. He couldn't look away from his reflection, from the green eyes so like his father's. Suddenly Gabe sensed he was at a crossroads and that he couldn't leave the restroom— couldn't rejoin his family—until God gave him an answer. It was an absurd idea, to think that a mirror in a public bathroom would reveal any deeper truth than he'd received during his sleepless night of entreating God's mercy—

It's not about you, man. Get over yourself.

His startled cry, mixed with a humorless laugh, echoed in the tiled restroom. This voice, so much more controlled and commanding, rang with a sense of purpose Gabe couldn't ignore. Who had spoken to him? As he continued gazing into the mirror, the words repeated in his mind . . . and as they sank in, he realized he'd been given a wake-up call.

With his father lying down the hall, cut open and totally at the mercy of the surgeon—and God Himself—this day was *not* about his tribulations or the deals he'd tried to make with Jesus. The ultimate issue was about Dat and about how important it was for him to pull through. All the worrying about what would happen if he didn't survive the surgery was worthless. And Gabe's whining about *I should've* and *If only I'd done* were even more useless.

It's not about you, man. Get over yourself.

Gabe's shoulders relaxed. His muscles loosened as he reconsidered the words that had brought his self-centered thinking to a halt. He needed to be the man of the family, to carry on while his father was laid up so Mamm wouldn't worry about their income—and so Dat would believe he'd made the right choice when he'd named Gabe as the foreman of Flaud Furniture.

It was no longer about keeping his distance or about giving up his guitar. It was about *being* there for his parents and his sisters—and his employees. And Red. He wanted to be there for her, too. It seemed she had a better handle on this repentance thing than he did. Perhaps he should take a few lessons from her, wise woman that she was.

After he composed himself for a few more moments, Gabe left the restroom. He fetched some real coffee from the cafeteria for his mother, along with soft drinks for his sisters. He asked God to guide the surgeon's skilled hands. Mostly, though, he held his mother's hand as he sat beside her, and he patiently paid attention to Lorena and Kate's questions about the mysteries—and miracles—that occurred behind the hospital's closed doors.

"It's best if we believe the doctors know what they're doing, and that God stands beside them in the operating room," he remarked softly. "If we shut down emotionally because we're afraid, we're not living our faith, ain't so? I don't know the answers to your questions, girls, but God does. That's all we really need to know."

When a surgeon in blue scrubs came through the doors

a short while later, Gabe's pulse pounded. Was this their Dr. Bosworth? He looked so different with a blue shower cap covering his hair. As the man approached the Flaud family, tugging off his head covering and mask, he flashed them a smile.

"Martin came through the procedure like a trooper, folks," Dr. Bosworth said. "He'll be recovering in intensive care while we keep him under observation, so this might be a good time to get something to eat or go for a walk to stretch your legs. He won't be awake for another hour or so, most likely—but he did *very* well."

"He's a tough old bird," Mamm quipped with a nervous laugh.

"Oh, but it's *gut* to hear you say these things," Gabe said as he rose to shake the surgeon's hand. "We can't thank you enough for all you've done to bring him through."

"I suspect your prayers played a big part in it," Dr. Bosworth said matter-of-factly. "God'll watch over you all as we monitor Martin's progress for a few days before we send him home."

After he gave them more information about what to expect during Dat's recovery, the surgeon strode down the hall as though life-and-death heart surgery was an every-day event for him. Kate and Lorena stood up, stretching, with hopeful expressions.

"Let's go to the cafeteria," Kate suggested eagerly.

"*Jah*, I want to try that dark chocolate pudding I saw in the dessert section yesterday," Lorena put in.

Their mother sighed wearily. "I'm not all that hungry, but I suppose it would be a different place to wait while your *dat* comes around," she replied as she, too, rose from her chair.

Gabe reached for his wallet and handed Mamm some money. "You go on down there," he suggested quickly.

"I've got some questions I want to ask a nurse. I'll see you in a bit."

Before his mother could quiz him, he took off down the hallway. He wasn't even sure where he was going, except he had to *move*—and he had to see with his own eyes that Dat was still alive and breathing. Over the past several hours, Gabe had come to realize just how much life as his family knew it depended upon the health and well-being of Martin Flaud.

He saw the hand of God at work when another fellow in scrubs came through some double doors wheeling Dat toward a room. Gabe followed a short distance behind the rolling bed. He gave the hospital worker a chance to get Dat into a small room with all the monitors and tubes rearranged to his liking, and as soon as the man left, Gabe slipped in. With all its observation windows, this room didn't seem as intimidating as the room he'd been in before—and Gabe figured he didn't have much time to waste on being nervous before a nurse realized he was in the room without permission.

He stepped over to the bedside. Dat was still pale and unconscious, his features slack, but this time Gabe didn't let his father's appearance spook him. He wrapped his hand around his father's, careful not to disturb the needle and tube taped to his wrist.

"I'm sorry I've caused you so much trouble, Dat," he said beneath the subdued clicks and beeps of the medical machinery. "I've been a pain in the butt, when I should've been more helpful and less concerned about keeping my music a secret. I was concerned only about my own wishes, when I should've been watching out for *you*."

His father stirred a bit, but he remained unconscious.

Gabe gazed at the man he'd idolized all his life, more aware of the deep lines and shadows life had sketched upon the face that had determined his own appearance. "I'm giving up my guitar for *gut* now—taking it to the thrift store today," he began again. "And it's all right— because we have lots more music to make with our voices, ain't so, Dat? We'll sing again soon, won't we?"

His father's bandaged chest rose and fell steadily.

For good measure—and so God couldn't help but hear him—Gabe repeated the words that were easier to say when Dat couldn't rebuke him.

"I'm sorry I put you through so much trouble, Dat," he said earnestly. "You deserve better from me, and if— *when*—you get out of here, I'll try not to upset you any- more."

His father's lips parted very slowly. "We're . . . not fin- ished irritating . . . each other, son," he wheezed.

Gabe stared at his father's face. Had he heard the words, or imagined them because he so badly wanted to know his *dat* was *in there* and fully alive?

One eye opened, barely. "Lemme sleep . . . willya? We'll talk . . . later."

His pulse thumped into overdrive as he gently grasped his father's arm. "I'm holding you to that, Dat," he whis- pered urgently. "Do what the nurses tell you, and we'll be here when you come around."

Dat moaned softly, turning his face away. For a blessed moment, Gabe caught a hint of a smile.

When he turned to leave, a nurse was watching him from the doorway—but rather than scolding him, she smiled compassionately. Gabe was too ecstatic to speak to her. All the way down the hall, he wanted to bounce and sing and rejoice because his father had heard and under- stood him—

Or had Dat been floating so high on anesthesia, he wasn't aware of what he was saying? Was it just luck that

Gabe had heard a promise that their father-son quibbling would continue?

It didn't matter. God had answered his prayers.

As he headed to the cafeteria, Gabe pondered the day's blessings. He still had misgivings about Old Order rules and regulations, but he believed with all his heart that God had brought his father safely through his surgery—and that He'd *cared* enough to give Gabe a wake-up call as he'd looked in that mirror.

On the way home from the hospital, he made a detour.

"Why are we stopping at the thrift store?" Lorena asked when he drove the buggy near the donation drop-off box. "It's too late to shop!"

Gabe winked at his mother. His nerves were a-jitter as he went around to his toolbox. Deep down, he still wished there was a way to continue playing his beloved guitar. But God had done him a huge favor, so it was only right to follow through with the promise he'd made during his confession.

As he removed his guitar from its compartment, Gabe's soul sighed sadly. "Find a home for this, Lord," he murmured as he gently positioned the instrument inside the drop-off box. "Help this guitar bless somebody else's life the way it's blessed mine."

Chapter Twenty-Six

As Gabe entered the Detweiler house Wednesday evening for Dorcas's visitation, he made his way toward Bishop Jeremiah—who was easy to spot because he was the tallest man in the room. Although folks didn't speak to him, he felt blessed: he'd just visited with Dat, who was gaining strength every day. There would be no funeral in the Flaud family, and for that Gabe was grateful to God.

Deacon Saul and Preacher Ammon stood near the bishop, within a few feet of Dorcas's plain pine casket. Gabe's heart stilled at the sight of poor Glenn, who held baby Levi to his shoulder as he clutched Billy Jay's hand. At seven, Billy Jay didn't understand the mysteries of death—or why his *mamm* was lying lifeless in a wooden box positioned on a sturdy drop-leaf table near the wall.

"Wake her up, Dat," the beleaguered boy pleaded. "All these people are here to visit with her, and she's supposed to be talkin' to them."

Glenn grimaced, trying to maintain his composure, but he—and most of the folks around them—choked back tears. Glenn's mother, Elva, whispered in Billy Jay's ear and led him toward the kitchen, while Dorcas's sister followed her with little Levi.

Gabe approached the bishop, hoping his idea wouldn't

be inappropriate. The last thing he wanted to do was upset Glenn and the others even more.

"What would you think if we sang a couple of songs?" he asked when Jeremiah leaned toward him. "Saul's here—and I see Matthias in the corner. Maybe a couple verses of 'Near to the Heart of God' or 'In the Sweet By and By' would be a nice offering."

The bishop's eyebrows rose in thought. He spoke to Glenn beneath the conversations that filled the crowded room. "Would you accept the gift of some music? It would be a few of us fellows," he explained. "If that would make you uncomfortable, we'll respect your wishes."

Glenn's expression lightened as he looked at Gabe and Jeremiah. "That might be nice. My soul could use some soothing about now."

Deacon Saul appeared doubtful about singing with Gabe at first, but because Bishop Jeremiah did the talking, he agreed. The four of them shifted toward the corner and chose two or three songs they knew. Gabe hummed a pitch.

As their united voices began "Near to the Heart of God," people around them looked up. No one had ever sung at a visitation—and because singing wasn't considered appropriate at funeral services or similar solemn gatherings, Bishop Jeremiah had planned merely to read the words from a hymn or two.

The lyrics about a place of quiet rest set just the right tone. When the singers came to the refrain about Jesus, the blessed Redeemer, they broke into four-part harmony—and Gabe's spirit soared with the profound simplicity of a hymn that had blessed believers for decades. Then they sang "Abide with Me"—a song about the evening of a day as well as the twilight of life. Gabe noted the rapt expressions on listeners' faces as the four of them continued into "'Tis So Sweet to Trust in Jesus." As they brought their singing to a close, the roomful of folks let out a calm, collective sigh.

It was all the thanks Gabe needed.

As he went to offer his condolences to Glenn, his friend's firm handshake surprised him because he was still under the *bann*. "You have such a gift, Gabe," Glenn whispered. "*Denki* for sharing some moments that I can replay in my mind later, when my spirits have hit bottom."

When Gabe stepped out into the summer evening, he was aware of the July humidity, the low drone of frogs at the pond, and the opalescent tint of the horizon as the sun sank behind distant trees. Such ordinary, everyday things these were, yet he cherished them. Dorcas could no longer take pleasure from them—and Glenn would be too distraught to enjoy them for a long time as well.

What a blessing it was to know his family had been spared the darkness of death and mourning. Because a surgeon's skill had given Dat a new lease on life, Gabe and his parents and sisters had everything to look forward to.

"Flaud, that was a fine idea," called a familiar voice from behind.

Gabe turned to see Deacon Saul, who—as always—appeared a bit better dressed than most folks even though he wore broadfall trousers, a dark shirt, and a straw hat like the other men. He was amazed that the deacon had initiated conversation, but who was he to question it?

"I think we did the Detweilers a favor," he remarked as Saul caught up to him. "Glenn has a hard row to hoe, raising those two boys without Dorcas."

"*Jah*, he'll lean on his friends and family for a long while," Saul observed. "It's a *gut* thing Elva and Reuben live in the *dawdi haus*—although, at their age, looking after two little boys won't be easy. Especially with Elva being diabetic."

After a moment's hesitation, Gabe seized the opportunity that had presented itself. "I appreciate the way you joined in the singing tonight, Saul—and I'm glad my being under the *bann* didn't come between us. After the remarks I made about your carriages, I can understand why you might resent my presence or—"

The deacon shrugged. "What you said that Sunday morning was true. Hartzler rigs are pricey because I have several employees to pay—but those specialty carriages I make for amusement parks are over-the-top. I build them for my own enjoyment, mostly."

Saul thought for a moment as they walked along the shoulder of the road. "Your remarks won't *stop* my building them or charging top dollar, but you made an interesting point about what is practical transportation and what counts as *art*," he explained. "And you said those things to support Regina's cause—and you confessed your own secrets despite the restrictions a *bann* would place on you. Most folks wouldn't have."

Gabe remained quiet, again surprised that Saul was speaking so positively.

"How's Regina doing, by the way?" the deacon asked with a knowing smile. "Jeremiah told us you were consoling her because her house had sold so quickly."

Gabe's jaw dropped. Did everyone from church figure they were a couple now? "Well, *nobody* would like having to give up their family home," he hedged. He didn't dare admit that he'd asked Red to jump the fence with him.

"Ah. So it wasn't *you* who made that offer on her house, to surprise her?"

Gabe suddenly wished he'd thought of that idea—and

wished he had the money to provide Red a home. "Some young English couple wants it, along with most of her furniture, I hear."

Saul nodded. "Well—give your *dat* my best. He'll be home soon, I hope?"

"Probably tomorrow or Friday," Gabe replied. "After that, our challenge will be keeping him from overdoing because he feels so much better."

As Saul took the fork in the gravel road that led to the Hartzler farm, Gabe continued walking toward the business district. The steeple of the Methodist church rose against the dusky sky like a finger pointing toward heaven, but Gabe resisted the temptation to go inside and listen to the Wednesday evening choir rehearsal. Instead, he walked another block and let himself in the back door of Flaud Furniture.

While Dat had been in the hospital, Gabe had gone to the factory a time or two to see how his crew was progressing on their orders. Thankfully, no one had reminded him that he'd been banned from the premises—and indeed, the men had been pleased to see him. After flipping on the gas lights, he ran his hands over a stately maple china cabinet and matching buffet that were nearly finished. He also noted a set of twelve chairs that were in pieces, ready to be assembled on Friday because the shop would be closed Thursday for Dorcas's funeral.

The growing pile of scraps in the corner bins gave testament to the increase in their orders since they'd opened the stall at The Marketplace. Gabe fiddled with a few odd slats and boards. He visualized how they could be made into a simple coffee table—with an irregular "distressed" top, because the largest plank had been rejected for its knots and imperfections. Setting aside this thick board, he rummaged through the bin for pieces that would become the table's legs.

Before he switched off the lights half an hour later, he'd sketched his table on a scrap of paper and had drawn the cutting lines for an asymmetrical top to be made from the cast-off plank. It felt good to work with wood again.

It felt even better to have a plan bubbling on the back burner of his mind.

Regina was pleased to see Martin sitting up in his hospital bed late Thursday afternoon. Considering the way he'd snapped and snarled at everyone before his surgery, she hoped he wouldn't get upset with her for coming—and if he stuck with the rules of her shunning by refusing to acknowledge her, she would respect that. But *bann* or not, hadn't Jesus instructed His followers to visit the sick?

She placed a wrapped piece of peach pie on his rolling bedside table. "This is from Dorcas's funeral lunch," she explained. "I could've brought you a whole plate of food, but I thought the nurses might—"

"And I would've wolfed it down, too," Martin cut in with a laugh. "They tell me I'm to be on a restricted diet when I get home."

"Ah. So eat your pie *now*, while you can," she teased.

Had Martin forgotten about her shunning because of his surgery? Regina didn't want to ask, because he seemed delighted to see her—and visiting him was a much better option than going home to do more packing. She tried not to dwell on the fact that her boss was an older, thinner version of his son—right down to the deep green eyes that she'd often seen in her dreams of late.

Martin's fingers trembled as he fussed with the cellophane and picked up the disposable fork, but otherwise he was recovering nicely. The cheeks above his dark, shaped beard were unshaven and his silver-shot hair had a serious case of bedhead, but his face glowed pink and his eyes held their old sparkle. "I guess we both have to behave ourselves for a while, ain't so?" he commented. "You're not hiding your paints someplace, are you? In case the mood strikes?"

Regina put on a smile to cover her momentary sense of loss. It had been difficult these past few days, living without her art and Gabe's company. "Nope—I took them to the thrift shop," she replied with more cheerfulness than she felt. "And I heard Delores saying that Gabe dropped his guitar off there, too, right after your surgery."

Martin sighed deeply. For several moments he gazed at his pie rather than at her. "Tell me straight-out, Regina, because I trust you to be truthful," he said in a subdued voice. "Have I been crotchety of late? Crankier with folks than I should've been? I've got some blank spots in my memory. I can't recall things I might've said—especially to Gabe, after he railed at me and Saul that Sunday morning."

Regina busied herself clearing the cellophane and some other food wrappers from his table, unsure of how to answer. But he'd asked for the truth, hadn't he?

"We all noticed how every little thing was upsetting you," she hedged. "After my shunning, I tried to stay in the staining room—"

"Because you were afraid of losing your job?" he interrupted softly. "Lydianne warned me not to let my attitude get out of hand, but Regina, it was never my intention to let you go. You do *gut* work, and I'd be hard-pressed to replace you."

Regina sucked in her breath. At last, she felt a hint of a silver lining behind the dark clouds that overshadowed her

life. It would be such a relief if she could still report to
work after she moved in with her aunt and uncle.

Martin shook his head ruefully. "I'm real sorry about
how things have soured because Clarence is making you
sell your house, too. Between you, me, and this table," he
added, knocking on its veneered surface, "I'd run screaming into the night if I had to live at the Miller place. But
you didn't hear that from me!"

Regina's eyes widened. She'd always gotten along with
Martin—until his blood pressure and heart had gone out
of whack—but he'd never expressed such concern for her.
"*Denki*," she murmured. "I appreciate your support. Your
generosity."

"See there?" he teased, raising his half-empty plate.
"Bring me pie and I lose all sense of control. You're a
peach, Red."

A short time later, as she pedaled home, Regina re-
viewed her conversation with Martin. She'd been delighted
to see that Gabe's *dat* was on the mend, but the deeper
joy came from his insistence that he valued her work and
trusted her. She treasured the sense of forgiveness she'd
felt because he'd been willing to talk to her.

*Let's hope he and Gabe can set things straight between
them, too, Lord,* she prayed as her house came into view.
*The inches between my TV tray and Uncle Clarence's table
are nothing compared to the chasm in the Flaud kitchen.*

Chapter Twenty-Seven

Gabe waited, trying to keep his eagerness in check, while his *dat* ate another cookie from the plate Mamm had placed on the kitchen table. He'd come home first thing this morning, and other than looking a little tired, Dat appeared to be doing well.

"Mighty nice to be here," Dat remarked as he smiled at Mamm. "I suspect I'll need a nap soon, because those nurses were always waking me up to take my blood pressure and poke pills down me—"

"*Jah*, you're to take it easy for a while," Mamm assured him. "We're grateful to God to have you among us again, Martin. If you feel woozy or disoriented, you're supposed to—"

"I'm fine," Dat insisted, waving her off. He glanced at Gabe, gesturing toward his usual spot at the table. "Take a load off, son. You look as twitchy as a long-tailed cat in a roomful of rocking chairs."

Gabe paused, proceeding carefully. "Um, my table's over in the corner—but I've got something I want to show you, Dat! I'll be right back!"

He felt a special excitement bubbling up inside him as he picked up the coffee table he'd left on the back porch.

When he set it on the kitchen floor where Dat could get a
good look at it, his father cleared his throat.

"Took me a minute to recall what you were talking
about, son, but before you go any further, how about if you
put away that card table?"

Gabe's heart skipped a beat. "My *bann*'s to last another
couple of weeks, so—"

"I want you back in your old spot where I can keep a
close eye on you," his father teased, tapping the kitchen
table beside him. "Life's too short to make my twenty-
seven-year-old son sit in the corner, ain't so? I'm in a forgiving frame of mind, so let's go with that flow, all right?"

Gabe's mouth dropped open—and then he grinned
gratefully. "*Denki* for seeing it that way, Dat, and for bend-
ing the rules to—to let me back into the family again."

"I'll put that card table away," Mamm said happily. "You
show your *dat* what you've been up to while he was gone."

Gabe perched on the chair to the right of his father.
"When I saw how big our scrap pile was getting, I wondered if it would be worth my while to use some of the
pieces that aren't perfect enough for our regular furniture,"
he explained, gesturing toward the two knotholes in the
table's top. "What do you think of selling irregular pieces
for less money? We could start a department called Flawed
Furniture—you know, *flawed* with a *W* instead of a *U*—"

Dat rolled his eyes, but he was smiling. "And you think
somebody'll buy a table with a top that swirls around like
a couple of commas instead of having four corners?"

"*Jah*, I do!" Gabe shot back at him. "And if nobody
snatches it up at The Marketplace for, say, fifty bucks, all
we're out is my time, ain't so?"

His father shrugged good-naturedly. "Why not? If you
can scare up some business from the scrap pile, who am I
to say no?"

Dat took his time choosing another cookie, and Gabe took a brownie. "The *interesting* business, however, is that your girlfriend came to see me at the hospital. She's none too happy about living at the Miller place."

Gabe nearly choked on his brownie. "No, she's not," he said cautiously.

Where was this conversation going? He'd have to mend some serious fences if he expected to get back into Regina's good graces.

Dat's laughter filled the kitchen. "A smart man would offer her an alternative," he said, holding Gabe's gaze. "You were on the right path when you stood up for her before you confessed, yet I didn't see any sign of *sparkle* while she was talking to me yesterday. Does your old man have to give you lessons on how to make a young lady *sparkle*?"

Gabe was wedged between a rock and a hard place. After his father had so graciously reinstated him to the kitchen table, he could *not* explain that Red had sent him packing because he'd wanted her to live English. When they heard a loud knock at the door, he rose to answer it— but Mamm hurried out in front of him.

"Keep him talking," she whispered. "Who knows what other miraculous decisions he might make?"

Gabe nodded. His *dat*'s turnaround of attitude was amazing, indeed, and he wanted to build upon it. "You're the one who's gotten his sparkle back," he remarked, squeezing his father's shoulder. "Did the doctor say how long you're supposed to be off work?"

Dat grunted. "I've got a follow-up appointment in a couple days, but I'm feeling too *gut* to sit around here at—"

"Martin, look at you!" Bishop Jeremiah's voice filled the kitchen. "I almost didn't recognize you without all those tubes and cables coming out of your chest. Welcome home, buddy."

As the two men shook hands, Gabe felt a wave of relief—because the bishop had saved him from explaining why he and Red weren't seeing each other anymore. And if anyone could convince Dat to follow doctor's orders, it was Jeremiah.

"*Gut* to be here," Dat replied, gesturing for the bishop to have a seat and a cookie. "And you might notice who's sitting in his usual spot at the table."

Bishop Jeremiah nodded at Gabe as he chose a brownie. "What brought this on, Martin? You're a couple weeks early—is your new medication affecting your decision-making skills?" His tone was light, but he expected a straight answer.

Dat cleared his throat. "Maybe that's part of it, seeing as I'm on *heart* medication," he replied. "All that time in the hospital gave me a chance to think things out, and I've had a change of heart about the *banns* on Gabe and Regina."

Gabe stopped chewing. His father had forgiven him moments ago, so he wasn't sure what to expect now that Dat was openly challenging Old Order ways.

"Delores tells me Gabe took his guitar to the thrift store—and he's apologized to me countless times," Dat continued with a nod toward Gabe. "I want to fully restore my son's standing in the church *now*, instead of waiting for his *bann* to end. Who knows if I might even be around by then?"

Gabe sucked in his breath. He wasn't ready to think that Dat might be dead in a few weeks. Or was his father trying to soften Bishop Jeremiah?

The bishop didn't miss a beat, however. "Which of us knows the day or the hour when God might call us home?"

he countered matter-of-factly. "I'm pleased to hear about your change of heart, Martin. I believe families should handle the details of a *bann*'s separation as they see fit."

"It should go further than that, Jeremiah," Dat insisted earnestly. "I want my son's return to the fold acknowledged at church this Sunday—and I want the same forgiveness and acceptance to apply to Regina," Dat continued before the bishop could respond. "If we turn our backs on our young people—if we shut them out for weeks at a time—we're telling them we don't want them around. If their families don't want to speak to them, they might come to think they should leave the Amish faith."

Gabe's mouth dropped open. As far as he knew, Martin Flaud had never questioned Old Order procedures.

Jeremiah's dark eyebrows rose. "Maybe I should ask you again if your medications are doing the talking, Martin," he said sternly. "You know full well that if I ask this question on Sunday, the preachers—and most of the congregation—will turn your idea down flatter than a pancake."

"Ask anyway!" Dat shot back. "These days, it's a lot easier for our young people to make their way in the English world. My son could start up a furniture shop in a snap—and Regina could make a *gut* income from her paintings," he pointed out as he held Jeremiah's gaze. "I, for one, don't want that to happen! We should show more concern—more encouragement—so we don't lose such valuable members of our church."

The bishop fell back against his chair, gazing at Gabe. "Have you considered leaving, son?" he asked. "You know the consequences of jumping the fence—both from a membership perspective and because of the way we Amish view eternal salvation."

Gabe sensed he might as well be honest. Dat was

sticking his neck out to keep him in the family and in the community, so he felt safe voicing his true feelings. "I've had that thought more than once of late," he admitted softly. "But when Dat could've died in the operating room, I realized how important it was for me to stay—and Red told me in no uncertain terms that she was *in* rather than out, when it came to the Old Order. So I'm still here."

Dat flashed him a knowing smile. "I was wrestling with my faith at your age, too," he murmured. "And even though I've been immersed in our ways all my adult life, I sometimes wish the noose didn't feel so tight. Other faiths change with the times," he pointed out to Bishop Jeremiah. "Why not ours?"

The bishop exhaled slowly. "All right, I'll do as you've asked, Martin, because I respect your concerns—and because I'm mighty glad you're still around to express them. But don't expect a welling up of acceptance and agreement from those other fellows seated on the preachers' bench."

As Jeremiah rose from his chair, he looked at the coffee table with the asymmetrical top. "Is this a new direction your product line's taking, Gabe? It's um, *different*."

Gabe laughed. "It's made from wood we tossed out because of those knotholes," he explained. "Sort of like Christ was the block the builders rejected, and then he became the chief cornerstone of something bigger than anyone could've imagined."

He hadn't intended to get preachy, but the bishop smiled as he shook Gabe's hand. "Point well made—and I'm glad you're still here to express your thoughts as well, Gabe," he added. "See you folks on Sunday, if not before."

Chapter Twenty-Eight

The first thing Regina saw as she approached the shops inside The Marketplace on Saturday morning was a glossy walnut coffee table situated outside the Flaud Furniture store. Its swirling, irregular shape appealed to her immediately. She felt so drawn to it, she ran her hand over its top, which was sanded and stained to perfection, letting her fingers explore the knotholes.

"That's Gabe's latest project, part of a new division he's calling *Flawed* Furniture—as in, imperfect," Lydianne remarked from the shop doorway. "It'll be interesting to see if it sells, or what folks say about it."

Regina sighed as she rose to her full height. "If I weren't moving, I'd snap it up in a heartbeat," she said wistfully.

"Any news on when you have to be out?" her friend asked. "We *maidels* will be over this week for that packing frolic we offered you, on whatever evening works best."

"I haven't heard anything from the real estate lady, so I should probably contact her," Regina replied. "Aunt Cora's been asking me the same question."

Rather than dwelling on such a downbeat subject, she smiled at Lydianne and removed the contents of the tote bag she'd carried in. "What do you think?" she asked as she unfolded one of the towels she'd been working on and held it up. "Embroidery's going to be my new—"

"Oh, Regina, this mallard is so—so amazing!" Lydianne blurted as she grabbed the towel's edges to get a better look. "This is different from any stitching I've ever seen! Look at the sheen on his head, and the way his feathers look so real!"

Regina's heart swelled. This was the first time she'd shown anyone the designs she'd sketched and embroidered on tea towels. "Once I got the idea, it really grabbed hold of me," she said as she held up towels with cardinals, rabbits, and an old barn on them. "It's an acceptable way for me to play with colors and designs, now that I've pitched my paints."

"Well, don't cut yourself short when it comes to pricing these," Lydianne advised. "It took a lot more time to complete one of these towels than it would the ordinary kind where the picture is just outlined. Show these to Jo—and the twins when they get here!"

"What've you got?" Marietta's voice came from behind them.

"*Jah*, let me set this box of noodles down so I can see— my stars, Regina!" Molly exclaimed. "That bunny looks so real I want to stroke its fur."

"These are just like your paintings," Marietta commented as she studied each of the four towels. "How long does it take you to stitch one?"

Regina laughed. "Well, painting went a lot faster," she admitted, "but stitching has kept my hands busy these past few evenings whenever I lost interest in packing."

"And I bet you'll get faster at the embroidery after you've done more of it," Lydianne suggested. "Let's show them to Jo before customers start coming in. She's been a busy bee this morning and she could use a break."

As Regina walked with her friends, she inhaled the aromas of snickerdoodles, sweet cherry pie filling, and the coffee that was brewing in the central commons. She paused to look around at the shop fronts, and at the Shetler twins as they set sugar, creamer, and napkins on the square tables. "Did you ever imagine The Marketplace would be such a success?" she asked in a faraway voice. "It wasn't but three months ago that we were walking past this poor, dilapidated stable and noticed it was for sale."

Lydianne nodded. "Pete's supposed to start on the new schoolhouse this week, now that the pole barn's finished," she remarked. "We've already generated so much commission from these shops that we've covered the cost of its construction as well as new desks and furnishings. Goes to show you what we can accomplish when we all work together—and when we have this gal running things," she added as they entered Fussner Bakery

Jo looked up from the pan of cherry pie bars she was frosting. "We couldn't have succeeded without both of you," she put in. "Our church folks objected to Regina's painting, but they sure have benefited from the money her pictures brought in."

"And look at what she's up to now!" Lydianne said as she and Regina held up the towels. "Aren't these the best embroidered pieces you've ever seen?"

Jo's mouth dropped open. "Have you sold that towel with the cardinal on it?" she asked in a rush. "Mamm's birthday is next week, and she loves cardinals. She tells me every year I shouldn't get her any presents—but *this*!"

"It's yours," Regina replied. It was gratifying to see and hear another friend's positive reaction to her new form of artwork. "I'd like to display it today, so folks get an idea of—"

"I predict you'll take an outrageous number of orders,

Regina," Jo interrupted with a nod. "Better stock up on floss and towels at the craft store!"

Regina's spirits soared, but one problem remained to be solved. "I know Martha Maude won't let me display these in Quilts and More, so is there a place I can set up? This is spur-of-the-moment, and I haven't paid any shop rent—"

"And you're not going to!" Jo insisted without missing a beat. "You can position a table from the commons between my door and the Helfings' shop this morning. Is that okay with you, Lydianne?"

"Fine idea!" Lydianne replied. "If you want to, we can figure out which vacant shop stall you can move into—whenever you're ready."

Regina left Jo's bakery with feelings as warm as the fresh snickerdoodle in her hand. She and Lydianne shifted a table and a chair into place just as Jo was opening the front doors for customers. From the back entrance, Gabe and Glenn came in at either end of a beautiful oak buffet, which they were rolling in on a low cart. Was it her imagination, or did both men seem more content, more settled?

When Gabe looked at her, his face lit up—and Regina got butterflies in her chest. His hair appeared freshly washed and cut, and she noticed a spring in his step as he and Glenn wheeled the buffet into the Flaud shop. She didn't want to ask if he'd driven past her house earlier in the week without stopping—and she felt inexplicably tongue-tied—so instead, she greeted the women who were coming to look at her towels.

As her friends had predicted, many customers ordered sets of two or three towels with designs embroidered on them. One woman was so excited, she asked if Regina could make a set of table linens.

"I'm so glad you're back, dear!" she said as she studied the display towels. "Three of your paintings hang in my dining room, and if I could have a tablecloth—and eight napkins!—wouldn't that be totally beautiful?"

Regina felt temporarily overwhelmed by this idea, yet she quickly saw its possibilities. "What paintings do you have?" she asked as she picked up her pen. "It might be best if you provide the tablecloth and plain napkins, so you get the color and fabric you want."

"That's a great idea. My name's Janice Akers," she said as Regina began to write. Janice grinned like a little girl at Christmas. "I have a raccoon with an apple, and a chipmunk with his cheeks full of food, and a lovely scene with an old red barn in a pasture. If I bring the linens next Saturday, we'll both have design ideas by then, so—oh! What if each napkin had a different small animal on it?"

Regina was scribbling so fast she could barely read her writing, but ideas for this project were simmering in her mind. "*Jah*, we can do that," she replied. "I'm thinking I might put animals and wildflowers on the tablecloth edges, and maybe a pasture scene in the center."

As Regina wrote some final remarks, Janice reached into her purse. When they shook hands, Regina felt some folded money in her palm.

"A down payment," Janice said with a smile. "We'll settle on a final price next week, all right?"

Regina thanked her profusely, slipping the money into her apron pocket. When she took a bathroom break, she was astounded to see that it was a one-hundred-dollar bill—and she had the sudden, impractical urge to buy the unusual coffee table displayed in front of the Flauds' shop.

But you'll soon have nowhere to put it, she reminded herself as she walked faster.

So what? Maybe you'll get a chance to talk to Gabe—

Regina stopped, her mouth dropping open. A hand-lettered sign on the table said, SOLD. FOR MORE FLAWED FURNITURE IDEAS, SEE GABE INSIDE.

Deeply disappointed, Regina gazed at the wonderfully quirky piece, trying not to think about the fact that she'd soon be leaving her furniture—and her home—behind. The conversations in the central commons echoed off the building's high ceiling as customers went from shop to shop or sat chatting over coffee and goodies at the crowded tables—so loudly that Regina almost didn't hear the woman who was calling out to her.

"Regina, is that you? Can we talk for a moment?"

Expecting it to be another of her previous customers, Regina turned. The tall blond English woman in a flowing red tunic and slacks stood out in the casually dressed Saturday crowd.

"Jessica, it's *gut* to see you," she said as she returned the Realtor's handshake. "I've been wondering when the folks who bought my house want to move in."

The agent pressed her lips into a line. "We've hit a snag, Regina," she said beneath the conversations that rang around them. "I'm really sorry, but the couple's loan didn't go through."

Regina frowned. "What exactly does that mean?"

Jessica sighed, frustrated. "The bank won't loan them the money they need—it can happen, especially with first-time home buyers. I'll remove the sign that says your house is under contract, and we'll put it back on the market," she continued in a businesslike tone. "And I'll contact the other folks who've called me about it, too. Don't worry, Regina, your home's adorable and it *will* sell."

As her pulse accelerated, Regina almost blurted, *Let's take down all the signs and call it* gut—*no harm done!* If her house didn't sell, maybe she wouldn't have to move in with her aunt and uncle.

Reality returned in a hurry, however. Uncle Clarence would soon be telling her to move in whether or not her home had sold. "I guess I'll have more time to pack up my stuff," Regina replied sadly. "And I'll need to decide how to get rid of my furniture, too."

"Again, I'm really sorry this happened. I'll keep you posted, dear," Jessica said. She glanced around at the people who were carrying sacks and merchandise. "Wow, this marketplace is really hopping! I'm going to take a look around while I'm here—and what a great table!" she added, pointing to the piece displayed beside the Flauds' shop. "Do you know this Gabe fellow? Do you suppose he'd build me a desk with an irregular walnut top like this, for my office?"

Regina pointed through the doorway. "See those two men talking at that dining room table? Gabe's the younger one—and the other guy's his *dat*, who just got home from the hospital and probably shouldn't be here," she added with a chuckle. "You can't keep a *gut* man down."

As Jessica entered the Flauds' shop, Regina took a last longing look at the coffee table and headed into Jo's bakery. She hadn't had time to eat lunch, and she suddenly craved some encouraging, levelheaded company as much as some comfort food. It was no surprise that Jo's glass display cases were nearly empty, but Regina took heart when she saw Jo lifting a large rectangular pan from the oven.

"Is that something really yummy and chocolate, I hope?" Regina said as she stopped at the counter.

Jo laughed as she carefully lowered the pan to the butcher-block worktable. "Brownies—with chocolate chips!" she replied. "I've gone through so many cookies in the commons today, I baked these to get us through the afternoon. So what's up, Regina? You look *ferhoodled*."

Regina nodded at her perceptive friend. "On the one hand, I've sold a lot of embroidered towel sets—not to mention a tablecloth and eight napkins," she replied. "But

I just now learned that my house hasn't sold because the couple's loan didn't go through."

Jo's eyes widened. "Could you just keep it?" she murmured excitedly.

"That was *my* first thought," Regina agreed. "But we both know Uncle Clarence won't change his mind."

Jo fetched a knife and a metal spatula. "Sounds like a fine time for a warm brownie and a cold glass of milk— which is in my fridge," she added with a nod in that direction. "If you'll pour, I'll bring our treats to that table in the corner. Chocolate makes everything feel better, ain't so?"

Chapter Twenty-Nine

As Gabe jotted notes for the flawed-top desk Jessica Mayfield had just ordered, his mind raced. Was it God's will at work? Just as he'd overheard Red through the slatted wall, telling Jo her house deal had fallen through, Red's Realtor had handed him her business card. Could he be holding his ticket to a happily-ever-after?

If you buy Red's house—surprise her with it—she'll love you forever!

The idea had come at him so fast, so unexpectedly, he had to get out and walk around to keep from exploding with excitement. They didn't have any customers at the moment, so his *dat* was stretching out on the bed in the corner of the shop, more fatigued than he would admit. Gabe flashed him a smile.

"I'll be back in a few, Dat," he said. "How about if I bring us something fresh from Jo's shop, for after your nap?"

Dat waved him off. "Just resting my eyes. If anybody comes in, I'll be on them like a duck on a bug."

Chuckling, Gabe strode out into the commons area. He saw that Jo and Red were still chatting over their brownies and milk. The treats smelled amazing, but he didn't want to go near Red for fear he'd give away his plan for sweeping her off her feet. He kept walking, past the

Helfing twins' noodle shop and the Hartzlers' quilting store, which were all busy. He saw that the last customer was leaving Glenn's woodworking shop.

Gabe stopped outside to observe his friend, who'd returned to The Marketplace much sooner after his wife's passing than anyone had expected. Glenn seemed to be holding up pretty well—while he was around other folks, anyway—but Gabe couldn't miss the weary droop of his shoulders or the deep shadow of sorrow that overtook Glenn's face as he dropped into one of his unique birch rocking chairs.

After a few moments, Gabe entered the shop. "Hey there," he said, pulling another birch rocker alongside Glenn's. "Are you sure you want to be here today? Lydianne can handle things if you want to go home—"

"It's not much of a home without Dorcas," Glenn put in with a sigh. "My folks are trying very hard to rise above it—to keep the boys busy and keep *my* spirits up—but I can't be in that house without seeing my wife making dinner at the stove, or picking up the front room. I kept waking up last night, hearing her voice."

Gabe blinked back a sudden tear. It seemed like the wrong time to hint about his happy plan for buying Red's home. "That's got to be tough," he mumbled for lack of anything more inspiring to say.

After a few moments of awkward silence, Glenn smiled a bit. "You know what else I hear, though? Those songs you and the other fellows sang at the visitation," he continued in a brighter voice. "Your singing really lifted me up. Your music is such a gift, Gabe, and you have a way of leading us to share the best of ourselves whenever we sing with you."

Gabe blinked. He recalled the night he'd been standing beside Dat's hospital bed and Saul, Matthias, and Bishop

Jeremiah had eased his troubled heart—even though they'd been singing for his father. "That's quite a compliment, Glenn—"

"What if we men formed a little musical group?" Glenn's expression brightened as he considered his idea. "We could sing at reunions or picnics, or even for folks who're sick. If you'd take charge, I bet Saul and the rest of our Friday night group would agree to perform now and then. It would give me something to look forward to, you know?"

As Glenn held his gaze, Gabe felt deeply moved—led by the Spirit to accept his best friend's challenge. "I would look forward to singing together more often, too, as a re-placement for times when I used to play my guitar," he said eagerly. "Let's do it! We can mention it to the other men tomorrow at church—although you'll have to do the talking."

Glenn let out an exasperated sigh. "Sometimes shun-ning causes more problems than it solves," he muttered. "I'll be glad when your *bann*'s over, Gabe."

"Me, too." Gabe rose from his chair. "I'd best get back, in case Dat's taking more of a nap than he expected. He didn't stay home today for fear he'd miss some *gut* gossip, you know?"

Glenn's laughter seemed like a good sign to Gabe as he left the wood shop—and the idea of performing songs with his male friends had struck a chord within him, too. As he passed the noodle shop, Red was surrounded by customers admiring her embroidered towels, and that pleased him, too. When he entered Flaud Furniture, his father was seated at their worktable in the back with a small plate of brownies in front of him.

"Jo's fresh goodies smelled so *gut*, I couldn't sleep," Dat teased.

Laughing, Gabe took the other chair as he snatched a brownie. "You've got to help me, Dat." He spoke softly so Jo wouldn't overhear him through the slatted wall. "Red's house is up for sale again, and I want to buy it for her! Can you go in with me on a down payment—like, first thing Monday morning? *That* will make her sparkle, *jah*?"

Dat's eyes widened. "The original deal fell through? This is a mighty sudden turnaround in your thinking, son, so—"

"I just overheard the news about half an hour ago," Gabe explained urgently. "I—I've come to realize that Red's got her priorities in order, and that I want to be with her. She makes *me* sparkle."

His father took his time chewing a bite of his brownie. "Does Regina know about your feelings for her, or are you springing this purchase on her as a surprise?" he asked cautiously. "What if she doesn't go along with your plans, Gabe? You'll have made a huge investment, and you might be stuck living in that house all by your lonesome."

"We'll take up where we left off! Red and I got really close after we were shunned together, and—and I love her, Dat," Gabe added softly. He gazed into his father's eyes, pleading for understanding as he'd never needed it before. "I'll be offering her a much better life than she'll have at Clarence's, after all."

After his father finished his brownie, he reached for another one. Gabe's pulse was pounding. Even though Dat might have a point about Red needing to know how he felt about her, buying her home seemed like such an obvious solution to most of the dissatisfaction that had plagued them both of late.

"When you and Red come to me and say you're courting, I'll consider putting some money on that house," his father replied after an agonizing pause. "After all, if you two marry, you could live at our place until you can build her a house on a plot of land—or you could buy a place from an Amish family that's leaving the district. The church leaders would consider that more acceptable than repurchasing her house in town, you know."

Gabe bit back his disappointment. He didn't know of any families planning to move away—and his heart was already set on living in Red's cozy little home.

Check your bank balance—maybe you can put enough money down to keep somebody else from buying the place.

Gabe sighed, because the bank wouldn't reopen until Monday morning. His father had always paid him a minimal salary for managing the furniture factory, but he'd never pressed for more money because the business would be his someday—and because, as a single fellow living at home, he hadn't been concerned about accumulating cash.

But he knew better than to pester his father about the matter. Martin Flaud said what he meant and meant what he said—and Dat had finished his brownies, so he was eyeing the bed again.

"Well, it'll all work out, I guess," Gabe whispered impatiently. "God is *gut.*"

"All the time," his father chimed in as he headed toward his nap.

Chapter Thirty

Sunday morning, after an uncomfortable meeting with the preachers while the rest of the congregation sang the opening hymns, Regina and Gabe were the last folks to enter the Waglers' front room for the church service. Following the Old Order way, Regina sat on a folding chair to one side of the preachers' bench, facing the congregation with her head low and her hand covering her eyes. This was by far the most painful part of shunning—being silently scrutinized by folks she'd known all her life, as a reminder of how her sin had separated her from the community.

This must be how zoo animals feel while visitors gawk at them.

Gabe had taken the folding chair on the opposite end of the preachers' bench, but Regina didn't glance in his direction. After enduring Preacher Ammon's terse questions about her sense of repentance during their meeting before church—and hearing Uncle Clarence state that she'd be moving to his place by the end of the week—she knew better than to give the church leaders any more reason to chastise her.

The Waglers' front room was smaller than most, and the humid July heat felt even more oppressive because Regina felt she was on display—an example of the misery that awaited members who strayed from the well-paved path to salvation. All during the three-hour service, she longed for the simple comfort of sitting among her *maidel* friends. As they sang the final hymn and Bishop Jeremiah gave his benediction, Regina couldn't wait to leave. She and Gabe were excluded from the fellowship of the common meal.

"Folks, we've had a request for a Members Meeting," the bishop announced. "I've been asked to suggest the possibility that Gabe and Regina might be reinstated to full membership today rather than waiting another two weeks."

Regina's head jerked up. When she stole a glance at Gabe, she wondered why he didn't seem surprised by Bishop Jeremiah's statement—but the flicker of hope in her heart was soon squelched.

"Out of the question!" Preacher Ammon blurted.

"*Jah*, we've been plenty lenient as it is, shortening their *bann* to four weeks rather than six," Deacon Saul pointed out.

Uncle Clarence scowled. "You should've brought this matter to our attention at our meeting before church, Jeremiah. This is highly irregular!"

All heads turned when Martin Flaud rose from his place, his face alight with a mission. "I'll speak to this because it was my idea," he said, gazing around the crowd. "While I was in the hospital with too much time on my hands—thinking how I'd regret it if I didn't live to reconcile with my son—I decided that our way of shaming and shunning members is the *opposite* of what we should be doing. Why do we turn a cold shoulder to those who have strayed?" he asked earnestly. "Shouldn't we be encouraging our members—especially our young adults—to *stay*, rather than giving them the silent treatment? How does that reflect Christ's commandment that we love one another?"

Regina held her breath. She'd witnessed a miraculous change in Martin's behavior—health-related, as she understood it—yet she hadn't expected him to speak out so openly against the age-old Amish ways.

"We're showing them tough love, Martin," Deacon Saul replied without missing a beat.

"*Jah*, Regina and Gabe have known all their lives that members of the Old Order are forbidden to paint and to play musical instruments," Preacher Ammon pointed out sternly. "They accepted such limitations when they joined the Amish church."

Bishop Jeremiah held up his hands to bring the conversation under control. "I've done as Martin asked, by bringing up his request," he said as he focused on the congregation. "We've heard the preachers' opinion, so what do you folks want to do? Do you wish to vote on ending Gabe and Regina's *bann*—or continue it for two more weeks?"

After a short silence, Drusilla Fussner raised her hand. "What's the point of having our *Ordnung* if we change its rules for every little thing?" she asked gently. "If we end Gabe and Regina's *bann* just because Martin wants us to, we'll soon be making so many exceptions to the Old Order ways that we might as well be Mennonites, ain't so?"

Several folks in the room nodded, whispering among themselves. Even though she was disappointed, Regina appreciated the way Jo's *mamm* had worded her observation— and she wasn't surprised that the other members agreed with her.

"Seems we've made our decision and we'll stick by it," Bishop Jeremiah observed. He glanced at Regina and then at Gabe. "We'll proceed two Sundays from today with your reinstatement. For now, I wish you well as you continue on your paths toward reconciliation and rightness with God."

Regina didn't have to be told twice. Avoiding eye contact and conversation, she made a quick exit down the side aisle, which was the fastest way to the Waglers' front door. It was a relief to be dismissed from the common meal, so she wouldn't have to listen to the remarks people were bound to make about Martin's attempt to change the age-old way Amish congregations chastised their errant members.

Once outside, Regina slowed her pace to avoid becoming overheated. As she walked from one shady spot to the next alongside the road home, recalling the difficult meeting with the preachers before church, one stern voice stood out in her mind: *We'll see you at the house by Friday, Regina. You've stalled long enough.*

She grimaced. Why did her uncle always make her feel like such an encumbrance—such an inconvenience?

If you told Aunt Cora the sale of your house fell through, could she convince Uncle Clarence to let you stay in it a little longer?

It was a useless question, however. As the intense afternoon heat pressed down upon her, and the issues of her shunning and her relationship with her uncle weighed her down, she was ready to burst into tears. Determined to hold her composure until she reached the privacy of her dear little house, Regina rounded the corner of Maple Lane and started to jog, gritting her teeth against a sob—

And then she saw Gabe sitting in one of her porch chairs.

The wretched expression on Red's face made Gabe want to rush to her, wrap her in his arms, and never let her go. He didn't want to push her too fast, however, or assume that she would immediately welcome his attention—not to mention his exciting idea for their future. After all, their last conversation had been more than an endless week ago, when she'd sent him away—believing that he no longer wanted to be Amish, and that he wanted her to live English with him.

"Hey there, Red," he murmured as he rose to greet her. "Tough morning, *jah*? I was pleasantly surprised when Dat and the bishop spoke in favor of ending our *bann* early—except now things feel even touchier because folks have rejected any chance for change."

She stopped at the bottom of the porch steps, eyeing him cautiously. "The whole point of shunning is to make us sorry we've sinned—to point out how alone we'd be if we didn't repent," she remarked with a hitch in her voice. "We're not supposed to like it."

Even as he resented the Old Order's insistence on shunning, Gabe deeply admired Red's willingness to accept the consequences of painting her beautiful pictures and then lying about it.

"While we're on the topic of forgiveness and reconciliation," he began, praying for the right words, "I came here because I offended you when I suggested we leave Morning Star to live English, and—and I've changed my mind. Changed my *ways*, Red," he added in a rush of emotion. "Please, can you forgive me? *Please*, can we be friends again and talk about it, honey-girl?"

A sob escaped her. Then it was as though the levee on a flooded river gave way, and Red began to cry as if she couldn't stop. Gabe didn't have much experience consoling women, but it seemed right to descend the stairs with his bandanna in his hand.

"I'm sorry for what I said last week," he continued softly as he gently blotted her wet face with his handkerchief. "And I'm sorry your uncle is being so hard-nosed about making you move to his place. But—I've got a solution for that!" he blurted, even as he sensed he was racing ahead at exactly the wrong time. "I'm going to buy your house, honey-girl! We can live *here*—get married and keep this place as ours!"

Red's eyes widened, yet Gabe sensed it was more out of shock than gratitude.

He kicked himself. What sort of idiot threw such a presumptuous statement at a woman when she was so upset?

"Red, my excitement got the best of me," he whispered, cupping her damp face in his hand. "I—I'd hoped to talk things through and show you how my thoughts and feelings have changed, but I've done it again! I've assumed you'd go along with my crazy ideas just because I *want* you to. Sheesh," he added with a shake of his head. "I've really stepped in it now, haven't I?"

Gabe closed his eyes in a wave of pain. Why had he blurted things out instead of saying them in a logical, practical order? Why hadn't he concentrated on Red—on making her feel better—before he'd launched into his grand plan for their future?

With a sigh, he turned. There was no putting the cat back in the bag, and there was no way to restate the ideas he'd bungled so badly. Maybe he really did need Dat's help when it came to making Red sparkle, because he'd only made her cry even harder.

"Okay, I'll see you another time," he said as he started down her walk. "Maybe when we've both had a chance to settle ourselves—"

"Please don't go."

Gabe's heart lurched. Had Red spoken to him? He'd been so intent on chastising himself, he wasn't sure if her words were real—or just wishful thinking on his part. When he turned, she was mopping her face with his handkerchief, hiccupping instead of sobbing.

Red let out a sigh that sounded every bit as *ferhoodled* as he felt. "I'm sorry I cut loose on you, Gabe," she said. "I could use a friend about now. Can we start this conversation again?"

Her smile looked as wobbly as a newborn colt and her freckled face was red and blotchy, yet Gabe had never seen a prettier young woman than Regina Miller. He reached for her hand—a hand as stained and calloused as his own—feeling intensely relieved when she wove her fingers between his.

"Really? You'll give me another chance?" he whispered.

Her smile took on more confidence as she gazed at him. "After all the stern words we endured during the preachers' meeting—and the way we had to face the congregation with our heads down during that endless service—why wouldn't I want to spend time with you, Gabe?" she asked softly. "We're partners in crime—kindred spirits, like you said before. Nobody else understands us the way we understand each other, ain't so?"

Gabe felt ready to melt, and it had nothing to do with the afternoon heat. "Red, you're the *best*, you know it? I—I really do love you, even if I've bungled things up telling you about it."

"Shall we get in out of the sun? I've got some bologna for sandwiches and some fresh lemonade," she said as she led him up the porch steps. "And while we eat, you can tell me about why you've decided to stay Amish—and your plan to buy my house."

To Gabe, her offer sounded better than any Sunday dinner he'd ever eaten. It sounded like an invitation to a beautiful new life.

Chapter Thirty-One

As Regina made their bologna sandwiches, her whole being thrummed with excitement. Not only did Gabe love her, he wanted to live in the house she so desperately hoped to keep!

"When I asked Dat to help with a down payment, he insisted on your coming with me—to prove we're courting, so I wouldn't make a big investment mistake in case you didn't want to—" Gabe sighed in exasperation. "There I go again, putting the rig before the horse. You must think I'm the biggest idiot on the face of God's *gut* earth."

Regina took her time pouring lemonade and taking the chair across the table from him. She'd always assumed Gabe was coolheaded and in control around young women—even suave enough to date English women—so it was almost fun to hear him tripping over his tongue as he expressed his feelings for her. But it would be cruel to keep him wondering where he stood.

"Shall we pray for a moment?" she asked.

When they bowed their heads for a silent grace, Regina peered at Gabe through the slits of her partially closed eyelids. *Lord, You've brought us this far and I'm so happy that I might pop! Help us make this dream come true—and help us do it the right way*, she added.

Gabe ended the silence with a sigh—and then laughed when he caught her watching him. Then he became serious. "What do you see in me, Red? Anything worth your time?"

Regina's heart pounded. It was a question that deserved just the right answer—but she needed an explanation first. Gabe didn't look any different on the outside, yet he'd apparently undergone a complete inner transformation. "What made you decide to stay in the Old Order, Gabe? Last I knew, you were totally frustrated with Amish rules and regulations and you couldn't wait to jump the fence."

He picked up a half sandwich and then put it down, sighing. "When Dat was in the hospital and we didn't know if he'd survive, I—I got a wake-up call that could've only come from God," he replied reverently. "I got *scared*, Red, when I realized how much I stood to lose if my father didn't come home . . . and what I'd forfeit if I left my family just so I could play my guitar."

His whispered admission gripped her heart. "*Jah*, life's not the same after you've lost your parents," Regina said softly. "If my friends from church—and Bishop Jeremiah—hadn't been there for me, I might've rolled into a useless, mindless ball and never recovered."

Gabe nodded. "I also realized what I'd lost after I suggested we jump the fence together," he said ruefully. "I was so focused on myself, I couldn't see how I was shooting myself in the foot. Losing you, Red, well—I finally saw that you are a woman of purpose and integrity, while I was skipping out on my vows for a very selfish, adolescent reason. When I grow up, I want to be like *you*. Strong and true."

Regina blinked, stunned by the sincerity of his confession—and his compliment. Words eluded her, so she simply gazed at him, basking in the glow of his deep green eyes.

"Do you see anything worth salvaging, Red?" he asked in a voice she could barely hear. "Could you be happy with me despite my tendency to speak before I think and—"

"Oh, Gabe, I've wanted to be with you for *years*—even when you didn't realize I existed," she confessed as she reached across the table for his hand. "After all, why would you choose me, when you could court girls who wear pretty, colorful dresses and who could cook you a decent meal—with their soft, clean hands?"

He relaxed and took a deep breath. "I guess it's like those words to 'Amazing Grace,'" he said. "The part about being blind but then able to *see*. And when I look at you, Red, I don't want to look any further. Will—will you let me court you?"

"Will you let me marry you?" she shot back before she thought about it.

Regina's hand flew to her mouth as her face burned with embarrassment. "I—I was trying to be funny, but I jumped in feet-first and stomped all over the words the *man* is supposed to say. I'm sorry, Gabe," she added meekly.

Gabe's face shone brighter than the July sun. "I'm not!" he said. "We're both on the same page, ain't so? I want to be with you, and you want to be with me—and we want to be here in this cozy little home, *jah*?"

"Oh, *jah*. You've said it all exactly right, Gabe."

Regina felt so full of joy she suddenly had to share something very special—something no one else would understand. She rushed back to her bedroom and returned to the kitchen with the pencil sketch.

"When you left last time—when I thought you would skip town to live English," she said in a rush, "I sinned yet again by drawing your face, Gabe. I thought it might be all I had left of you. I—I was worried I'd never see you again."

Gabe gazed at the sketch. "This is how I look to you?" he asked in an awed tone. "You surely can't believe I resemble this fellow with the determined look in his eye. *This* man has everything all figured out, and he knows exactly how to create the life he wants—without making stupid mistakes."

Regina shrugged, gratified by his reaction to her work. "It's you," she insisted. "So now that you've seen it, you don't have to doubt how I feel—because I love you, Gabe. I loved you even after I thought I'd lost you."

Gabe blushed, looking flustered. "Well, then," he mumbled, seemingly at a loss for more words.

After a moment, however, he met her gaze as though he couldn't possibly look away. "*Well then*, Regina Miller," he said, teasing yet sounding extremely serious. "You've committed an even worse sin than painting wildlife by sketching my face, ain't so? And I'll carry your secret to my grave, honey-girl," he added softly. "You have *no* idea how your talent touches me, and how grateful I am that you shared this picture with me. You're amazing, Red."

How could she possibly respond to such a compliment? Regina had a feeling she'd remember this moment with Gabe until her dying day. She swallowed half of her lemonade to settle her runaway emotions. "So, you're thinking to buy the house?"

"Before anybody else can snatch it away from you," Gabe said, nodding eagerly. "We can talk to Dat about a loan first thing tomorrow—or I'll take money from my bank account for a down payment, then go straight to Jessica's office to start the paperwork. I was hoping to have it signed, sealed, and delivered before I *surprised* you with it—"

"And that's the sweetest thing I've ever heard, Gabe," Regina said as she picked up half her sandwich. "But—but why don't we just tell Jessica it's not for sale anymore? Why should you have to pay for a house I already own?"

Gabe looked thunderstruck. "I hadn't thought about that," he admitted. "I was trying to prove I could take care of you and—and I figured your uncle wouldn't have a thing to say about it if *I* bought the house," he explained. "He couldn't accuse you of defying his wishes."

Regina chuckled. "I can't wait to see Uncle Clarence's face when I tell him I'll soon be living here with *you*, Gabe," she said. "But that'll happen no matter whose name is on the deed, so why not just take the house off the market?"

"It would be simpler," he agreed. "We can use my down payment as plan B, if Jessica's got some legal reason she has to keep the place listed."

Regina suddenly felt as though the whole world had changed course—because it had. Someday soon she'd be Gabe's wife, and they would begin their life together in this home they both loved. It was a far cry from believing she could never marry because she wanted to keep her painting a secret. "We've come a long way in a short time, Gabe," she whispered.

"We have," he agreed as he clasped her hands on the table. "It'll all work out now. We'll court for a while, and then we'll set a date to begin our happily-ever-after, Red. Me and you. Right here, honey-girl."

Gabe arrived with Red at Jessica's office just as the Realtor was opening her door on Monday. "We'd like you to take Red's house off the market!" he began jovially.

"We're getting married soon, and we plan to live there ourselves!" Red put in with a big smile. "This changes everything, *jah*?"

Jessica's key stopped just short of the lock. She resembled a deer blinded by high-beam headlights. "Uh—congratulations on your engagement," she began, swallowing hard. "But I sold the house yesterday afternoon. The buyer's paying full price for it, in cash, including an allowance for all the furniture. I—I was coming to tell you about it first thing this morning, Regina."

Gabe exhaled hard, clutching Red's hand for support. "You *sold* it?"

"How could that be?" Red demanded with a frown. "We were *there* all yesterday afternoon, and nobody came by to look at it or—"

"The buyers and I were here, filling out the papers," Jessica hastened to explain. "I couldn't argue with the fifty thousand dollars of earnest money they laid on the table. And you'd given your consent to accept a full-value offer, Regina, because you were certain you had to be out of your house. I had the impression that changing your mind wasn't an option."

Gabe's thoughts swirled like a tornado, and Red's expression told him she was as flummoxed—and as keenly disappointed—as he was. "Who bought it?" he demanded. "We can return their money—persuade them to back out."

Jessica got an odd look on her face. She studied Gabe closely. "I'm not at liberty to say," she replied. "The buyer insisted that the transaction be kept confidential. Sometimes that happens when ex-spouses are involved, but—"

"Ex-spouses?" Gabe blurted. "We don't know anyone who's divorced! We don't believe in it."

"Must've been somebody English," Red suggested

ruefully. Her sigh sounded like a balloon with a slow leak. "Are you sure it's a done deal, Jessica? We had our hearts set on living in that house, and I was delighted about keeping my furniture—and telling my uncle I wouldn't be moving to his place. So now . . . "

Gabe tucked Red's hand in his elbow, trying to sound more in control than he felt. "So now we make plan C," he said under his breath. "I don't have a clue what we'll do, Red, but we'll work it out. I promise."

As they walked back to the rig, Jessica called after them. "Congratulations anyway, kids! Keep the faith—this will turn out exactly the way it's supposed to."

Gabe shook his head and kept walking. "*Jah*, we've kept our faith," he muttered.

"Even after we got turned out," Red chimed in. "I guess God's not finished testing our mettle yet."

Chapter Thirty-Two

Regina gazed straight ahead, not really seeing the familiar buildings they were driving past. She hugged herself hard to keep from crying in front of Gabe, who was every bit as disappointed as she was. Just when they'd thought their plan for happiness had fallen into place, they no longer had a home.

"I don't feel like going to work yet, do you?" Gabe asked.

Regina blinked. "We have a lot of furniture orders to—"

"The other folks can carry on without us for a while," he interrupted, his voice tinged with bitterness. "I'm in no mood to deal with people right now—especially Dat. I was all ready to announce that we'd be living at your place because we'll be getting hitched someday soon . . . "

Regina's eyes widened. "Um, that *getting hitched* part hasn't changed, has it?"

Gabe hugged her close as the rig continued down Morning Star's busy street. "Of course not, honey-girl! I'm just really bummed about this news. It seemed like everything was finally going our way—and I was hoping you wouldn't have to move in with Clarence and Cora," he added sadly. "I doubt your uncle would allow you to stay with Lydianne or one of your other friends. And it wouldn't look proper if you took the guest room at *our* place."

"*Jah*, that would be pushing it," Regina agreed. She thought hard, hoping to lift Gabe's spirits. "I'd be fine with living at your parents' place after we marry, though. That's how a lot of couples get started."

"It's not how *I* want to start out," he shot back. He sighed, falling back against the seat. "Sorry I'm so cranky. Where would you like to go for a while, so we can get past this mood we're in?"

"Let's go home," Regina insisted. "I'll only be staying there until Friday—and I was so surprised by the sale, I didn't ask Jessica when the new owners will take possession."

Gabe turned the rig, and they were soon at the house on Maple Lane. It seemed odd to offer him lemonade and cookies from the bulk store this early in the day, yet the humidity and the lack of a breeze made coffee seem like the wrong choice. As they sat down in the kitchen, Regina turned on the small battery-operated fan on the counter.

"Here's another example of my baking skills," she teased. "I'd cook more, but with working at the factory—and my new embroidery projects—I don't spend much time in the kitchen. Maybe that'll make you rethink your decision to marry me."

As she'd hoped, Gabe waved off her remark. He bit into an oatmeal cookie that was so stale it shattered between his teeth—and then he began to laugh. "I know just how that cookie feels," he teased as he brushed its crumbs into a pile. "Soon enough you won't be working at Flaud Furniture. You'll be staying home with our babies, *jah*?"

Regina couldn't help smiling at the pictures his statement brought to mind. "I never thought I'd see that day, and I'm looking forward to it, Gabe. You'll make a wonderful *dat*."

His eyes widened. "You think so? Sometimes—like yesterday when I was tripping over my tongue, telling you I loved you—I wonder if I can pull everything together and support a family," he admitted. "It's time to ask Dat for a raise, now that we'll be house-hunting."

"At least he's still around, so you can ask him," she pointed out.

Gabe grasped her hand. "That's what I love about you, Red," he said. "You see the *gut* in everything and you handle setbacks—like our shunning—with a positive attitude. You'll be the anchor of our marriage, honey-girl. The rock I build my life on."

Her cheeks tingled as he gazed at her. "I'm blessed to have you, Gabe. We're two of a kind, even though we had no idea about that until the chips were down, *jah*?"

He finished his lemonade, appearing renewed. "What if we take the long way back to the factory? We could ask Jessica for information about lots or houses that are for sale, *jah*?" he asked, brightening. "And I could treat you to pizza before we make our entrance at work—which will cause a stir, most likely. Are you up for that?"

Regina laughed, feeling better already. "A *stir*? I can be the spoon—as long as you're the hand that's holding it."

"That makes us an unbeatable team," Gabe stated as he rose from his chair. "Let's find another place to build our nest, Red. If we're there together, it'll be the best home ever, ain't so?"

When he kissed Red lightly on the temple before she headed for the staining room, Gabe caught the speculative glimmer in his father's eye.

"I was wondering if you skipped town, son," Dat remarked as he fell into step with Gabe in the main workroom.

"But when I realized Regina was gone as well, I got my hopes up. You won't give me a different excuse for missing work, I hope?"

Gabe motioned for his father to follow him into the office, where they could speak privately. "Truth be told, we went to the Realtor's office to take Red's house off the market this morning, but somebody snatched it up on Sunday afternoon," he began with a shake of his head. "So we're regrouping. Drove around a bit, looking at other places that're for sale—because now that I'm engaged, I need to provide my future wife a home. Which means we need to discuss a hefty raise in my pay, Dat."

His father swiveled in his wooden desk chair, laughing—but it was joy Gabe heard in his voice, rather than ridicule. "*Gut* for you, son! Congratulations!" he crowed. "Your mother'll be mighty happy to hear that. And I'm pleased that you and Regina are figuring out how to handle setbacks together. But I'll not be raising your pay."

Gabe blinked. A protest was on the tip of his tongue, because he'd worked for his father all his adult life without asking for more money—yet something in Dat's expression made him pause. It was a fine sight, watching his father laugh as though he'd made the best joke ever.

Dat tented his hands under his chin. "So you talked to Jessica this morning? And she broke the startling news?"

Gabe frowned, wondering where this odd conversation was headed. "*Jah,*" he replied softly. "Red and I were so disappointed we couldn't see straight—"

"Can you keep a secret?"

Gabe stared. Could his *dat* be having a reaction to his medication? Why else would he be downright giggly after learning that his son and future daughter-in-law had been dealt such an emotional blow—and after flatly turning him down for a pay raise?

Dat rolled his chair around the desk so he was sitting close to Gabe. "Your *mamm* and I bought Regina's house for you, son," he whispered. "We want the two of you to have it, so—"

"You paid cash, too!" Gabe shot back. "We could've saved you all that money, if you'd let us take it off the market."

"But we took it out of Regina's name, mostly so Clarence can't cry foul," his father explained. "Now she'll be a traditional Amish wife, allowing her husband to support her, and you won't have to spend your early years in a bedroom between your parents and your sisters. Your *mamm* thinks she'll have grandkids sooner—and more of them— if you have your own place. If you get my drift."

Gabe nearly choked. His mother *never* mentioned such things. "*Mamm* said that?"

His father shrugged. "She and I spent several months living with her parents before we could afford a home," he explained. "What with her grandmother and two brothers in their twenties in bedrooms adjoining ours, it wasn't exactly a newlywed couple's dream."

As Dat's information sank in, Gabe's heart swelled with hope. "Well—wow," he murmured. "*Wow.* That's quite a gift—way better than a raise, or any other place you could've picked for us. *Denki*, Dat. I'm—*we're*—delighted!"

"But keep it under your hat," his father insisted, suddenly serious again. "This sort of announcement—including your engagement—is best saved for after you've been reinstated into the congregation. If folks realize you've been courting and having such a fine time while under the *bann*, it won't sit well with Clarence and Ammon. Those two preachers are starched so stiff, I wonder if they *ever* have any fun— or ever give their wives anything to smile about."

"Even so, Red has to go to the Millers' on Friday—"

"But not for long—and not forever," Dat put in quickly. "Meanwhile, you and I can fix anything in Red's house that might need attention, *jah*? Does she have hardwood floors that could use a face-lift?" he asked eagerly. "Or maybe the rooms need some fresh paint—and your *mamm*'s offered to sew new curtains. We could even build new kitchen cabinets, or fronts for them—"

"Out of the flawed wood in the scrap bin!" Gabe put in excitedly. "When Lydianne told me Red was so taken with that swirl-topped coffee table, I put a SOLD sign on it so I could give it to her as an engagement present. She'll *really* sparkle if we replace her cabinet doors to include a few knotholes and irregularities in the grain!"

When Dat rocked back in his chair, he looked happier than he had in a long time. "You're getting the idea, son. I can't wait to see Regina's face when she finds out about all these surprises you'll have for her."

Chapter Thirty-Three

Because they had no church service Sunday morning, the Miller family stayed at home for a day of quiet contemplation   and after only two days at their house, Regina was already going crazy, shrinking into herself. Her young cousins had been eagerly trying to engage her in conversation all weekend, and she'd tried to be patient with them, but she felt her fuse growing shorter.

How could she explain to Emma, Lucy, and Linda that she was upset about having to leave her home—mourning the loss of her independence? They were young enough to obey their *dat*'s every command without question, because he had absolute authority over them and their mother—and because, as a preacher, he expected nothing less than complete compliance. More than once Regina wanted to tell her young cousins that there was another way to live, a freer lifestyle that still conformed to the Old Order way. But with her uncle and aunt following her every conversation with their impressionable daughters, Regina knew better than to encourage the girls to ask questions or think for themselves.

Because her small room didn't have a window, Regina couldn't stand to spend much time there. Despite the July heat, the windows in the rest of the house remained closed to prevent the odor of Uncle Clarence's hogs from permeating the indoor air. Battery-operated fans ran in the kitchen and front room, but they were just moving hot air. Aunt Cora was making meals that didn't require the oven— or even much time at the stove. Uncle Clarence didn't seem to notice the stifling heat as he read his big King James Bible in his recliner.

At a loss for something to do in the endless stretch of time between washing the breakfast dishes and setting out their cold Sunday lunch, Regina carried her embroidery into the front room. She sat on the end of the sofa nearest the window's light, focusing on the brilliant crimson of the cardinal she was embroidering on a napkin for the customer who'd ordered the tablecloth set. She tried to ignore the way her dress was sticking to her damp body.

Uncle Clarence looked up from the big Bible in his lap. "You know better than to work on the Sabbath, Regina," he scolded her. "You're selling that handiwork for money, so you must put it away. Perhaps reading the *Martyrs Mirror* will put you in a proper frame of mind."

Regina closed her eyes against tears. The huge volume her uncle pointed to held a place of honor in the center of the coffee table. It contained stories of early Anabaptists who'd been persecuted—even burned at the stake—for following their faith during the centuries before believers had migrated to North America to seek religious freedom. Written in Dutch, in 1685, the accounts of such violence and hatred had always depressed Regina rather than giving her any spiritual guidance.

But what else was there to do? Aunt Cora and the girls were also reading their Bibles—or pretending to—so Regina had little choice but to follow their example. She carried her embroidery into her airless room and stood for several moments with her hands on the top of the old dresser, desperately trying to compose herself.

Someone knocked at the front door. A few moments later, Bishop Jeremiah's greeting filled the front room, and he exchanged small talk with Uncle Clarence and the others. "And where's Regina?" he asked pleasantly.

"She's putting away her embroidery," Uncle Clarence replied sternly. "I have half a mind to forbid her to do any further business at The Marketplace. We've seen how spending so much time among English, engaged in earning money she doesn't really need, has skewed her priorities, after all."

Panic filled Regina's soul as she gripped the top of the dresser. If her uncle no longer allowed her to spend Saturdays at the shops with her friends, how would she survive emotionally? At Martin's suggestion, she and Gabe had agreed that it was better for him not to call on her at her uncle's home until after they'd been reinstated into full church membership—a week from this morning.

It was going to be the longest seven days of her life.

"Regina? How's it going, dear?"

Bishop Jeremiah's gentle voice nearly made her blurt out the truth, but somehow she held her emotions in check. When she turned, she saw that the bishop had stopped in the doorway, filling it with his tall, sturdy form as he took in the daybed, the three pegs on the wall where her dresses hung, and the small dresser behind her. His scowl could've curdled milk.

"I had no idea—" he muttered before striding back into the front room. Jeremiah Shetler was the most patient man Regina knew, but waves of his anger washed around her in his wake.

"Clarence, that's the most deplorable thing I've ever seen!" the bishop exclaimed. "You and Cora and the girls have normal-sized bedrooms upstairs—with windows!—yet you've confined Regina to a dim, airless space the size of my mother's pantry. Why is that? And how does it reflect any sort of hospitality, much less *love* for your niece?"

Regina's eyes widened and she held her breath—mostly so she could hear her uncle's answer. She sensed it might be better if she weren't present when he replied to the bishop's outburst—

And then she walked into the front room and resumed her place on the couch. She might know better, but watching Uncle Clarence squirm was the best entertainment she'd had in days, and she didn't want to miss a moment of it.

Aunt Cora and the three girls sat riveted in their chairs, not daring to speak.

Uncle Clarence seemed unable to get out of his recliner. His complexion was somewhere between the red of a raw beefsteak and the color of a turnip. "The upstairs rooms are all—all occupied," he sputtered.

Bishop Jeremiah frowned. "As I recall from being up there for pre-church preachers' meetings, you folks have at least four bedrooms—yours and Cora's, and two for the girls," he said, counting them off on his fingers. "What about the other one?"

Uncle Clarence glanced quickly at Aunt Cora, whose jaw was clamped shut. She seemed as fascinated by the men's conversation as Regina was—and she was letting her husband respond, as was proper.

"It's a sewing room," Lucy put in quietly. "Mamm has her quilting frame and both of the sewing machines in there."

Uncle Clarence shot his daughter an irritated glance. The bishop seemed to conclude that although Aunt Cora had claimed the room for her own use, she'd followed her husband's instructions about where their too-independent niece would be staying.

After an uncomfortable pause, Bishop Jeremiah said, "Clarence, your current arrangement is unacceptable. You may either shift your wife's equipment into the space where Regina is now and allow her to have that upstairs bedroom—or, Regina, you may come and stay at my place."

The bishop lowered himself to the other end of the sofa so he could speak with Regina at eye level. "Mamm and I would be happy to have you in one of our spare rooms," he said kindly. "I understand that your home has sold very quickly—for sure, this time—so if you'd like to shift some of your belongings to my house before you let it go, we'll be fine with that. You've been through a lot these past few weeks."

"But Regina's my responsibility," Uncle Clarence protested weakly. "I've done the right thing by bringing her into my home—"

"Your niece is a responsible adult," Bishop Jeremiah pointed out. "She has a job that allows her to be self-supporting, and—until you made her sell it—she had a perfectly acceptable home. Regina confessed and gave up her artistic pursuits of her own accord, and I see absolutely no need for her to keep paying for her perceived sins simply because you believe it'll keep her humble and compliant with the *Ordnung*. End of discussion."

Regina forced herself to breathe so she wouldn't pass out from sheer joy. She could leave! She could live out the remainder of her *bann* at the bishop's house—and Uncle Clarence couldn't make her stay.

"I accept your generous offer, Bishop Jeremiah," she said before Uncle Clarence could say anything further. "It won't take me but three minutes to pack."

Regina hurried to her room, stuffed her underthings and *kapps* into her suitcase along with her embroidery, and grabbed the dresses hanging on the wall pegs. "*Denki* for taking care of me," she said to her family as she followed the bishop to the front door. "I'll see you in church."

Just like that, she was free! Regina clambered into the bishop's buggy. She held her breath until they reached the road, wondering if her uncle would come outside to have the last word.

"*Denki, denki, denki*—from the bottom of my heart," she blurted. "I don't know what brought this on, but—"

"I'll tell you how it came about, but you have to keep it under your *kapp*," Bishop Jeremiah put in as he turned onto the paved road.

Regina crossed her heart with her fingers, nodding eagerly.

"Your Aunt Cora told me a while back about where you were to stay when you got to their house. She said Clarence had insisted that she not clear out her sewing room to accommodate you," he added softly. "She knew you were going to be miserable—and that she would be, too."

Regina's heart softened. She'd often thought of her aunt as regimented and set in her ways, but she owed Aunt Cora a huge debt of gratitude.

"I stopped by today with the hope that Clarence had changed his mind," Jeremiah continued amiably. "I'm sincerely sorry he's remained so hard-hearted, Regina. Do you want to swing by your house and pick up anything else?"

Regina nodded gratefully. "When the other *maidels* helped me pack Thursday night, we put my personal belongings in a couple of boxes—and I know right where they are," she added. "The new owners want my furniture, so there's not much else to claim."

The bishop smiled as he guided his mare toward Maple Lane. "The Bible tells us the Lord makes all things new," he said kindly. "You're still going through some rough waters, but soon your troubles will be behind you. Do you believe that?"

As Gabe's handsome face—and their plans to marry— came to mind, Regina nodded. "I'm ready for a fresh start, Bishop. I can't thank you enough for helping me get it a little quicker."

Gabe sighed with satisfaction as he stepped away from the ladder Tuesday evening to look at the kitchen walls he'd just painted a deep apple green. He'd kept Red's color scheme because it was fresh and vibrant—and because he loved every detail of the home that expressed exactly who Red Miller was. He saw no reason to change the palette of her life when she became Regina Flaud.

When the sound of the sander died away, Gabe called toward the front room. "How're you coming with that floor, Dat?"

"Just finished," his father replied. "We can apply the new stain tomorrow evening—"

"Or Thursday," Mamm put in firmly from the back bedroom. "You've exerted yourself enough for now, Martin. We want you to be around for the wedding, after all."

"*Jah*, we do," Gabe agreed as he tapped the lid onto the paint can with his hammer. "Won't take me but half an hour to put up the new cabinet doors, and I'm calling it *gut* for the evening. How about if you sit out on the porch and wait for me?"

His father let out a few disgruntled words in German. "What I need is a few more folks bossing me around."

His sisters, who were helping Mamm make the new

curtains, laughed. "We just finished hemming this pair, so we'll pour some lemonade and join you out there, Dat," Lorena said.

"*Jah*, we want you around for our weddings, too!" Kate chimed in.

Gabe began driving the screws into the cabinet hinges with his battery-operated drill. As he mounted each new oak door, he thought about how tickled Red would be when she saw the beadboard insets he'd chosen, as well as the interesting knotholes and irregularities in the wood he'd salvaged from the scrap bins.

"This home is so cute," his mother said behind him. "It'll make you kids the perfect place to start out."

"Who says we'll ever need to leave?" Gabe asked as he hung the final cabinet door. "What with the two big rooms upstairs—and a backyard large enough that we can add on as more kids come along—we'll be here till we're old and gray. Or at least as old as you and Dat," he teased.

"It's a joy to hear you saying such things, son," Mamm said as she slipped her arm around him. "And it's such a blessing that you and your *dat* are working together again, as close as you ever were."

"It is," Gabe agreed as he hugged her. "You two have given Red and me an amazing gift, Mamm. Not just the house, but your forgiveness. Your acceptance and belief in us."

His mother blinked away the dampness in her eyes. "That's what *family* is all about," she whispered. "One of these days, when you've got kids of your own, you'll know even better what I'm talking about, Gabe. I wish you and Regina all the best."

"*We* can't wait to come over for Sunday visits," Lorena said as she moved a chair toward one of the kitchen windows. Tall as she was, she easily reached the brackets to put up the fresh pair of royal blue curtains Kate had slid onto a curtain rod.

"And what about overnights, too?" Kate's dimpled face lit up. "It would be great fun to set up a tent in your backyard, ain't so?"

Gabe smiled, loving the glow that filled the kitchen as his *mamm* and sisters finished hanging the curtains. When he and his family left for the evening, Gabe felt tired—but he'd never felt more blessed.

Chapter Thirty-Four

At long last the Sunday service ended and Bishop Jeremiah called the Members Meeting. Although Regina didn't doubt their *bann* would be lifted, she prayed that their responses would be deemed acceptable as she and Gabe went down on their knees. The preachers asked the necessary questions: *Do you believe your punishment was deserved? Do you believe your sins have been forgiven through the blood of Jesus Christ?*

After assuring the congregation of their penitence, the two of them stepped outside so the congregation could vote. The shade gave some welcome relief from the noonday sun as they stood behind Bishop Jeremiah's tall white house.

"A lot has happened since we first confessed," she remarked softly. "I'm a different woman, with different dreams—because you decided to stay, Gabe."

Gabe's smile suggested that he knew things he wasn't telling her. "I had nothing to lose and everything to gain, honey-girl. I still have some reservations about Old Order ways, but you were right. Leaving you—leaving my family—would've been the biggest mistake I could ever have made."

He glanced toward the door behind them. "How about if we make quick work of the common meal and take a little ride this afternoon?"

Regina's eyebrows rose at his secretive tone. "Folks will want to congratulate us after you announce our engagement—"

"And they'll have plenty of time to do that," Gabe insisted. "I—I've got a little surprise, and I can't keep it to myself any—"

"You two can come inside now," Jo Fussner announced from the doorway. "Let me be the first to welcome you back!"

Regina hugged her friend tightly before entering the Shetlers' mudroom with Gabe close behind her. As they stepped into the big front room, folks rose from the pew benches with warm smiles on their faces. All the way down the center aisle, their friends welcomed them—and Aunt Cora reached out to pull Regina close.

"*Denki* for *everything* you've done for me," Regina whispered in her ear.

Easing away, Aunt Cora winked. "Happy to help out," she murmured. "We girls should stick together, ain't so?"

As Deacon Saul and the two preachers watched their approach, Uncle Clarence's smile was not the brightest of the three, but he was nodding. To him, her reinstatement marked his success at leading her back into the Old Order fold, so he'd done his duty. Regina could leave it at that, without any lingering resentment about why he'd treated her so harshly for the past month. And what did it matter, now that she and Gabe were together?

The Flaud family was smiling, too—especially Martin, who stepped out of his row to clasp Gabe's hand. "It's a great day, kids!"

"We're pleased to have you both back," Bishop Jeremiah

joined in as Regina and Gabe reached the center front area where he stood. "And I believe Gabe has something further to announce."

Regina's stomach filled with butterflies as Gabe grasped her hand and they turned to face the congregation. "This beautiful young woman has agreed to be my wife!" he said proudly. "We'll keep you posted when we've set our wedding date—"

The applause was so loud, Gabe didn't try to talk over it. He beamed at Regina, his dimples making his smile even more handsome as his deep green eyes held her gaze. Her heart was pounding so hard she could barely breathe. She knew she'd never forget this moment—which might not have come about if Gabe hadn't made a fateful guess about her identity as the painter who was hiding behind a fake name.

And think what I gained by giving up my secret and my paints. I would've been content to remain a maidel, *but now I have so much more to look forward to—and to thank You for, Lord.*

As the applause receded, Bishop Jeremiah gestured for folks to sit down. "We have another matter to discuss, which came up rather suddenly," he announced, his resonant voice becoming more somber. "We need to keep Teacher Elam in our prayers, as his *dat* suffered a debilitating stroke a few days ago."

The faces in the congregation fell. Folks murmured their concern as Regina and Gabe took seats on the front pew bench.

"Elam will be moving his family to his parents' farm in Illinois so he can care for them," Bishop Jeremiah continued, "which leaves our school in need of a teacher before the new term starts up on the first Monday of September. If you know of a qualified person to fill this vacancy—"

"I'll do it!" a young woman behind Regina blurted.

Regina's eyes widened. When she turned, Lydianne was standing up with an earnest expression on her face. Gabe appeared as surprised as Regina about her best friend jumping at the chance to teach—and to leave her job at Flaud Furniture.

"I'd be delighted—honored—to work with our scholars," Lydianne said earnestly. "I'm grateful to Martin and Gabe for hiring me at the furniture factory, but I have other abilities I'd like to share with the children of Morning Star—if you folks will have me."

Bishop Jeremiah appeared thunderstruck. He recovered quickly, however. "We'll call a meeting of the school board and have you come for an interview, Lydianne," he said with a nod. "Shall we set Monday—a week from tomorrow—as the final date for applications? We need to give our new teacher time to prepare for the coming year, and to set up the new schoolhouse, which Pete will have finished by then."

Everyone nodded, smiling at the burly blond carpenter who sat near the back of the men's section. After the bishop declared the meeting adjourned, everyone rose to prepare for the common meal, which was to be a picnic beneath the big trees in the Shetlers' backyard.

"Let's duck out *now*," Gabe whispered into Regina's ear. "We'll grab some lunch later—"

"Folks will speculate about why we're leaving so early—especially Uncle Clarence," Regina pointed out.

"Let them talk! Why should we stop being the topic of hot conversation just because we're not shunned anymore?" he teased. "Besides, my folks can set them straight. They know exactly where we're going."

Regina sensed she shouldn't object any further. Gabe's surprise was piquing her curiosity, and she was eager to share whatever was making him so happy. Most folks were heading toward the kitchen, so he led her quickly through the door to the bishop's attached *dawdi haus* and then outside. He hitched up his horse, and they were clip-clopping down the road at a brisk trot a few minutes later.

"You've got a bee in your bonnet, Mr. Flaud," Regina teased. The breeze that blew her *kapp* strings back felt wonderful as they rolled through the countryside.

"Oh, it's much more than a bee, honey-girl. It's a wedding gift that can't wait for the big day."

Regina's heartbeat accelerated. They'd had their first date four weeks ago, on the day they'd been shunned. For some couples, such a quick decision to wed might've been an invitation to a lifetime of regret and heartache—yet she believed she and Gabe were making the right move. They were indeed kindred spirits, and that closeness had deepened since they'd gone through their *bann* together. She'd known the Flauds before Martin had hired her years ago, so she felt comfortable with his family, too. Many new brides didn't have that advantage.

As the rig approached Maple Lane, Regina licked her lips nervously. She hadn't been to the house since she'd fetched her boxes with the bishop—avoiding the pain of knowing someone else would soon live there. When Gabe turned the corner, she saw that the FOR SALE sign had disappeared. The lawn was neatly cut and everything looked tidy and well cared for.

"Um, why are we stopping here?" she asked in a thick voice. "I don't care to see how the new owners have—have made it their own."

Gabe halted his horse and set the brake. His expression was an odd mixture of emotions Regina didn't dare interpret, for fear she'd be in for a big disappointment. When he smiled full-on at her, however, her heart began to pound.

"You remember how sick we were when we learned somebody else had snatched up your house before you could take it off the market?" he asked softly.

Regina nodded. Her hands were clasped in such a tight knot that it took a couple of attempts before Gabe could pry them apart to hold them.

"My parents bought it—for us!" he blurted exuberantly. "They didn't want any quibbling with Clarence about your name being on it, so they've signed it over to me as our wedding present, Red! You—you've got to look inside!"

Regina's mouth dropped open. First she felt numb with disbelief, and then she could only stare at Gabe, waiting for the other shoe to drop. "But we could've arranged one of those sales where you sign over a property for a few dollars, to change ownership—"

"You know Dat. He did it his way, without asking me," Gabe pointed out. "When I requested a raise last week, he refused me—dropped this surprise in my lap instead! He *adores* you, Regina. He's grateful for the way you convinced me to stay Amish."

Regina's mouth closed and then fell open again. When she burst into tears and started laughing at the same time, Gabe gently blotted her face with his handkerchief. "I—I don't know what to say," she whispered.

"Come inside," he urged as he helped her down from the buggy. "I think you'll like what you see."

All the way up the walk, Gabe prayed that Red would appreciate what he and his family had done—the gifts of time and energy they'd devoted to the home he looked forward to sharing with her.

"The swing looks really nice in white," she said as she paused on the porch. "And it has new cushions, and—"

Her eyes widened as she took a closer look. "You painted the whole porch! I—I hadn't realized it was looking a little tired."

"Mamm and the girls are handy with paintbrushes, and they were here a lot during the week," he said as he reached for the doorknob. "Now—humor me, Red. I'm going to cover your eyes while we head to the kitchen first."

She appeared doubtful, but he covered her eyes with his bandanna and guided her through the front room before she could protest. When they'd entered the kitchen, he removed his handkerchief with a flourish. "What do you think, honey-girl? Notice anything different?"

Regina sucked in her breath. "Fresh paint—my same favorite shade of green! And new curtains," she said as she hurried to the windows to finger the fabric.

Gabe remained in the doorway, having the time of his life watching Red's reactions. When she glanced at the cabinets and then did a double take, it was all he could do to let her speak first.

"Look at these!" she exclaimed as she ran her fingers over the new cabinet doors. "Beadboard! And you made the outer edges with *flawed* wood—and these little glass knobs are the coolest hardware I've ever seen! These doors are *perfect* for a bungalow!"

Gabe thought his heart might pound out of his rib cage. "I—I was hoping you'd see it that way," he admitted. "Let's look at the bedrooms."

Once again Regina allowed him to cover her eyes. "It's like a treasure hunt! Only better," she added as they headed toward the back of the house.

When they reached Regina's bedroom, she pressed her hands to the sides of her face. "A new quilt and curtains! And fresh paint in here, too! My word, you Flauds worked your tails off this week."

"Keep going," Gabe suggested. It was a joy to hear the excitement in Red's voice as she discovered the freshly painted walls and rag rugs in the bathroom and second bedroom, as well as the way a coat of cream-colored paint had brightened the walls of the stairway leading to the attic.

When they reached the room on the front of the house, which had been Red's studio, she let out a long sigh. "I'd be lying if I told you I never miss my painting," she confessed softly.

"I know the feeling," Gabe murmured. "Sometimes my fingers itch to press into guitar strings."

Red nodded. "*Denki* for taking down my picture-hanging lines—and you cleaned the spilled paint and stains off the floor, too," she remarked as she crouched to run her fingers across the boards. She looked up at him, realization dawning. "Did you *refinish* this floor? And all the floors downstairs, as well?"

"Bingo!" Gabe cried out. "That was Dat's special project. They only needed a quick sanding and a new coat of stain—"

"But what a difference it's made." Red shook her head, appearing dazed. "I guess after you live someplace for a while, you don't see all the stuff that needs to be done."

"Like the way I worked around you for so long without really seeing *you*, eh?"

Red's face softened with a smile. "But I made you look, ain't so?" she teased.

"And by the way, these soft yellow walls are perfect for when our kids are old enough to be sleeping up here, *jah*?"

Butterflies fluttered in Gabe's stomach. "Can't tell you how many times this week I've heard about those grand-kids Mamm's wanting."

As they descended the wooden stairway, Gabe hoped

Red would pick out the detail he'd saved for last—and that she'd love it as much as he did.

"Your *dat* made these floors look better than new," she remarked as they headed for the front room. "It's such a blessing to see my comfy chairs and lamps in place, just the way I liked them, and—"

When she stopped to stare, Gabe thought he might split at the seams.

"The *coffee table*!" she cried out. "You—you didn't sell it! You—"

"When Lydianne told me what you'd said about it, I couldn't let anyone else have it, Red," he explained as he joined her alongside his flawed, swirl-topped creation. "If you didn't forgive me for expecting you to jump the fence, I figured to use it as an enticement to lure you back—"

When Red threw her arms around his neck and hugged him hard, Gabe knew the meaning of pure joy. He held her close, knowing every ounce of effort he and his family had put into the house had been repaid five times over.

Red kissed him, long and soft and sweet. When she came up for air, her eyes were misty and her freckles glowed on her flawless face. "I love you so much," she whispered. "Gabriel Flaud, you are one amazing man."

Her words were sweet music to his ears.

And Dat had been right: it was all about the *sparkle*.

*Please read on for an excerpt from the next book in
Charlotte Hubbard's
The Maidels of Morning Star series.*

First Light in Morning Star

Hope fluttered like a butterfly in Lydianne Christner's heart as she parked her rig in the pole barn just north of the new white schoolhouse. It was barely dawn and she was more than an hour early for her interview with the members of Morning Star's school board, but she needed time to collect her thoughts and plan her answers to the questions she anticipated from the five men who would decide her future. It had been a spur-of-the-moment decision when she'd blurted out her wish to apply for the teaching position at the Members Meeting after church a week ago—but in the days since, Lydianne's soul had reconfirmed her impulsive outburst.

She *really* wanted this position. The trick would be replying to the school board's questions without hinting at the very personal reason she wished to become Teacher Lydianne.

Did she stand a chance?

Lydianne had no idea whether anyone else had applied for the position in the past several days. Morning Star's previous teacher, Elam Stoltzfus, had already left town to assist his family in the wake of his father's debilitating stroke, so there was no chance he would return. She didn't know of any other married Amish men who'd likely fill the position—nor did she believe any of Morning Star's other single Amish women aspired to teaching.

Her close friend Regina Miller had just become engaged to Gabe Flaud, so she'd be ineligible to teach. Jo Fussner sold the baked goods, canned vegetables, and jellies she and her *mamm* made—and she'd taken on the challenge of managing The Marketplace, the renovated stable where local crafters sold their goods. The Helfing twins, Molly and Marietta, ran the noodle factory their mother had begun as well as renting out their *dawdi hauses* to tourists—and they kept a shop at The Marketplace—so neither of them seemed a likely candidate for the teaching position.

Lydianne grimaced when she thought about either of the middle-aged Slabaugh sisters managing a classroom. Esther and Naomi lived on a farm just outside of town, and their main occupation seemed to be sharpening their *maidel* tongues on tidbits of other people's business.

Pity the poor children who had one of them for a teacher! Lydianne thought as she gazed across the large grassy lot between the new white schoolhouse and the red stable that housed The Marketplace shops.

She warned herself not to pridefully assume the school board would hire her, however. After all, she had no teaching experience. She'd taken a job as bookkeeper and finisher at the Flaud Furniture Factory when she'd first come to Morning Star, and she was also the financial manager for The Marketplace, so maybe the men on the board would believe she should remain in her current positions. Martin Flaud, who owned the furniture factory, was the school board president. He hadn't directly challenged her about leaving her job with him to teach school, but his speculative gazes during the past week had given Lydianne plenty to think about while she'd been staining furniture and tallying orders.

But with God's help, you can do this! Your heart's in the right place! Lydianne reminded herself fervently. *Just look at what you and your friends accomplished over the summer. The stable across the way was falling in on itself, and now it's full of successful shops that attract hundreds of shoppers to Morning Star every Saturday—and its commissions have funded the new schoolhouse.*

Lydianne and her *maidel* friends felt extremely pleased about the businesses that now thrived because they had believed in the power of their positive intentions—and because the church had bought the property as a place to hold its auctions and build a new schoolhouse. In the first light of this August morning, the white geraniums, purple petunias, bright green sweet potato vines, and yellow marigolds filling The Marketplace's window boxes glowed in the rays of the rising sun. The stable's deep red walls shone with the care she and her friends had lavished upon the building.

Inspired by the sight, Lydianne firmly believed that her ability to manage money, solve problems, and deal effectively with people would be her finest assets as she took on the challenges of teaching Morning Star's Amish scholars. It was her deepest desire to share her love of learning— to share the best of herself—with the children who'd be charged to her care . . . even if one child in particular was the reason she especially craved the position.